For Devon
& Hank

THE
HUMAN
TRIAL

Love you
and so appreciative of all
your support!

AUDREY GALE

A Gale

ISBN: 978-1-95386570-0(Paperback)
ISBN: 978-1-95386571-7 (eBook)
ISBN: 978-1-95386572-4 (Audiobook)

Library of Congress Control Number: 2023911157

Cover Design: Eric Labacz
Typesetting: Stewart A. Williams
Photo by Starla Fortunato

Although inspired by historical events, any references to historical events, real people, or real places are used fictitiously. All characters, incidents, and dialogue are drawn from the author's imagination and are not to be construed as real.

Books Fluent
3014 Dauphine Street
New Orleans, LA
70117

For J –
for the adventure of a lifetime

CHAPTER ONE

JOE COLLEGE

1921

Randy Archer skulked low in his seat in the overcrowded class-room, hanging his head so his black tangles concealed the angry lump on his forehead. If the bullies who enjoyed making his life a living hell caught sight of it, they'd be on him like ravenous dogs on the scent of fresh blood. Ignoring the teacher, Archer focused on hiding all signs of vulnerability.

But the pretty blonde seated beside him who headed the baton twirling squad—Julie, Julia?—was struggling with the science review conducted from the front of the classroom. She mumbled her confusion under her breath. "The smallest solid particle in the universe is a-a what?"

As if he'd heard every word, Mr. Ehn singled her out. "Miss Julie," he began, grinning as he paced through the rows of students, "there's been quite a bit of upheaval in the scientific world of late. Recount for the class what we've been learning about the dramatic new hypotheses advanced by physicist Niels Bohr and others. Please stand."

"Um," she hedged, coming to her feet slowly as Mr. Ehn drew

closer. Taking pity on her, Archer slid a note over for her to read. "Yes, Mr. Ehn," she stalled, "yes, well, we've been studying, a-a new understanding . . . of the atom!" The last word gushed out with her relief as she plopped back onto her seat, mouthing a too-obvious thank-you to her seatmate.

Archer winced, knowing what was to come. On cue, the teacher called his name. "Randy Archer, you generally have a depth of knowledge that *on occasion* seems to elude your classmates." That grin again as Mr. Ehn's eyes, weirdly magnified behind thick lenses, swept the room before coming to rest on Archer. "Describe for *all* of us the evolution of our understanding of the miniscule atom."

Archer could easily recite that evolution from the very beginning when the Greek Democritus invented the name centuries BC. *What else could I do to avoid my family but spend long hours in the library studying?* He rose carefully, moving nary a hair on his head.

For a moment, Archer considered minimizing the resentment his brainpower often inspired. But, in the end, just like at home, he couldn't hold back exhibiting his one superior trait. *Father, brothers, and bullies be damned.* "I believe, Mr. Ehn, you are referencing the atom, considered for centuries as 'the basic building block of nature.' In other words, the smallest, invisible, and indivisible solid unit in all of nature. However, in the two-and-a-half decades since Thomson, in 1897, discovered particles within the atom, the first being the electron—"

"Thank you, thank you, Mr. Archer, that will do. Leave some of these sensational discoveries for your fellow fledgling scientists here to expound upon." The instructor perused the classroom for his next victim, enjoying the squirming it evoked. "Mr. McGrevey, would you care to elaborate on—"

The bell signaling the end of class clanged loudly, interrupting Mr. Ehn's inquisition. Varsity linebacker Jimmie McGrevey, Julie's boyfriend, led the class in clambering for the exit while

Archer hung back—hoping, like any battered pugilist, that the bell would save him.

But the moment he entered the hallway, overflowing with students bantering during the short break between classes, trouble awaited. McGrevey shoved Julie behind him possessively to challenge Archer head-on. One fist clutching his collar, McGrevey screamed in his face, "How many times I got to tell you, Archer, steer clear of my girl?"

Julie rattled an explanation from behind her boyfriend's huge frame, insisting she'd asked for Archer's help. But it had no effect. McGrevey's other fist latched onto Archer's collar in his drive to teach him yet another lesson about parading his knowledge at the expense of everyone in the classroom, when a button popped off in the big thug's face.

"What's this?" he cried, spying the welts and bruises now exposed beneath Archer's shirt.

Mr. Ehn chose that moment to exit the classroom, stepping between the pair to break them up. McGrevey whined, "I didn't do nothing, Mr. Ehn. Honest. Those marks, they were there. I swear, I hardly even touched him!"

Ehn peered closely at the bruises while Archer shrugged his clothing into place. "Who did this to you, son? Mr. McGrevey here? Did this just happen?"

Archer pulled back from them both, clothing straightened and checking his bangs. "No. I-I fell, before school this morning. Now can I go?"

Mr. Ehn considered for a moment. "You may go directly to the counselor's office and explain to her how you 'fell.' I'll expect her explanatory note delivered back to me within the hour. Go on now, Archer."

He raced down the hallway toward the counselor's office at the far end, catching only the beginning of the exchange between the science teacher and McGrevey. "No, honest, I hardly touched him . . ."

§

'Miss Fidella Dolkowski, Student Counselor,' read the removable cardboard sign in its metal frame centered on the door. 'Miss Della,' as most students called her, brightened upon seeing Archer enter. From behind her small desk, her delight crinkled the skin around her blue eyes and scrunched up her liberally freckled nose.

"Randy! I'm glad you— Oh good heavens, now what's happened?" She leapt to her feet for closer inspection. "Randy, you're hurt. More than before!" She examined him, though he resisted her prying, unable to successfully cover his neck, hands, face, and arms at once.

"Stop, Miss Della, stop! It ain't— It is nothing. I fell before school. There was ice on the stairs. And then that bastard, McGrevey, 'scuse me, tried to rough me up for helping his girlfriend pass science. Mr. Ehn says ya gotta," Archer again stopped himself and took a deep, steadying breath, "that is, you need to report your findings, and I am to deliver them to him within the hour. Just say I fell, will you? Please don't make it worse. Please?"

Miss Della plunked back onto her desk chair, shoving back sandy bangs and pointing Archer to the seat before her. She sighed, blinking fast and biting her lip. "I've turned a blind eye too many times already, Randy. *I'm* involved now, even implicated. How long are you going to put up with this? How long *can* you put up with this—this violence?"

His intense, black-brown eyes faltered as he fidgeted with the positioning of the dark curls over his forehead. When he met her gaze directly, he asked, "I'm sixteen years old, Miss Della. What choice do I have?"

"You've completed all requirements for your high school diploma, and in record time. You have an unparalleled scholastic record in addition. Many colleges would fight to have you. Let me help you, Randy. Let me make inquiries. Let me—"

"Dam—darn it, Miss Della. I'm underage, have no money, and no hope of support from anyone, especially my family, especially for college. How can you possibly help me overcome all that? Honestly, Miss Della," he huffed in resignation, "as if it's not hard enough."

"You can accomplish whatever you set your mind to, I know it, Randy. You have within you everything you need to go anywhere you want, do anything you really wish to."

Archer sat, sullen and unconvinced, assessing which of his wounds would be most likely to show and how to compensate for it now that he'd lost some buttons.

"Look, Randy," the counselor continued, "I've been thinking about your situation, and I have someone who I think could help us, a distant cousin of mine. Let me look into it. Give me a week, and stay out of harm's way during that week, you hear?" She dashed off the report Mr. Ehn required. "I will not lie for you again, Randy, after today," she stated, coming around her desk to hand him the note.

As he rose, the young counselor impulsively hugged the battered boy, her sudden nearness shocking Archer. Beneath her rigid collar and baggy skirt lived a soft, pliable femininity he had never before experienced, with a scent that was spellbinding. He leaned into her embrace until she drew back, stepped away, and cleared her throat. "And—and promise me you'll do all you can to keep your distance at home? Any more such evidence of your family life, and I'll be forced—"

"Promise," he cut in. Archer snatched up the report and, folding it into his pocket, nodded. "I will try. Thank you, Della. Uh, *Miss* Della."

§

One week later, Marty Archer, Randy's father, the burly antithesis of his youngest son, filled the doorway to Miss Della's office.

Spying his son slunk low in a chair, he growled, "If you're in trouble here, boy, you'll be in a heap more when we get home!" Once inside, Mr. Archer spied the counselor, previously hidden by the door, seated at her desk. He paused in obvious surprise and amusement at her sandy-haired, freckled-faced youthfulness. "*You're* the high school counselor? Ain't this somethin' new," he laughed out loud. "Mighty big title for such a little girl."

"Mr. Archer," Miss Della stood, straightening her diminutive frame to full height, "that won't be necessary. Your son is in no trouble, at least here at school." Randy heard a sharpness in her tone he'd thought Miss Della incapable of, especially in the presence of his rough-cut father. "Please take the chair beside your son." Once all were seated, she began again. "I am Miss Fidella Dolkowski, Eastside High Counselor. And yes, I suppose I am something 'new.' For your information, this school district has embraced the modern trend in counseling which goes beyond vocation to students' broader needs. I'm pleased and honored to represent that change."

She paused for Mr. Archer to introduce himself, which only led to another off-comment from him. "Polish, right? There's some Dolkowskis at work. At the steel mill."

She smiled stiffly and nodded. "Allow me to get directly to why I've called you here today, Mr. Archer."

Marty Archer sprawled back in his seat, which creaked and squealed beneath his weight. He cracked the thick knuckles on his work-toughened hands, making the space suddenly sound and feel suffocating. His son leaned as far from him as their seating allowed.

Miss Della considered the hardened man before her, weighing how to begin and how to accomplish her goal. "Actually Mr. Archer, I have very good news for you today. As you know, your gifted son has not only completed all high school requirements in two years *less* time than normal—" She stopped, startled by the widening of the elder Archer's black, deep-set eyes as he sat forward. "You—you did know, that is, you were aware Randy had officially completed high school?" His answer was clear in the scowl the man leveled on his son, who determinedly ignored it.

Miss Della gathered her thoughts. "Randy has in fact not only completed high school requirements, but has done so with a *perfect* scholastic record, Mr. Archer, a fact nearly unheard of around—almost unheard of. You should be so proud."

Mr. Archer grunted, finally taking his eyes off his son and with his personal version of belated charm said, "Marty, Miss. You can call me Marty."

"Marty," she repeated, deciding to state her business and get this disconcerting behemoth of a human out of her office once and for all. "Mr. Archer, Marty, I am pleased to tell you that, due to your son's scholastic excellence and demonstrable aptitude, *Harvard University* in Boston, Massachusetts has offered him a full scholarship to attend!"

Staring blankly, Marty Archer appeared not to understand.

The counselor filled in the silence. "Because of his age, I need only your signature of consent on this form," she pushed a paper toward him, "giving your son permission to accept this incalculable opportunity. You can be certain, Mr. Archer, an offer like this with no required monetary contribution is so very rare. You should be extremely pleased with and for Randy. I certainly am!"

Randy's father stared at the paper laid before him until his narrowed eyes drilled into his son before shifting to Miss Della. She swallowed with difficulty but held his gaze. Abruptly, Mr. Archer screeched back the chair and stood. "No son a' mine needs a fancy education, Miss—Miss Dolkowski. Ya did say you're related to the Dolkowskis at the mill, right? Pollacks. Your folk work the steel? Then you know. What's a puny kid from around here goin' to do with more schooling? At *Harvard?*"

He chuckled before abruptly beckoning his son. "Let's go, kid, now!" He charged for the exit.

Miss Della, surprisingly quick not to mention courageous, blocked the large man's passage. Resolved, though tiny and fighting back fear, she shouted, "Mr. Archer! You will leave me no choice should you fail to sign this release form for your son and this singular chance for a bright future. I shall be forced to go to the authorities to report the physical abuse your son has experienced in your home. Those authorities will determine just punishment for the repeated acts of violence in evidence all over his body. Not only could you lose your son, Mr. Archer, you could face prison time. And how will your other children survive?"

While the elder Archer gawked in disbelief at the petite female counselor blocking his way, young Archer's mind flashed to the hulking gang of older brothers always at the ready to teach him his 'place' and 'toughen up' their 'puny' youngest, the 'runt who thinks he so smart.' Somehow, Randy decided, the other 'children' would survive just fine.

"Now, you listen to me, *Miss* Dolkowski," Marty Archer threatened. "I run a house fulla boys all on my own. Yeah, it's rough, but they're boys, just havin' some fun. And doin' Randy a favor—toughening him up! My youngest here who's been pretendin' to attend high school," he paused to glare at him, "avoidin' pullin' his own weight at the mills like the rest of us, needs t'learn what it takes to get by in this world. Where better to learn how hard life is than at home?"

The senior Archer summed it up. "Expect nothin' from anyone and ya won't get disappointed. That's my motto and it serves me well, I gotta say. Now don't get all mothery and go tryin' t'protect him, Miss. It's just the way it is—fight or die. You from around here, right? Ya know it's truth. Now step aside. Come on, kid!"

"The scars, wounds, and bruises on this boy's body look like a lot more than 'fun,'" Miss Della exclaimed after catching her breath. "*Years* of fun evidently. Tell me how it's fair that the bigger, older boys, and you yourself, ganging up on the youngest and smallest teaches anyone anything but fear, brute force, and abject humil—"

Mr. Archer stepped in closer to cut her off. "No son a' mine is gonna run to the counselor and hide behind her skirts. Now stand aside, Miss. I got no time for this foolery. Come on," he spat at his son.

But Miss Della did not relent. "Mr. Archer, no one wants trouble for anyone, least of all your son. Sign this document, and the rest of it goes away forever. At the same time, know you will be doing him the greatest favor of his young life, granting him an invaluable chance for success. And you'll be giving all your children the reassurance of a family intact." She held the paper before him where it wavered as if caught in a gusty wind.

After a long moment of unbearable tension, at least for Randy and Miss Della, Marty Archer snatched the document, slammed it down, and scrawled his name. Leaving it on the desk, he rounded on his son. "There. Signed. Got what ya want? But I warn ya, you don't come home right this minute, don't ever. Never come home again, ya hear?" Mr. Archer's smoldering anger flamed to a splotchy crimson boil as he stomped past Miss Della into and down the hallway, thundering footfalls from his work boots emphasizing his threat.

Miss Della grabbed the paper and folded it carefully, holding it with both hands against her heart. Seeing young Archer gone pale, she reached out to touch his arm. "Randy?"

He looked from her to the figure of his father, the only parent he'd ever known, shrinking in the long hallway, footsteps fading. When Miss Della repeated his name, Archer's dark eyes zeroed in on her freckles before he lurched after his father.

At the far end of the corridor, Randy Archer hesitated, glanced back once, then vanished around the corner.

§

The knock came late that night. "Who is it?" Miss Della asked through the locked door to her small apartment. To the indistinct mumble, she repeated, "Who's there?"

She could barely make out a soft, "Miss Della, please. Open up."

She cracked the door cautiously, then pushed it wide, yanking Archer from the hallway and the sight of her nosy neighbors, praying they hadn't heard. She closed and locked the door behind them, tightening her bathrobe and knotting it as she faced him.

The two stood staring at each other. She appeared to be gauging as always where he hid further abuse, and he was wondering if he'd lost his mind in coming. Did he really think she might . . . they might . . . He took in her sandy locks pulled back in a ponytail, making her appear even younger. *Where could this lead?* he'd been pondering since her spontaneous hug the week before.

Archer beseeched her, "He signed it, right? I can still take the offer from Harvard? It's still on, right? I'm not too late? I can still say yes?"

"Oh Randy," she hugged him in profound relief, and he willingly succumbed, welcoming the softness and scent he'd been obsessing about since their first physical contact in her office. "Yes, oh yes, of course," she grinned, standing back at arm's length. "You're not too late. I'm so glad you changed your mind. But . . . how did you know where I live?" she asked, suddenly aware of their questionable circumstance, and she in her bathrobe.

"Then I can go right away, to Boston I mean, to Harvard? I dare not go home again, Miss Della, ever . . ." In the dimness of the apartment, he rubbed his eyes, opaque black in the low light, as though wiping away dark visions.

"Come sit down. I'll get you some tea. You're safe now, Randy."

When she returned to the miniscule room where her convertible sofa had been transformed into her bed for the night, she was struck by how small, young, and helpless he looked with his strange dark eyes and disheveled black hair. She tried to imagine him on a buttoned-down campus like Harvard's as she handed him the hot cup, which he accepted with unsteady hands.

"I can't do it anymore," he suddenly cried, "pretend to be less to make them feel like more. I can't! I'm not cut out for the mills. They'll be better off without me. And me them, do you think, Miss Della?"

"Certainly the latter. Randy, you can always return to Pittsburgh if things don't work out in Boston. There will always be jobs at the steel mills. But you'll never know what you are capable of until you try. Plus, to refuse such a scholarship offer would be a travesty, Randy, especially for someone of your abilities.

"Now," she said, sitting lightly at the far end of the sofa-bed, "we'll get you the bus ticket you need first thing in the morning." Studying his frayed clothing, she added, "and a few things to wear on campus." She smiled. "I'll consider them, along with a bit of pocket money, a sound investment in your future as an MD!" She giggled at the thought. "You do still plan on becoming a doctor? I assured my contact at Harvard that was your intention."

"My dream, yes. But-but tonight . . . I mean," he hesitated, "I cannot go home."

"You have no friends who would take you in for the night?"

Randy shook his head, biting his lip. "No one in my neighborhood would risk crossing my father or my brothers, Miss Della. But," he brightened as though at a sudden solution, "I could sleep at the bus station."

"Have you seen the kind of people who sleep overnight in the station? No! Over my dead body. I got you into this and I'm going to make sure you see it through, in one piece.

"So no friends," Miss Della concluded. "Then—then you'll just have to, that is, you'll have to stay here for the night. We'll get you outfitted first thing, and tomorrow I'll see you off to Boston myself. I'm sure they run every day, the buses, even on Saturdays."

She gazed at him, and her brow wrinkled. "*How* did you say you knew where I lived, Randy?"

"Oh, I snitched an envelope addressed to you here from your desk. In case of emergency," he said as if that explained it, "which this is," he added, surveying the small room. The recollection of her scent and suppleness distracted him as his eyes traveled over her bed and back to her. "So, uh, where shall I sleep, Miss Della?"

§

An auspiciously bright sun burned through the grit spewed night and day from the steel mills' towering smokestacks. Randy Archer and his high school counselor stepped into the light of the busy bus station early the next afternoon. He proudly carried an inexpensive suitcase containing a few slightly used things Miss Della had purchased for him, at no small expense to herself given her meager salary. Yet, the belief shining in her eyes when she looked at her protégé expressed every confidence in her 'investment' in Archer's future. Or was it another emotion shining there?

Randy felt like an adult, going off on his own for the first time, ready for Harvard and the world in a confidence-bolstering shirt and tie and his first-ever jacket, though secondhand. He'd parted and slicked down his hair with water in a style he'd seen on grown men, although disobedient waves were already springing free. But it was his first sexual encounter with a woman much older than himself—Miss Della had to be at least twenty-one, he guessed—that bolstered his confidence like nothing before.

Stolen glimpses at her brought to mind their tangled limbs rumpling her narrow bed late into the night, to be repeated before parting in the morning. The boggling pleasure she'd guided him to, not to mention the thrill of seeing his effect on her, both embarrassed and stirred him. He colored and glanced away. Whenever their eyes met, they both blushed, gazing off awkwardly. Young Randy Archer had gained in one night a whole new world of experience and a budding self-assurance unimagined.

The bus to Boston was called over the loudspeaker, and Miss Della handed him the ticket. He faced her, still reddening. "I don't know, that is, how to—"

She cut him off, grabbing him in a brief but smothering hug. "I believe in you, Randy. Now go out and find your dream and don't stop until you do." She continued blushing as she stepped back primly to send him on his way. "You have the instructions and contacts I wrote down for you?" He nodded, touching his breast pocket to be sure. "My second cousin left your name with the head of student housing, so start there. Go set the world on fire," she said in a tremulous voice, her eyes misting as she further distanced herself.

"Thank you, Miss Della. Thank you for all of this. And," he flushed deeply as he thought of sweet Della abandoning herself to passion, "for—for last night."

Burning an equally hot shade of red, the counselor gently nudged him toward the bus. "Goodbye, Randy. Let me know you got there safely, and how you're doing from time to time. A postcard perhaps? Good luck," she called after him.

Eyes firmly on his future, he entered the bus without hesitation, its dark interior instantly swallowing him. With a number of seats to choose from, Archer surveyed the passengers settling in, drawn to a young copper-haired beauty sitting alone. Now, when he looked at a woman, his imagination carried him to possibilities he'd only learned of the previous night. Without further vacillation or a backward glance at the well-wishers waving the bus off, he slowed at the young woman's row to inquire, "Is this seat taken, Miss?" His first taste of sex and the heat two bodies can generate tingled throughout his frame as he smiled innocently at her.

The girl tossed copper ringlets over her shoulder and made room beside her for Randy Archer on the bus ride to a promising future.

§

The bronze statue, surrounded by campus elms fading to their fall colors, glared down menacingly. 'Who let the likes of you onto Harvard's sacred soil?' was what the scowl seemed to express.

Archer gazed up into the cold, empty-eyed stare, feeling his confidence slip. He read aloud the identifying placard at the base of the statue. "Ansley Bradley Prescott Perrish, Steadfast Proponent and Guiding Influence in the Establishment of Harvard College, Anno Domini 1636."

"Well, Mr. Perrish," Archer proclaimed, squaring his shoulders beneath the statue's glower, "I'm here by invitation of Harvard itself, and at the expense of this great institution of yours. I aim to show you, your peers, and the abundant descendants of founders such as yourself who populate this campus that my presence is no fluke nor accident. I will belong, no matter what it takes. Sir," he added with emphasis.

The commotion all around him drew Archer's attention. He observed the busy campus, aswirl in students, singly and in boisterous groups, traversing its green knolls in every direction. No one but the intimidating statue paid Archer any mind.

§

He tried not to ogle the sumptuous new dormitory to which he'd been assigned in what was referred to as the Gold Coast, a name he found fitting. But his troubles began immediately. An upperclassman approached him as he wandered the hallway, searching for his assigned room.

"You need some help?" the gawky stranger with thick glasses and a remarkable spread of acne across his face asked. "That's my job, helping freshies find their way." The boy stopped, removed his glasses, and cleaned the lens with a handkerchief. He eyed Archer while resetting his spectacles on his nose. "You are a freshman? Correct?"

Archer nodded, standing as tall as his five-and-a-half feet allowed.

"Name please. I'll check my list and help you find your room."

"Randy Archer," he replied as the upperclassman scanned his papers.

"Archer, Archer. Oh yes. Here you are, indeed a freshman, not that I doubted you. And pre-med? Impressive, Archer. Follow me." He turned on his heels and hurried along the hallway, forcing Archer to trot to keep up with his long-legged pace. When the man stopped suddenly, Archer nearly collided with him. "Wait," he said, pivoting around, "where are your things?" When Archer indicated the satchel in his hand, the upperclassman questioned, "That's it? No other luggage? Trunk? Boxes?"

"Um, just this for the time being," Archer replied, feeling the familiar taste of humiliation sour his mouth.

"You do travel light, don't you, unlike most freshmen, I must say. Well, come along." When they reached the room Archer would occupy his first year at Harvard and his first time away from home, the door stood ajar. "This is it, Archer. Go on. I think your roommate is already laying claim to the place. Better get in there and make a stake before the best is taken." He shoved the door wide open before taking his leave by explaining, "Other freshies to help, I'm afraid. Welcome to Harvard, old man. And good luck, Archer."

Archer peered in cautiously before stepping inside. "Hey kid," a freshman in a high-collar shirt, tight to his neck with a tie jauntily tossed over his shoulder, called out. Looking more like a professor than freshman, his new roommate unpacked a microscope from a large, open, well-stuffed trunk. He carefully placed it on a desk before facing Archer directly.

The young man was of average height, though still inches taller than Archer, but that's where 'average' ended. He was extremely handsome with a cleft jaw, dazzling white smile, bright blue eyes, and parted, pomaded blond hair. "You lost?" he asked Archer. "Here with your older brother? Helping him check in?"

He might have traveled miles from his Pennsylvania home, but Archer was learning his mere sixteen years, abetted by his short stature, had traveled right along with him. "Um, no. No brother. I'm checking myself in. This is the room I was assigned, I think. I'm, uh, Randy Archer." He puffed out his chest and extended his hand in what he hoped was a college-man manner.

"You're Archer?" the roommate repeated, seemingly dumbfounded as he scrutinized the new arrival and his attire with obvious disdain. Archer shifted uncomfortably. "You're, that is, *you* are to be my roommate? Well you look, ah, younger than I was expecting, but well, welcome . . ." he added, trailing off. "Oh, I've taken the window-side, so stow your belongings over there." He peered behind Archer. "Where are your things?"

"Being shipped," Archer lied, taking in the windowless side of the two-person room and slinging his bag emphatically onto the narrow bed. It was going to be a long day, he realized. Perhaps a long number of years.

§

The balloon filled with water barely missed his temple before splatting against the wall beside him. Giggles broke out from the boys ducking into their respective rooms and closing their doors. "Sorry, Junior," he heard from one of them. "You should be more careful!"

It had been little more than a month of freshman living, but Archer already wearied of the pranks and foolishness that accelerated as cliques formed on the dormitory wings and floors. It was beginning to remind him of the home he'd left behind, though far more privileged and far less brutal. Besides the water balloon fight he'd barely avoided, there were the football games played in the hallways; the raucous singing, loud and out of tune, that disrupted the nights; the short-sheeting of his bed; and the water balloon stretched beneath the toilet seat, which wreaked havoc on his few clothes and only shoes as well as on the bathroom floor. All of it ended in giggles and crude comments until Archer's only defense was to spend as many hours in the library as possible, another reminder of home.

The boys had taken to calling him 'Junior,' and, once aware of his actual age, taunted him with 'sweet sixteen, never been kissed, Junior?' Such endless childish puns which only grew meaner and more frequent once he'd been publicly singled out by a senior professor in the medical school.

§

Archer trailed a group of boys in neatly buttoned blue jackets and perfectly-knotted ties on stiff, white collars. After crossing the campus, they entered a large lecture hall. He had been warned not to miss the opportunity to hear from senior faculty at the Medical College at the freshman introduction to the medical track. He could only assume it was Miss Della's second cousin, who'd helped with his entry and scholarship, who'd sent word to his dormitory.

Yet, even among other freshmen, Archer stood out. He looked much younger than the two years that separated him from the majority of freshmen. He noted how the others wore their jackets, blue blazers they called them, and their ties non-chalantly, almost negligently, yet still managed to appear neat down to their slicked and parted hair. Was it his imagination that they all seemed to know each other as well?

When he entered the arena-like lecture hall and gazed down into its pit, he was shocked to see how many freshmen had evidently expressed interest in the medical curriculum, given its many additional years of required study. At the same time, he noticed those gathered eyeing him skeptically. His youthfulness? His questionable haberdashery? He himself could see how cut-rate his jacket looked in comparison, dirt-brown against a sea of navy blue. But it was too late, and this was the best and only jacket he possessed.

He spied his roommate, Alton Peabody, in the crowd, but as soon as their eyes met, Alton ignored him, joking with his comrades nearby. They could have been his relatives in their similar striking appearance, the epitome of Joe College.

Willing himself not to blush, squaring his shoulders in imitation pride, Archer scuttled into the nearest aisle seat and purposely ignored the glances shifting his way. The august presence of the day's lecturer, entering the pit from its rear and standing up to the podium, finally distracted his fellow attendees.

Clad in an impeccable three-piece charcoal suit, high white collar, and a flawless bowtie, the speaker carefully surveyed the gathered crowd. He looked to be a good six-foot-plus, even with his salt and pepper hair flattened by gel against his scalp. Archer was awed. Given the first impression, he was hardly surprised when the speaker's welcome boomed and echoed around the large hall.

"I'm Dr. Errol Dole, a senior professor at the Medical College. I'm pleased to see so many freshmen, new to Harvard, already interested in our little college," Dr. Dole proclaimed. "Of course, it's a long road ahead to get there. Four years of difficult preparation for the even tougher four years to follow on your journey to a doctorate in medicine."

He leaned in confidentially. "Frankly, some of you won't make it that far, and the long road will weary most of you. But I promise each and every one of you this: those who hold fast to your dream of earning a medical degree from Harvard will be richly rewarded. Not just monetarily, not that it's unimportant," he added with a chuckle, "not just with the opportunities that will beat a path to your door, but in the pride you will feel for the rest of your lives being associated with our grand alma mater. Harvard University is the oldest, and dare I say most prestigious, institution of higher learning in these vast United States, if not the world."

When the speaker paused, clapping and cheers spontaneously arose. The attentive audience sat up straighter in their seats, none more so than Randy Archer, underage kid from Pittsburgh stepping into the greater world of his no-longer-secret ambitions.

Dole admonished those present to work diligently on the preparatory studies presented in their undergraduate years before he highlighted the rigors to follow. "For those of you who do well in your undergraduate studies, and are lucky enough to qualify *and* be accepted into the Medical College thereafter, you'll be struck immediately by an obvious difference unique to the medical field. The level of detail you must master in a medical setting requires you to apply that knowledge *in crisis mode*. What could be more stressful than a work environment that demands on-the-spot decisions, often of life-and-death consequence, suffused by the emotions of the sick as well as their loved ones?"

For some reason, the speaker's words called up the warm memory of Della Dolkowski standing up for Archer against his intimidating father and his bullying anger. Archer appreciated the bravery of the small young woman who would not be deterred in her support of him. Would he have such courage and commitment? It sounded like he'd have to in order to be a good MD, which he fully intended.

Archer tuned back in when he noticed hands raised around the hall, realizing he'd missed the lecturer's question. But the lecturer hadn't missed him or his daydreaming. "Young man," he heard, "on the aisle there, in the brown jacket. Yes, you," he responded when Archer, glancing side-to-side, pointed at himself. "Stand please, and state your name."

Archer came haltingly to his feet, pointing to himself again to verify whether, in fact, Dr. Errol Dole had meant him. Seemed he did. "Young man, state your name and tell us what specialty you might wish to pursue should you succeed to the Medical College and survive four years therein. As evidenced by your un-raised hand, you're disinclined to heed my advice to consider as much extra exposure to the pharmacological fields as can fit into your training, fields one senses are poised to dominate the future of medicine. So tell us, where might your interests lie at this early stage?"

Archer answered meekly, "Pathology. Sir."

"Speak up, man. We can't hear you. What specialty, you say?"

"Pathology, sir."

"Pathology? Is that it? Well now, all the subspecialties hold importance, but why the study of disease?"

Archer could feel his body-heat rising but gathered his strength to respond. "My first view through a microscope has haunted me since. The teeming life-forms in a riot of existence right at your fingertips and yet completely invisible and ignored as we live our day-to-day lives. Until, of course, those invisible forms can no longer be ignored."

"Rather poetic, Mr. . . . . Mr.? Do state your name, young man."

"Randy Archer, sir."

"Archer . . . Randall, you say? See me immediately after the lecture today, Randall. You may be seated." As Archer quickly reseated himself, he noticed those around him taking note of the inexplicable attention he'd garnered, the surprised eyes of his roommate amongst them.

The rest of Dr. Dole's introductory lecture fought with the buzzing in his ears as Randy, dubbed Randall, wondered what explained that attention from among the crowd of freshmen. But with a quick glance about the room, he recognized he would hardly be mistaken for just one of them. More than the clothing, it was an assurance, a sense of belonging he'd have to develop, and fast. He gulped, knowing he would soon find out what had drawn Dr. Dole's notice, fleeting glances reminding him that 'standing out' too often came at a very high price.

CHAPTER TWO

ISOLATIONISM

1922

Archer never got on with his roommate, Alton Peabody, an insufferable snob from Connecticut, even though he too was pre-med. The microscope Alton had unpacked that first day should have been the first clue. After discovering that unhappy coincidence and after the attention Professor Dole had lavished on Archer for whatever his reasons, dorm pranks became more mean-spirited, even cruel. He'd had to miss class when the weather turned bitter and the crossfire of water-balloon warfare had 'inadvertently' drenched his only jacket and pants. Archer had been forced to hang them over the radiator and wait for them to dry.

But nothing prevented Archer being called upon in the large lecture halls when no one could supply the answer a professor was looking for, something that had singled Archer out from his earliest school days and continued in Cambridge. He considered pretending not to know the answers, but given his 'inferior' background, age, and appearance, his reliable and agile brain was the only weapon he possessed. However, it further cooled things between the roommates.

Until the last straw. Archer returned from the shower to find his few articles of clothing missing from the closet. Peabody, deep into his studies, pretended not to notice. "All right, Alton, joke's over. Where are my clothes?"

He glanced up from his studies, looking convincingly perplexed. "Your clothes, Junior? Why, I haven't the faintest. In your closet, one would assume."

Archer opened wide the closet door, and both young men stared into its emptiness. "If not you, Alton, who has been in our room in the last thirty minutes? Surely you would have noticed that, despite your unswerving concentration on your studies."

Archer could see by his soured expression that he'd gone too far with that sarcastic reference to his roommate's scholastic difficulties. "Can't say I have, Junior. This biology course has me enraptured. I've seen no one. But hey, look, they'll be too large and long, but I can lend you a few things until the culprit is found." Alton opened his closet to a vast array of rich clothing and reached in. "Good heavens, man. These are not mine," he exclaimed emphatically, pulling out Archer's worn jacket and shoes, holding them as if they'd spread disease. "Here, take these before they infect mine. Or fall to pieces." He tossed them toward Archer, who caught them in a bundle.

That's it, Archer determined. Tomorrow, he would go to Dr. Dole and beg him to help him relocate. Anywhere would have to be better than here.

§

Dole's secretary, an eyebrow raised in suspicion, observed Archer as he begged for a few minutes of the doctor's time. "No appointment, young man? Dr. Dole is very, very busy. I'm not certain he'll—"

The office door suddenly opened, and Dole himself stepped out. "Look, Miss—" He stopped when he spied Archer. "Well, this is a surprise. How's the laboratory job working out, Archer?"

"Very well, Dr. Dole, thanks to you." Dole had offered him the plum position in the medical lab after his introductory lecture, surprising no one more than Archer himself. "But there is something I'd like to ask you. If you have a moment?"

The secretary jumped into action. "I was just telling this young man that, without an appointment, I was quite certain you wouldn't have time today, Dr. Dole."

"Just a few minutes, Dr. Dole, please. It's important."

Dole pulled out his pocket watch from his vest pocket. "That's all I have, Archer. A few minutes. Come in."

Archer came right to the point, so desperate was he to find a little peace in his living arrangements. "Dr. Dole, I don't wish to appear unappreciative of all you've already done for me. The laboratory job is a lifesaver, both in experience and the spending money it allows me. But I just don't get on well with my roommate, nor the rest of the boys in the dormitory actually. I've toughed it out most of freshman year, but if at all possible, I'd like to make a change. Could—could you help?"

"Who's your roommate, Archer?" When he told him, Dole snickered. "Ah yes, of course, Alton Peabody II. His father, Alton Peabody I, graduated medical school, and his son is attempting to follow in his father's footsteps. And let me guess, he finds your excelling where he struggles a bit much to take?"

Dole seated himself behind his desk, smiling to himself. "Problem is, Archer, you're living in the so-called Gold Coast. Those dormitories, built originally for wealthier students, became President Lowell's pet project in addressing the inequities between those well-off and those, well, less well-off. The other dorms I might get you moved to are in the 'Yard.' Most have no reliable heat or running water. Some don't even have indoor toilets! Are you truly that desperate?"

Archer reconsidered the cold Boston winter before replying, "Yes. Yes, sir, I am."

"Well then, I'll see what I can do. I take it you wish to move right away and not wait until your sophomore year or until the end of the semester? It's not that far off."

Archer gritted his teeth and nodded, rocking from foot to foot.

"All right then, I'll look into it. But while I've got you, Archer, there is something you could do for me in exchange. Have a seat."

He sat as directed before Dole's desk, wondering how he would survive an unheated dorm through the long Boston winter if that was what he'd just talked himself into.

Dole cleared his throat. "I'm pleased to have someone like you in the medical lab. It should help prepare you for medical school and give you a leg up, not that you appear to need one." He chose his words with care. "Anyway, I like to keep my fingers in all the goings-on around this college, and I'd like you to make it your business to keep your eyes and ears open in the lab. Find out what people are working on and how they're progressing or not, who's behind which studies and projects, what's working, what isn't, that kind of thing. Could you do that for me, Archer?"

"Well, of—of course, Dr. Dole. I could show interest in others' work there, watch their methods and progress. Is it something specific you're interested in?"

"No, no, just what's going on in general as well as the specifics when projects warrant. Nothing formal, Archer. No written reports. Just a verbal account, say, every month or so? We can establish a regular meeting time and keep our little discussions to ourselves. What do you say, Archer?"

"Sure, Dr. Dole. I can do that."

"Good. Knew I could count on you. Now then, let me get to work on your move. I'll reach out when I have good news for you."

§

After his first night in his single room in his new dormitory located in 'the Yard,' cramped but blessedly alone, Archer knew he'd either freeze to death or have to find a way to bundle himself against Boston's winters, which tended, he'd been told and now experienced, to drag on and on.

Dole's description was right about these, the oldest buildings on campus, some dating almost to Harvard's founding, the late seventeenth and early eighteenth centuries. They lacked modern amenities, the worst of which was lack of heat except from large fireplaces in strategic locations, one of which was *not* in his tiny single room at the far end of a hallway. The cost of the room, beside his agreement to keep Dole informed of doings in the medical laboratory, was oversight duties on the floor of his new dormitory.

"Keep the student shenanigans to a low roar," he'd been advised by the upperclassman who showed him his room. "That's basically all that's required of floor monitors. Just about anything except target practice with live ammunition goes, as you'll soon see." When Archer laughed, assuming hyperbole, the pudgy, short man in a suit bulging at the waist said, "I don't exaggerate. It's happened. And if it does again, remember to keep your head down!"

He studied Archer for a moment from intense brown eyes which betrayed a hint of mirth. "A blind eye might be your best weapon, Archer. But, if you take a stand, don't back down. Don't ever let them see you back down. That's my best advice from someone who has been in your shoes. Good luck. Oh, and where's your stuff? You need help moving in?"

"No, I can handle it. I'll go back to Mass Hall for it later, thanks anyway."

Before the door to the hallway swung closed, several large, beefy freshmen in their long johns crowded the doorway to get a look at the new authority figure on the floor, charged with keeping a semblance of order. The tallest had a football he tossed and caught repeatedly as the three stared at Archer in apparent surprise. All three burst into raucous laughter as they peered down on him, younger and nearly half their size.

The tallest one introduced himself. "I'm Jamison, and you're the new floor man, Mr.—Mr. . . . well, what is your name? I don't mean to sound disrespectful, but are you old enough for this job?"

"Randall Archer." He extended his hand and shook with all three, whose giggles repeatedly erupted before being partially subdued.

"You play football, Randall?" one asked. When Archer shook his head no, he added, "Too bad really. It's one way to stay warm around here. Be mindful when you leave your room. Hallway football can get rough. We wouldn't want you caught up in a mass tackle, though officially it is called 'touch' football. On occasion, we do get carried away. Come on, boys," he added to his teammates as all three swaggered back into the hallway.

Despite such veiled threats and worries these encounters stirred, when Archer stepped from the building into the Yard, the beauty of the wintry scene banished them. Red brick and white-trimmed buildings wore majestic crowns of glistening snow. The icing of white also covered the towering trees and stretching lawns crisscrossed by walkways. The elm trees, impervious and far above it all, looked regal and untouchable, like they'd stand forever. The imposing spectacle was what he'd anticipated since the first time he'd heard Harvard mentioned as an outside possibility in his young life, and he'd looked up the university in the library.

The scene provided a moment of stability and serenity, unlike the life looming before Archer in his new capacity in his new dormitory. Had he been too hasty in asking for this transfer?

But the wind and cold chased away his reflections and

reminded him of his mission. He hoped to sneak off campus undetected and into the nearby church where he'd been told secondhand goods could be had for a pittance, which was all he could come up with.

At least something warm to sleep in. And maybe, just maybe, his own blue blazer?

CHAPTER THREE

PROHIBITION

1924

When he'd begun work in the medical laboratory back in 1921 in his first-semester as a pre-med freshman, Archer was assigned the most menial of tasks. Disinfecting lab equipment, checking supplies and sorting them into useable allotments, and storing them as designated. He sterilized tables, floors, and equipment as necessary. But he caught on quickly, and Dole seemed more than pleased with his work.

Now, several years into his tenure at the lab and the college, he'd moved onto more important tasks. Dr. Dole still expected special reports on a regular basis. For example, to check on the progress of a drug for which animal tests were in progress.

"You know where the results are stored, Archer. Copy the significant findings to date and bring them directly to me. And as always, Archer, keep this between us."

Archer rationalized that the level of oversight Dole maintained had mostly to do with his deep concern for human health.

In what should have been his junior year of pre-med—though with summer classes he was moving through the curriculum an

entire year ahead of the norm—Dole informed Archer he was
being assigned to the backup team, testing a drug that would
enter human trials as soon as its last hurdle of animal testing
had been cleared. Thrilled, Archer knew it was a big leap in
responsibility and that it demonstrated Dole's tremendous trust
in his abilities. Archer was working alone, straightening up after
a review session on the project, when Dole appeared in person
in the now-deserted medical lab.

"There was an anomaly in the results of that animal test we
spoke of," Dole began. "I'm afraid it's going to set us back significantly with the human trial stage which we were expecting to
begin next week. That presents bigger problems for the College.
As you know, payment for our testing services is tied to specific
trial stages and time frames. I'm sure you'll agree, based on test
results from each prior stage, the final outcome is a foregone
conclusion. Every step has clearly pointed to it. So it would be a
great service to the Medical College as well as the University if
you would tweak that anomaly so we could move forward and
remain on schedule."

"You're asking me to *change* the results of the animal trials,
sir?"

"You record the data." Dole cast a meaningful glance at the
stack of papers in Archer's arms. "Fix the single anomaly posted
therein until its retesting proves the result. You'd be buying us
the funds and the time necessary to stay on track while what
is most likely an error in amount dispensed or an improp-
erly selected rat from one of the sub-groups has been worked
through, as we know it most certainly will.

"What I'm asking," continued an increasingly testy Dole, his
face flushing as he took in Archer's disbelief, "is that you rectify an obvious error which will be borne out in the concur-
rent retesting. Otherwise, we'll fall behind by months. Hasn't
each prior stage—specimen slides and cultures—shown strong,
repetitive, and positive results? I'm asking no more than to

eliminate the time to rectify an oversight which has occurred and which will be ruled out at the same time we move forward. That's all."

"Shouldn't the lead researcher, Dr. Cecil, be the one to handle—"

"Archer! What I'm telling you is I don't have time to fool with this. Either you'll do me this small favor, or you won't. Which is it?"

"Of—of course, Dr. Dole. I'll do as you ask. And I'll volunteer to help run the retesting behind the scenes to confirm it after the fact. If—if that's what you wish."

"Good man, Archer. You'll make a fine pathologist. Deliver the rectified data to me personally by tomorrow. Again, just between us. Good day."

§

Tercentenary Theatre was the vast central green space, resembling an undulating parkland, where graduations and other ceremonies were held at Harvard. Today saw it dappled by shade trees and sunlight, sectioned by walkways, superimposed with chairs and a dais for Archer's pre-med graduation ceremony. His graduation was taking place a full year earlier than the boys he'd begun pre-med with three years before.

Did that explain the dirty looks directed his way from what had been *upperclassmen* with whom he was graduating? Or was it that he looked and felt ridiculous on this sweltering spring day in the voluminous black gown that caught and swirled around him as he scurried down the row, stepping over and on their feet, seeking his assigned place?

Or was it simply because he was late and the ceremony had begun? Could he help that he had been summoned to a special meeting of all dormitory and floor personnel after the fire that had partially destroyed Massachusetts Hall? Couldn't they have chosen another morning to review and tighten emergency procedures? And why did it not matter that his duties monitoring his dormitory floor had ended that very day? And good riddance!

Seated in the beating sun, he tuned into the ceremonial speeches of both back-patting congratulations and rousing exhortations for the future, while thoughts about medical school crowded his head. He'd made it. He'd been accepted as Dole had assured him he would. He found himself one step closer to his dream of becoming a noted and honored doctor of pathology. Years of hard work lay ahead, to be sure, but he'd accomplished something no one in his family had before him. He'd graduated college. With honors. And now a doctorate in the offing. Ha! So much for 'Mr. Thinks He So Smart.' Gazing around at the sea of black gowns in orderly rows, Archer, for the moment, regretted not sending the printed graduation announcement home to Pittsburgh, to be certain they all knew.

Oh, and one to Della! Miss Della, who had opened not only this world to him. Thinking back on her now, years later, Archer was surprised at the tightening in his groin beneath all that black fabric. Her pliable and welcoming body had opened an equally profound door, but one he'd effectively shut at Harvard. It wasn't simply the lack of women in his classes. His drive to stay ahead of the jealous naysayers who would relish witnessing him fail forced all else into the background. Where it would have to stay for another six years, at least.

Pondering Della now, he realized how strange it was that he'd never met her mysterious second cousin who had facilitated it all. He'd never even learned his name. She'd given him only the information for the housing administrator when he arrived in Boston. Initially so overwhelmed, Archer had put it out of his mind, until now at his graduation years later. He'd have to ask Della about her cousin the next time he was in contact.

What next time? He'd never even sent a single postcard as she'd requested. Three years ago.

CHAPTER FOUR

CRASH

1929

"I say, old boy, you look to be quite proficient at that," came a clipped voice so unexpected and close by, Archer froze, laboratory implements clutched in his gloved hands. Above the surgical mask that concealed half of his face, his black brows pinched low over his dark eyes as they shifted toward the voice. His unkempt hair and soiled lab coat completed the impression of 'mad scientist.' His was a look cultivated by both his general disinterest in appearances and his notable lack of financial wherewithal, had he been interested.

Archer stared at the tall stranger, a man he'd noticed before, though they'd never spoken. The man invaded the late-night medical laboratory far too frequently, disrupting the usual emptiness Archer preferred. Since the stranger had set up a research project at the far end of the laboratory, rows of high-top tables and covered equipment had kept the two men at a distance. Archer had noted, however, that the man surrounded himself in his workplace with microscopes.

With a mere nod of acknowledgment once or twice as they

passed in the night, neither man had considered carrying rela-
tions beyond minimal politeness, until now evidently. 'Point-
less' was the unspoken assumption Archer had held. *What's
this crossing of the lines anyway?* he wondered, mindful of his
frayed and stained scruffiness. The stark contrast the stranger
provided irritated him.

The interloper had undoubtedly noticed Archer's status sig-
nals, or lack thereof. *Isn't this why people work so hard to present
themselves—to forestall wasted time without the necessity of
meaningless words? Had the recent financial collapse opened
minds on the other side of the divide?* he questioned himself.

Archer had consigned the lanky gent to a type far too familiar after years at Harvard, a residue of prep school and privilege
worn proudly for all to see. Fastidious in a spotless lab jacket, high
starched collar, and bowtie, the man's erect carriage added to that
indefinable quality Archer still struggled to develop. Was it confidence in his superiority—his former roommate, Alton Peabody
II, coming to mind? An ingrained assumption of belonging?

As Archer studied him up close for the first time, the man's
watered-down blue eyes and lacquered-blond waves, gleaming
beneath overhead lights, distracted him. But the guileless smile
Archer observed suggested a certain innocence, or perhaps an
anticipation of only good things to come. Imagine that . . .

The intruder cleared his throat before straightening his
bowtie and tugging at his tight collar, both of which seemed
ridiculously excessive to Archer, given the deserted late-night
lab. He himself had no time for such status-bound irrelevan-
cies. He had a career to pursue!

"By the looks of it," the preppie said, further to his opening
comment, "you've been at this for quite some time."

Archer shifted his attention away from the stranger and back
to the area where he assembled study slides, intending to finish
the one he had begun before this interruption. On a thin rect-
angular piece of clear glass, he placed a small sample taken from

either tissue or fluid-draws from the day's biopsies. After adding a fixative solution, he topped it all with a 'coverslip,' another thin rectangle of glass, to complete a specimen slide ready for study via microscope. Before placing it aside, Archer held the finished slide up to the light. To the naked eye, it looked like no more than a small piece of smudged glass.

"I should be good at assembling these slides," Archer conceded through puffs in his mask. "I've been doing this, making slides, for eight years now in this lab, throughout my tenure at Harvard, long before I entered the medical school and worked my way to intern."

With his intended path to a pathology specialty, Archer had always considered the chance to work in the medical lab a privilege as well as a bit of uncanny luck. He marveled again at Dr. Dole's plucking him from a lecture hall full of pre-meds, still unsure of why, besides the clothing that caused him to stand out. His initial conversation with Dole that followed had quickly laid bare Archer's humble background, his full scholarship, and Archer's obvious lack of sophistication and affluence. Did that explain why Dole instantly offered Archer part-time work in the lab? Because he clearly needed it? Though he thought of it often, he'd probably never know all of Dole's reasons.

Dole, on his rise through the Medical College's hierarchy toward becoming its dean, had only admitted to being 'on the lookout' for outstanding young men who, with time, guidance, and his insider knowledge and connections, might win his trust. Surprised but flattered, Archer had pinned his future on the one who promised to become the most powerful man in the College. After all, he figured, brains and ambition carry one only so far in the real world.

"You—you are an intern!" The tall man's shocked comment brought Archer back to the late-night lab. "You've *completed* medical school? I thought you were, uh, that is, I assumed . . . you—you look younger to me, that's all I'm trying to say." The man seemed flummoxed by his *faux pas* and hastened to cover it. "Please excuse me, we haven't met. I'm Adam Wakefield." He extended his hand.

Archer indicated his gloves, which conveniently excused him from a handshake.

"Well," Wakefield paused, apparently interpreting Archer's non-introduction as a brushoff. "Sorry. Didn't mean to intrude. As the only two here every night, it just seemed unneighborly not to at least introduce ourselves."

With still no response from Archer, Wakefield mumbled, "So then, I'll leave you to your important work." Wakefield snaked through the semi-lit tables to his own workspace on the far side of the lab.

§

"It's Adam, right? Adam Wakefield, I believe you said yesterday."

Clattering a small tool onto the table beside a microscope he appeared to be constructing, Wakefield looked up in astonishment at the ill-mannered young man from across the lab whom he'd not quite met the night before. Without his protective face-covering, Archer's cherubic face reinforced a youthful first impression, offset by the intensity of his dark-eyed gaze.

"I asked around about you," Archer admitted, "at the Medical College."

"Really?" Wakefield leaned against a stool. "And what did you find out that you couldn't have asked me yourself last night in our rather abbreviated conversation?" Wakefield's irritation bled through his words.

"Well, I—ah, I heard you're from an important family around here, called Boston 'Brahmins' for some reason. And you're *not* part of the Medical College. I mean to say, we are in no way competitors here or anywhere." Wakefield's forehead wrinkled at that comment as he huffed. "I was a little rushed last night,"

Archer continued, "and hope I did not come off as impolite. I'm Dr. Randall Archer, Intern." He extended his hand, and Wakefield eventually shook it.

"Charmed," he added ironically, which Archer didn't catch.

"So, Mr. Wakefield, what is it you do here at the medical laboratory every night, if you're not part of our College? Apparently you have unlimited access?"

"Technically, it's 'doctor.'" To Archer's confused expression he explained, "*Dr.* Wakefield, the PhD variety. And what I do around here is merely groundbreaking research and development of the humble microscope. Despite three hundred years of usage, there's been little improvement to the microscope's two most vital features, magnification and resolution or clarity.

"Both my master's and PhD were devoted to said improvements," Wakefield went on, perusing his handiwork fondly. "My dissertation was wordily entitled, 'The Optics of the Microscope, Limitations and Potential for Improvement.'" He smiled at a thought. "I count myself lucky to have won this post-doctoral opportunity to put my theories to the test here at my alma mater, especially after my second sabbatical.

"The dean was none too happy about either of them, my sabbaticals that is—the first, the requisite 'Grand Tour,' following my master's; the second, traveling the western United States after my PhD ..."

Seemingly lost in pleasant memories, Wakefield recalled himself to the late-night lab and Intern Archer's continued confusion. "Sorry. I do go on. Anyway, Dean Bainbridge at Physics interested your dean in my work. And easy access to this lab, which abounds in the study slides needed to test my technical improvements, was meant to speed things along."

Wakefield glanced at Archer. "I'm not boring you, Randall, am I? I tend to digress." Once Archer shook his head hesitantly, Wakefield spoke again. "So, as a lab tech finished with both pre-med and medical school, you of course understand the basics of the microscope. Both aspects have historically been limited by the lighting source used to illuminate those study slides you assemble." He again trailed off in thought.

"Will you ever forget your first view of the microscopic world?" Wakefield abruptly switched subjects. "I've owned, dis-assembled, and reassembled probably a hundred microscopes in my youth. My roommate at St. Paul's was none too happy about the row of them cluttering our dorm room." Wakefield chuckled at his visions.

Archer inserted into the meandering conversation, "I've used hundreds of microscopes over the years, but I've never seen one that looked anything like yours. What is all this?" he asked as he circled the large, complex scope under construction.

"Oh, right, just getting to that, old boy. To address the lim-itations of the lighting source, along with other improvements, I've built into my scopes multiple illumination sources like a monochromatic beam, polarized light, dark- and light-field capabilities, infrared, slit lamp, and so forth. The result is a greatly expanded 'useable spectrum,' that is, the range of light frequencies my microscope can utilize."

Archer continued his perusal of the microscope before him as he considered its physicist-creator's words. "So, *Dr.* Wake-field, what do you expect to gain with this strange-looking con-traption and its expanded useable spectrum?"

"Adam will do. Unless you prefer the honorific '*Dr.* Archer'?" Archer just snorted. "Right, so Randall, this 'contraption' as you call it, already reaches unheard of levels of magnification." Wakefield glanced around the lab at the many shrouded micro-scopes, near and far. "Of the scopes in this medical lab, most magnify one to two thousand times, correct? Twenty-five-hun-dred times tops?"

Archer nodded. "Most magnify around one thousand times."

"Well," Wakefield smiled broadly, displaying perfect, white teeth, "I am well past such paltry numbers and still aim for more."

"Like?" Archer asked, his brows raised skeptically.

"Like sixty thousand times, give or take." Wakefield anticipated at least an astonished whistle, but Archer only stared at
the scope, then at its creator, in disbelief.

"Really? Adam," he finally reacted, "why, that could change
everything in medicine. Potentially everything . . ." Archer's
mind spun scenarios, factoring in the advantage such powers
to perceive might provide him on his way to becoming *the*
world-renowned pathologist.

Both men took seats across the lab table with Wakefield's
unfinished microscope between them, lost in their own
thoughts, until Wakefield began, "It's perplexing though, I
must confess, Randall. With all the leaps I've made in magnification and resolution powers, there simply haven't been the
astounding new discoveries I'd anticipated.

"Perhaps I expected too much," Wakefield considered. "Given
the profound discoveries made this century by the great physicists like Einstein and Bohr, particularly the latter's discovery
of the numerous subcomponents within the atom, I suppose I
dreamed of similar revelations via my scope."

After a brief pause, Wakefield continued, "You'll recall that,
until Bohr, the atom was widely accepted as *the basic and indivisible building block* of all solid matter throughout the entire universe." The hulking frame of Jimmie McGrevey flashed across
Archer's mind with that statement. "With Bohr's discovery, the
field of physics, as known since Newton, was upended."

Wakefield trailed off into his mental wanderings, and Archer
checked the wall clock. That prompted Wakefield to withdraw
his pocket watch. "How I do run on," he conceded, seeing the
hour well past midnight.

Archer stood and stretched. "Fascinating, Dr. Wakefield, I
must say. I'd be happy to assist in any way I can toward your
ultimate success. But for now, duty calls. Slides await assembly.

Unfortunately, they won't assemble themselves."

"I do hope I haven't bored you, Randall. I'm hard to stop once I launch into my favorite subject."

"Actually, not at all, Adam. You've inspired me to ponder new possibilities. Well," he said, eyeing the microscope one last time, "let me know if I can help." With that, Archer crossed the darkened laboratory, weighing the incomparable tool he might have stumbled upon to further distance himself from the medical pack.

Wakefield, watching him go, thought, *There is something you might help me with, Randall. But it can wait for another day.* "Tomorrow night then, old man."

§

Archer's years on campus had perfected his ability to move through it unnoticed. From the first, he'd learned he had enough challenges fitting-in without spotlighting them.

Bundled in all the clothing he owned against a frigid wind scudding snow across the frozen earth, Archer kept his head down and his shoulders hunched against the wintry gusts. Moving fast retained some bodily warmth while lessening his time in the unforgiving elements. In the evening gloom of the short winter day, he scurried toward the medical lab feeling invisible and enjoying the anonymity.

But despite the frigid weather, he was not alone. Dodging all obstacles which could slow him, disjointed snippets of crunching footsteps and muffled conversations, even bursts of laughter, infiltrated his scarf-bound ears. He trudged determinedly onward even when he heard what sounded like his name, assuming it was no more than a trick of the howling wind. It was far too cold to stop anyway. Until ice-crushing footsteps forced him to a halt.

"Randall!" It was unmistakable. Archer glanced up into the

face of Adam Wakefield, barely visible beneath a warm-looking fedora which Archer eyed enviously. With a thick scarf knotted around his neck and ears, Wakefield looked impervious to the cold. A heavy woolen coat extended the length of his body. *No,* Archer concluded, *the coat's more luxurious than wool. Cashmere?*

"Whoa there, Dr. Archer. It's me, Adam. Adam Wakefield from the lab."

Archer gritted his teeth, rich layers of wool and cashmere close enough to touch adding to his physical discomfort. But the threadbare scarf he'd tied around his own face made his expression invisible. "Hi," Archer mumbled through the wool, the cold already overtaking him.

"Where have you been?" Wakefield demanded. "Haven't seen you in the lab in a couple weeks."

"An extremely demanding rotation," Archer replied, risking the uncovering of his face to do so. "But it's over now, and I have time for my extracurricular lab work again. I'm heading there now. You?" He drew the wrap back over his face, shifting from foot to foot to force his already-coagulating circulation.

"Shake a leg, Adam," a female voice behind them called out. "We're freezing here!"

Both Archer and Wakefield glanced toward the voice coming from the small group Wakefield had detached himself from. He nodded at them and turned back to Archer, who stared long-ingly at the assemblage in their insulating furs, hats, boots, and gloves. *You're freezing?* he grumbled inwardly, shifting faster and hugging himself, aware his meager layering looked ridicu-lous compared to real winter clothing. *Who are these overly tall people?* he wondered crossly. *Is everyone in Adam's world as tall and lanky, and yes, regal, as he?*

"No lab for me tonight, I'm afraid," Wakefield answered Archer's forgotten question. "My best friend since childhood, we attended St. Paul's together, is celebrating his birthday with a few of us and his sister. I've known the family my entire life and well, I'm taking the night off. My microscope will have to wait."

"Adam!" A fur-bedecked presence inserted itself. "We'll die if we don't get out of this wind. What's the holdup here?" When Wakefield acknowledged the female speaker, his blue eyes softened perceptibly, and Archer noticed.

"Sorry, Elizabeth. Be right there." When she didn't retreat, instead staring at Archer curiously, Wakefield said, "Oh, I forget myself. Elizabeth, this is a friend from the medical lab. He likes off-hours as much as I do. We tend to share the empty lab between us most nights. Elizabeth Perrish, meet Randall Archer, Dr. Randall Archer, MD, interning just now, but still keeping hours in the lab." He nodded at Archer. "You must need no sleep if what one hears about medical training is true. Randall, meet Elizabeth Perrish."

With a fuzzy cap tightly fitting her scalp, a few dark brown waves framing her striking face, the young woman offered Archer her gloved hand, a smile lighting her large eyes. "Pleased to meet you, Dr. Archer. Any friend of Adam's is a friend of mine."

Though it pained him to loosen an arm from his body, the cold instantly invading its place, he took her hand and smiled through his physical misery. Those eyes were dark and expressive, he saw, perhaps a deep blue, though it was hard to tell in the evening dusk. But definitely amused or of good humor. "Hm-mm. Nice to meet you, Miss Perrish."

Perrish, Archer contemplated. Like the glaring statue he passed regularly on campus? Likely related, he decided, based on her expensively clad, angular body, and that indefinable quality again—a self-assured bearing. He remembered to release her hand.

"Elizabeth," she corrected him. "I'm sorry but really Adam, we must be going. We'll all freeze to death if we don't. Prescott will never forgive you if his twenty-ninth birthday should prove his last."

"Be right with you, Elizabeth. You go on. I'll catch up."

Wakefield pivoted to Archer. "Glad you'll be back in the lab when I return tomorrow night, old boy. I worried I'd scared you off with my verbal meanderings. I will see you then, correct, Randall?"

Archer nodded, feeling frost tingling his toes, fingers, nose, and ears. He dragged his eyes from Elizabeth's retreating figure. "Uh-huh. I'll be there."

"Good!" Wakefield exclaimed before dashing to catch his companions, who loudly complained that his 'dawdling' had given them all frostbite.

As Archer hurried off in the other direction, Elizabeth, the only female in the group, could be heard asking, "Who was *that*?"

As he fled for the shelter of the laboratory, it never occurred to Archer to wonder at her meaning. He'd been reminded over and over again of his obvious otherness which her question implied.

§

Pleased to find Archer assembling slides from the day's biopsies and fluid-draws, Wakefield stopped the next night at his worktable, sniffing at the strong odor of sterilization which always permeated the space. "I say, Randall, it is good to find you hard at work again. Welcome back, old boy." Archer nodded, but didn't slow his tasks.

Wakefield seemed content to observe. After Archer completed a number of slides, Wakefield interrupted, saying, "Ahem, I do hope you recall offering to help me with my microscope's development. Actually, I've been thinking you very well could help. When you stopped showing up here in the lab, it alarmed me a bit. I am pleased your rotation ended and you're back. For a while, do you think?"

Archer nodded again as Wakefield studied his neat workspace, drifting off in thought before asking, "Tell me exactly what steps you take in assembling those slides."

"What?" Archer stopped for a double take, suspicious eyes above his mask leveled at Wakefield's. "You mean . . ." Archer set aside his implements, loosened the upper tie on his mask, and allowed it to fall around his neck. "As if *you* would have to ask, Adam. You know perfectly well, since you use them for your own project, what it is I do here."

"Humor me, just for a moment."

Archer paused to consider possible humiliating traps, and harrumphed. "I place a small sample of biopsied tissue or drawn fluids from patients at one of our affiliated hospitals—mainly Mass General—on a slide in preparation for study by micro-scope. We can also test potential remedies on these samples." Archer's black eyes narrowed. "But you know all that, Adam, so why inquire? And why now?" *Is this the moment when, subtly or otherwise, I'm reminded I'm not one of you? And never will be?* The imposing assemblage of friends he'd seen Wakefield with the night before in their rich, warm outerwear mocked him.

"Yes—yes, of course I know all that," Wakefield replied dis-missively. "I've used specimen slides continuously to test the powers of my microscopes. I was questioning what *else* you put on those slides, besides the tissue or fluid. I've watched you apply a liquid—a chemical, a wash, a setting solution of some sort—on top of the specimen on the glass base before you overlay it with the coverslip, correct?"

Archer nodded, confused but still wary.

"What I was getting at," Wakefield explained, "is a ques-tion which has been bothering me for some time. Specifically, what effect do those preparatory solutions have on the samples themselves? I know, as you do, that solutions have been used historically to fix, solidify, or preserve specimens, but espe-cially to augment visibility. The limited magnification powers of common microscopes require it."

Wakefield sank onto on a stool, an act Archer had come to recognize meant he anticipated taking some time on this

subject. "You've undoubtedly read about the possibility of utilizing electrons to greatly increase the magnifying powers of
the microscope. It's still in development in Germany and else-
where, and no prototype has yet come to market. However, I've
followed the concept's progress closely. If it bears out, an electron microscope promises to far surpass even the magnification powers I anticipate with my microscopes.

"But experiments with the evolving electron microscopes,
even at magnification powers multiples of the sixty thousand
times I now approach, has *not* to date unearthed the unexpected, let alone the revolutionary. Of course it's early, but I've
been obsessing over that disappointing *non*-revelation for as
long as I've been following it. I have mentioned that even my
new microscopes' large leaps in magnification powers have
borne similarly *underwhelming* results.

"Then, I read a research paper about the electron microscope that started me thinking. In it," Wakefield went on, "the
author speculates that microbial life-forms might not survive
the electron bombardment such microscopes use to illuminate specimens under study." He gazed blankly right through
Archer. "At minimum, one could assume a shower of electrons
would change a microbe's inherent charge ... which would then
initiate subsequent changes in cell shape and function ..."

Wakefield, brow crinkled in concentration, took his time
as usual getting to the point while Archer deliberated over the
phrase 'electron bombardment.' Scanning his recollections from
undergraduate physics, he recalled that all matter contains an
inherent charge, a vibration likened to energy or electricity. And
that moving matter creates ... But he couldn't call up any more.

"So," Archer carefully formed the question he assumed
Wakefield would eventually get to, "speculation about the effect
of electrons bombarding the study specimens caused you to
wonder what effect the preparatory chemicals I use in assembling study slides might also have on—"

"Precisely!" Wakefield jumped excitedly to the point. "At the risk of stating the obvious, the field of medicine does not study living samples, does it? Your preparatory solutions 'fix' the sample. Or put another way, those solutions extinguish life."

Archer's heart beat a little faster at the implications of these dangerous ideas bandied about so freely. He realized he too needed to sit to carefully consider. He scraped a nearby stool closer and sat facing Wakefield as his mind traveled back in time to Dr. Dole's classroom.

"Of course the specimens are dead!" Dr. Dole had retorted, outraged at Archer's 'impudent' question put to him before the crowded lecture hall. Archer was still confused and embarrassed by how an innocent query—how did medicine expect to learn the secrets of life by studying dead specimens?—had drawn such ire.

"The specimens are 'set,' young man, 'fixed,'" Dole had decreed, intent on the public humiliation of the ungrateful student he'd selected as his personal protégé. "May I remind you that these methods have been tested and used for hundreds of years? Unless you have something superior to offer the field, medicine has found no better way to utilize the microscope for study. Pretreatment chemicals to enhance visibility are necessitated even today, by our most advanced microscopes. Unless again, you have a better idea to offer us?"

Archer hadn't and didn't. But, scrutinizing the man seated opposite him, he thought Wakefield just might. He, a physicist, demonstrated no hesitation in probing established medical canon as Archer had inadvertently, and only once. The resulting public shaming had silenced him. He still could not erase the sound of the tittering medical students, happy to witness the deposing, or at least the demoralizing, of Dole's *wunderkind* who, all the while, could not suppress his blush.

Archer gazed across the lab to Wakefield's unfinished microscope, personal dread of further mortification and erosion of

Dole's favor at war with Wakefield's intriguing ideas, which had been stifled but never fully repressed in Archer's analytical mind.

He was still debating his response when the laboratory door clattered open, banging against the wall. Both men started at the unexpected disruption of the deserted lab at the late hour, which ushered in a large, well-tailored man with a full head of silvering hair, rushing toward them. "Archer!" the man shouted, dodging laboratory tables on rapid approach.

"Dr.—Dr. Dole!" Archer blurted, reddening and aghast. Had his crushing memories at this man's hands conjured this sudden appearance? Was Dr. Dole just in time to remind Archer yet again of *established* medical tenets?

The man closed in on Wakefield and Archer at the worktable like a tempest, and automatically, they both braced. "It's—why, it's uncanny," Archer choked out as Dole clamored to a halt before them, "but—but I was just thinking about you, Dr. Dole, and your advice which I—I always found, uh, beneficial."

"Evening," Dole offered brusquely to Wakefield. "Or morning I should say." Dismissing him, he addressed Archer. "Sorry to interrupt, Archer, but there's a bit of a problem I know you'll remedy for us. We need someone to cover the lab over the Christmas break. Immediately, I thought of you. You're not going anywhere, right? It's not like you have a family you'd dis-appoint. And I doubt you'd mind a few extra hours added to your pay now, would you? Times are tough and only getting tougher."

Wakefield observed the fluster the potent man, large in stature and overbearing in presence, evoked in Archer, who shrank before his eyes. Wakefield came to his feet, saying, "You'll excuse me, gentlemen, but I must get back to work. See you tomorrow night, Randall."

"Who's *that*," Dole asked after Wakefield had left. When Archer answered with his name and college affiliation, Dole repeated, "Wakefield. Yes, I'm familiar with the name, the family.

How did a 'physicist,'" the title sounded distasteful in Dole's mouth, "gain late-night access to the medical lab? And why haven't I heard about it in your reports?"

"He's working on a project that could radically improve the microscope. The Dean of Physics believed it best he work where the necessary testing slides proliferate. I assumed you or the dean had granted him access. One of his prototypes is across the way there."

"Hmm," Dole replied, eyeing Wakefield's strange-looking microscope from a distance. "Well," he refocused the full weight of his attention on Archer. "We have a deal then, correct, Archer, over the break?" Without waiting for a response, he added, "Our trade knows no holidays, I'm afraid.

"And just between you and me," Dole leaned in and lowered his voice, "now is a very good time to help out the dean in any way we can. It's not public knowledge yet, but he's planning to step down and is finalizing a succession plan as we speak. Meaning, it behooves us both to be helpful just now.

"Play your cards right, Archer," Dole continued, "and perhaps I can get you assigned to the human trial for the pharmaceutical company's new drug we've agreed to test. Such an assignment is a bit premature at your stage, but it would nicely feather your cap." Archer said nothing, the warm fedora Wakefield had worn the night before rising before his mind's eye.

Dole wound up his mission. "All right then, good lad. I'll see the schedule reflects you standing in over the holidays. Good holiday, Archer," he added, melting into the twilight of the semi-lit lab. "You need more light around here," Dole tossed over his shoulder as he dashed for the exit. "And no more omissions of the lab's doings! I'll decide what's important or not."

CHAPTER FIVE

TRICKLE DOWN

1930

Even at a distance, Wakefield's uncharacteristic slump, seated before his microscope, broadcast dejection. He stared into space, even after Archer arrived tableside.

"What's wrong?" Archer asked.

Finding Archer beside him, Wakefield startled from his deep contemplation. "Oh! Randall! I didn't see you come in. I was thinking about something . . . unrelated to microscopy, I'm afraid." A long, slow sigh followed. "That stock market dive last October, the plunging economy, it's given everyone the jitters, I suppose. But I was just informed by my father that he'd invested most of the family money in the biggest banks. At dinner last night, he warned that many high-ranking officials think even the largest, most powerful companies will, sooner or later, succumb to a severe squeeze—if not complete failure. And worse, he said, 'A major shareholder pulling funds out now only invites an earlier catastrophe.'"

Wakefield sighed again. "I'm not well versed in monetary concerns but as I understand it, he's trapped, *we're* trapped, along with most of our wealth as the financial sector teeters on collapse.

"Of course," Wakefield conceded, "the entire country and the world are failing as well." Another forlorn exhalation slipped out. "Strange, I've never paid much mind to the family fortune—until now, when it's slipping through our fingers."

"No use wallowing, is there?" Wakefield sat up and focused his translucent blue eyes on Archer, who paid more attention to his microscope than a problem he could only wish for—enough money to worry about losing. Wakefield turned to better news. "At least it's done, my microscope, and I think we've exceeded the sixty-thousand-times magnification powers I promised. Here, take a look at this influenza specimen."

"Influenza?" Archer drew back at the slide in Wakefield's ungloved hands. "After the epidemic that killed twenty million people a dozen years ago? That slide must be handled with more care, Adam!"

"Twenty million . . ." Wakefield repeated, shaking his head, "and that on the heels of the Great War which ended the same year." Wakefield's voice grew hoarse. "Nineteen-eighteen . . . the year I lost both my siblings. My brother was killed in France as the war was coming to a close. And my sister died right here at home of influenza. One of the twenty million."

Archer had no idea how to navigate such emotional waters, so he squeezed Wakefield's shoulder tentatively and muttered, "I'm sorry, Adam. That's—that's sad."

"Yes," Wakefield agreed, dabbing his eyes. "It is sad. Seems there's never a shortage of bad news.

"So anyway, take a look through my scope," Wakefield offered, brightening at the reintroduction of his pet subject. "You know better than I, Randall, the pretreated flu sample on this slide is no longer infectious. It's as dead as its victims."

Happy for a change of topic, no matter how macabre, Archer peered down the viewer, made adjustments to it for height and vision, then studied the greatly magnified disease sample, arrested and frozen in place for as long as the slide would be used. He stared for some moments before sitting back. He glanced around the room and said in a lowered voice, "You know, Adam, you may have made a valid point. *Over* sixty-thousand-times magnification should surely reveal something science hasn't before seen. That's thirty to sixty times *more* magnification power than in most microscopes in this lab—Harvard's *state-of-the-art* medical laboratory.

"Maybe," Archer guardedly allowed, "*maybe* your theory about fixative solutions, applied to study slides for various reasons, is correct. Maybe they do in fact have unwanted side effects, like those bombarding electrons you mentioned, used by the electron microscope. That's what originally started you wondering. Do common setting solutions added to specimens erase, kill, or otherwise affect the life of the very microbes medicine seeks to study?"

"Awfully glad to hear you say that, old boy!" Wakefield's mood lifted again, money worries elbowed aside by his overarching desire to prove the value of his radically improved microscope. "I've waited to make this suggestion, Randall. But might I suggest a little independent research of our own? You prepare a few slides for us to study 'fresh' from the biopsies and draws that come in tomorrow? No pretreatments or additives of any kind applied? That is, still-living specimens?"

Archer carefully scanned the lab again for unwanted ears. The mere suggestion of skirting laboratory protocol, something he had been recognized and rewarded for assiduously enforcing all these years, conjured Dr. Dole's ruthless rebukes. The guffaws of his fellow classmates still rankled. Both had redoubled Archer's paranoid avoidance of rule-breaking.

"Well," Wakefield pressed, "can't you? What's the harm in taking a look at living specimens, Randall? Make your slides as you've always done, just leave out any and all additives. Isn't this what research scientists do? Explore the unknown?"

"That is not permitted, Adam!" Archer exclaimed in a sharp tone as he rechecked the lab's emptiness. "What you're asking is totally outside laboratory procedure. Doing so would invite tremendous trouble for me, and I still need this job. I may be an MD in title, but not yet in practice. And I won't be for years." Archer's flitting eyes finally came to rest on Wakefield. "Unless I could procure advanced permission, which would be highly unlikely."

Huffing and incredulous, Wakefield considered his hoped-for partner-in-crime. "Really, Randall? All right, how about this. I don't tell if you won't?" But Wakefield could see the shifty-eyed nervousness of his collaborator's deep conflict. "Look, old boy, have we ever run into the doctor in charge of this facility, let alone faculty, or even other students at this hour? Never. All right, once, when Dr. Dole wanted you to cover the lab over a holiday. Once! What could it hurt to take a fresh sample, put in on a slide, cover it with a slip of glass, then walk it over here for a quick look-see?

"Who knows, old boy, it might be the opening of your route to pathology greatness." Wakefield elaborated the theme. "Imagine the headlines:

HARVARD'S TOP MEDICAL RESEARCHER,
DR. RANDALL ARCHER,
UNCOVERS NATURE'S DEEPEST SECRETS
Byline:
Made Possible by the Innovative Microscope
Created by
DR. ADAM WAKEFIELD, PHD, HARVARD COLLEGE OF PHYSICS."

Archer was unaware he grinned at Wakefield's flight of fancy. Double-checking the room a last time for intruders' ears, he, despite reservations, agreed. "Okay, Adam. As long as it's just you and me alone in the lab, I can put a few slides together tomorrow night from the specimens we acquire during the day and utilize no additives or pretreatments on them whatsoever.

"As you said, who knows?" Archer reiterated, seduced by the alluring vision of his personal path to glory. "Perhaps it will prove revelatory."

§

Relief flooded Wakefield the next night upon finding the lab empty, save for his hoped for collaborator-in-crime. He prayed Archer was still game to tweak the rigid laboratory rules of conduct, which, in Wakefield's mind, served only to hamper scientific discovery. But it remained to be seen if Archer, hunched over his worktable, was able to move beyond his palpable fears.

"Evening, old boy," Wakefield said, stopping before Archer's workplace. "Busy as ever, I see. What are we going to study tonight?"

When Archer looked up, his surgical mask bulged and sank eerily with each spoken word. "Keep your voice down, Adam! No telling when someone might drop in. We don't have to broadcast our—"

"Rule-breaking?" Wakefield helpfully supplied.

"Protocols, but yes. The freshest biopsy I have tonight is from the lung of a moribund tuberculosis patient. His samples are on these slides." He indicated a half dozen completed slides. "Let's start with these. Get your gloves and mask on."

Wakefield proceeded to don the protective wear Archer had laid out for him. He crossed to his microscope, which he uncovered and prepped while Archer followed with the slides, separated on a tray borne in his gloved hands.

Archer carefully placed the slides next to the microscope and double-checked Wakefield's protective gear. He insisted they sterilize the microscope as an added precaution to effectively working with live samples. It took both of them, working together with a solution Archer provided, about ten minutes to disinfect the entire area, to the tune of Wakefield's exaggerated sniffing at the offensive odor throughout.

"Well then," Wakefield said upon completion of sterilization, "would you like to do the honors, Randall? Be the first to see what's hidden in these untreated disease samples? Untreated and *alive*, I should add."

"*If* anything is hidden," Archer stressed, managing expectations. "I would very much like to be first. But it is your microscope, Adam. Go ahead." It pained Archer to be so generous, a fact Wakefield easily recognized.

"Technically, it's Harvard's microscope, Dr. Archer. And she's all yours," he insisted, "the key to your entire future as you've alluded to many, many times."

"We'll need to thoroughly disinfect your scope as well as ourselves after we're finished here, Adam," Archer commented, selecting a slide, slipping it onto the stage, easing onto the high stool, and making final adjustments to the scope before bringing the specimen into sharp outline beneath the viewers.

Archer fell as still and silent as an oddly posed corpse. He even appeared not to breathe for so long that Wakefield finally prodded him, "Well, Randall?" But Archer either ignored or didn't hear him. With a sudden movement, Archer exchanged one slide for another, immediately reverting to a convincing imitation of comatose.

Wakefield had experienced Archer's capacity for concentration before, but this performance sorely tried his patience. It *was* his invention, after all, even if the microscope had been built with University funds.

Archer bolted upright on the stool and away from the viewer. "Your turn, Adam. Look at this slide I've been observing." Wakefield heard the barely contained excitement in Archer's tone, but was too eager to see for himself to question it. The two men changed places.

Wakefield brought the sample into focus. What he saw literally took his breath away. He fell as mute as his friend had. Stunned by what he witnessed, he could only stare.

Wakefield sat back with a whistle of astonishment, his pale eyes above the mask wide with wonder, his breathing beneath it pulsing rapidly. "Was the first slide like this one, Randall?"

Archer nodded, relieved Wakefield had observed what he had. "Exactly!"

"Good heavens," Wakefield managed, peering into the viewer repeatedly as though expecting the visual to change or disappear. "What are we looking at? Have you ever—"

"Have you?" Archer cut in. "You've likely looked at as many sample slides as I have, maybe more. Have you ever seen anything like this?"

"Never," Wakefield responded, gazing down the viewer in disbelief.

Archer instructed him, "Tell me, describe to me precisely, what you see."

Wakefield observed for several moments before complying. "I see . . . microbes of some sort, in a kind of frenzied dance. Certainly alive. Wildly so!" Wakefield glanced at Archer who, despite his mask, seemed to be grinning from ear to ear, more exhilarated than he'd ever seen. "Let me try a new slide." Wakefield made the switch and spent several moments staring down at it before sitting back in a state of ecstatic wonder. "It works, Randall old boy, just like I said it would." His eyes traveled lovingly over his microscope. "It works, Randall. This slide, like the previous two, teems with life."

Archer organized his uncharacteristic giddiness into scientific deduction. "Okay. We're seeing something beyond surprising, shocking actually, on our very first fresh, untreated specimen slides," he glanced around and lowered his voice, "at the magnification strength of approximately sixty thousand times, correct?"

Wakefield nodded, crinkles around his pale eyes indicating smiling happiness.

"What we must do, Adam, is duplicate these findings—the first step of any credible research. However, we must be far more methodical in the biopsy procedures. I will volunteer to do the actual biopsies and draws myself in the hospital tomorrow. Then again in slide-assembly and at every stage of handling, I'll personally work to eradicate all potential contaminants. We'll disinfect your microscope and work area before and after as well.

"*Sterilized* must be our byword at every stage," Archer continued as if walking himself through necessary next steps. "We must be certain no impurity interferes with or skews our findings. Something in the lab, on my worktable, the glass slides themselves, anything that touches the actual specimen," he said, enumerating possibilities. "Or even an anomaly with the patients themselves."

Wakefield was coming to respect Archer's rigorous, step-by-step logic as he listened. "Assuming we again find these microbes," Archer concluded, "these 'teeming life-forms' as you aptly called them, especially if we find them in specimens from other tuberculosis victims, we must repeat these steps with other biopsies from other patients with other diseases." In an aside intended only for himself, Archer added, "I will collect as many different disease samples from the spectrum of hospital patients as opportunity presents."

Wakefield continued to glance time and again into the viewer while Archer seemed more distracted by possible intruders in the lab. "But what do you think we're looking at here, Randall?"

"Too soon to speculate. First, let's be certain this astonishing occurrence can be reproduced, Adam. However," Archer paused, succumbing to the irresistible temptation to speculate, "these microbes are too small to be bacterial. No," he stopped himself. "Let's just see where this goes tomorrow night."

"Wouldn't miss it for the world," responded a euphoric Wakefield, head in the clouds at the premiere performance of his powerful microscope, which appeared to have revealed a brand new life-form in its first observation of *living* disease specimens.

§

After the incomparable discovery of a previously undetected microbe gyrating in a living tuberculosis sample, the phenomenon was rediscovered by the two scientists night after night for weeks and weeks as rigorous scientific methodology required. Until finally they could rule out extraneous contaminants as the cause.

Expanding the study, the researchers moved onto a wide range of 'living' diseases for many nights following. As long as each specimen was fresh and untouched by any preparatory solutions, similar although not precisely exact replications of microbial life were found to dance madly on the slide—regardless of what disease was under study. Wakefield began to notice that these additional and unexpected confirmations, instead of exciting his partner, seemed to disquiet Archer increasingly. He grew taciturn and testy.

"Unbelievable!" pronounced Wakefield, his pale eyes alight above his mask. "That's the seventh different disease we've observed tonight, and as in all the nights preceding, microbes resembling each other with small variations in color and movement patterns appear in every single one of the living specimens."

Archer made no comment, concentrating on the viewers of the microscope, observing what Wakefield described. After double-checking the lab for eyes and ears, Archer surprised

Wakefield with these words. "Adam, we're going to need to move our study into a securable section of the lab. I've spoken to my supervisor and was able to obtain permission to use a space vacated by a drug test we've concluded." He pulled keys from his pocket. "I'll make arrangements to have your microscope moved in tomorrow. We'll meet there hereafter." He handed a key to Wakefield, who stared at it and then him, speechless.

Blinking as if he'd missed something, Wakefield quizzed, "What? What are you talking about? 'Securable'?"

"I told my superior that the Physics College wished to keep under wraps your unique insights into greatly enhanced magnification and clarity. Until such time as it was thoroughly tested and understood by those who had funded it, Harvard and its College of Physics."

"But—but that's not true."

"I know! But we must be cautious with what we're finding here, Adam. It flies in the face of medical orthodoxy. Until I understand it and why, I'd rather we kept it to ourselves. Remember, I'm the one at risk here. *I'm* the one who's making living specimen slides without the required advanced permission for such an exception to strict laboratory rules."

Archer faced his partner, dark eyes shifting above his mask as if expecting spies everywhere. In a near-whisper he added, "What started as an innocent-sounding observation of untreated specimens has literally taken on a life of its own. Unknown microbes, similar in size and movement characteristics from disease to disease? But present in every disease? Why, I'd be laughed out of the medical school, Adam. Medicine as traditionally taught and practiced labels all of this—this phenomena—as impossible, and would likely attribute our results to poor research practices."

Dumbfounded, Wakefield could barely form a response. "Really? You wish to move to a space we keep locked? Is that necessary, Randall?"

"It's a precaution, Adam. Let's give ourselves the time needed to fully understand what we've happened upon before our collaboration is either shut down, becomes the center of heated controversy, or I get expelled."

§

The next night, Wakefield used his key to enter the space his study with Archer now occupied in a corner of the medical lab. But although his microscope, notes, drawings, and related equipment had been relocated, Archer was nowhere in sight. Nor did he show throughout that night, nor the next. He had risen from intern to medical resident by this time, and residents were paid, though minimally. But Archer's constant struggle with money had kept him at the lab, at least so far.

When his partner's absence dragged on for weeks, Wakefield became alarmed. Had Archer's fears gotten the best of him? Could he just walk away from the opportunity which had presented itself because it conflicted, albeit seriously, with his medical training and practice? Because it was too politically charged—at least in his somewhat paranoid mind?

What kind of research is limited by 'orthodoxy'? Wakefield puzzled over. *A brand new life-form! What researcher wouldn't die to explore such an unexpected opening into the mysteries of life?*

With no fresh study slides to work with, Wakefield locked and left the space and wandered through the dimly-lit lab, a place he found not only of great intellectual stimulation and exciting revelation, but a welcome buffer from the day's worsening financial news. Collapsing banks and businesses, panic rising in all sectors, the cancerous growth of farms and homes in default, jobless multitudes mushrooming daily. Desperation trickled down into every facet of life. He didn't want to go home, where financial tensions charged its atmosphere.

There was only one thing to do, he decided, given he had no idea where Archer lived. Go ask after him at the Medical College in the morning and hope the asking didn't cause him problems. Wakefield turned to leave the lab and ran headlong into Archer, who had silently materialized in the gloom of the low-lit lab. "Ye gods, Randall! Where have you been?" Wakefield scolded like a worried parent. "It's been over *two* weeks! You just disappear? Without a word? In the middle of our fantastic journey? Again?"

"Good to know you missed me," Archer teased, boyishly grinning and coloring at the same time.

Wakefield's cheeks reddened as well. "I—I, well yes, I admit I have missed our scientific debates. Frankly, Randall, I'd begun to fear you'd lost interest in microscopy. Or that I'd bored you to death with my wild opining. I do get carried away by possibilities. Then I began to fear that this research was simply too far beyond the medically acceptable, and too risky for you."

"'Lose interest in microscopy'?" Archer mimicked. "Never!" He laughed out loud at Wakefield's embarrassment. His unguarded laughter was something Wakefield had never before heard from his collaborator. "Seriously, Adam," Archer continued, "you know the microscope, yours in particular, holds the key to my future as *the* medical researcher I intend to be. There is no possibility of my losing interest. But the research is . . . well, let's just leave that subject for now. It's still so new and inexplicable."

Wakefield tamped down the irritation which replaced weeks' worth of unnecessary worry. "So what, then? Your schedule changed? A new rotation? Your nights are no longer free?"

Archer's stalling only fanned the flames of Wakefield's annoyance at his wasted time and worries. "Explain yourself, old man," he demanded. "You've been a constant in this lab for as long as I've worked here. And after what we've been witnessing, something important must have happened. It better have."

Archer smiled self-consciously. "I've been," he began, sliding onto a stool and glancing away, "uh, with patients. That is, one patient in particular."

Wakefield's jaw dropped as he watched Archer fidget like a schoolgirl. "'*One* patient'? You mean a girl? You've met a girl? A girl capable of luring Dr. Archer from his celibate path toward medical fame and fortune? Now *that* I never would have guessed," Wakefield confessed, not entirely convinced, "not in a million tries, not after your much discussed single-minded effort to climb to the very top of your profession. Which actually is consistent with what I've observed in you."

Looking as though he might burst from holding in his secret, Archer remained determinedly tight-lipped.

Wakefield took a seat nearby as he studied his errant colleague more closely and noted several changes. For one, he'd cleaned up. Though his shoes remained worn and scuffed, his lab coat looked new, fresh, and white. His frizzled dark curls had been pomaded almost into submission. "Out with it now, Randall. Who is this temptress who's enticed dogged Dr. Archer to forego his favorite hours in the medical lab with his favorite partner, unearthing never-before-dreamed-of microbial life?"

Having grown used to it, Archer ignored Wakefield's excess. "Actually, Adam, you know her, and she you. She's from Boston too."

Wakefield had to prod for every word. "Okay, old boy. So she is?"

Archer prolonged his admission, knowing once out, it would likely invite infuriating innuendo, if not outright insults. Until finally, he released his breath, prayed Wakefield would be different, and declared, "Elizabeth. Her name. Ah, Elizabeth. Perrish." Archer allowed no time for Wakefield to react. "The acute appendicitis which landed her in Mass General occurred during my surgical rotation. I assisted in her surgery. Sewed her up myself! It was the nastiest, near-to-bursting appendix I hope

I ever see."

Archer barely took a breath. "Afterward, I checked on her and my personal handiwork and continued to do so throughout her recuperation, more often than necessary. But that's what it took for her to notice me. It helped when I reminded her you'd introduced us one frigid evening on campus. *Finally*, Adam, she took note," he exclaimed in awe. "Over her weeks of forced rest in the hospital, she and I uncovered common ground. For example—" Archer stopped himself, correctly interpreting Wakefield's flabbergasted expression, jaw dropped, blue eyes wide, as utter disbelief. It was precisely what he had both feared and anticipated. "What?" he demanded.

"Elizabeth Perrish?" Wakefield enunciated each syllable. "You and *the* Elizabeth Perrish of the Brahmin Bradley Perrishes? You've found 'common ground?'" He snickered. "Sorry, old chap, but like what?"

Archer bit his lip as he studied Wakefield. "I should have spoken to you in advance, Adam. I'm sorry. I saw the way you looked at her, despite the darkening evening. Is there something between you two I should know about?"

Wakefield instantly flustered. "No! No, of course not. We're just lifelong friends and, well, you were saying? You two are dating? You plan to see each other again?"

Archer's self-protective barriers sprang up around him. Not a muscle moved as he stoically awaited instruction on their obvious class differences. *Who the hell am I to even dream the likes of Elizabeth Perrish of the Boston Perrishes would look twice?*

Wakefield guffawed at the ridiculous notion until he noticed Archer slipping behind his impenetrable shield. His intense gaze diffused to blankness. Wakefield recalled seeing this act of self-preservation, witnessed when blustery, overbearing Dr. Dole had stormed the lab late one night.

Still, Wakefield struggled to banish the amusing visual of

short, frayed Randall Archer of Pittsburgh aside tall, willowy, unattainable Elizabeth Perrish of Boston, of *Old* Boston, in fact the *oldest* Boston. At last, Wakefield sobered. "You're *not* kidding?"

"If, Adam, you imply a woman like Elizabeth is out of my league, there's really no need." Straightening himself on the stool to maximum height and indignation, Archer stated, "It's not like I didn't know who she was, at least her family's historical importance. I pass that towering statue of Ansley Perrish and his sinister glare every time I cross campus. Even in bronze, the artist captured a lofty sense of superiority. I'm well aware a beautiful, smart woman from the uppermost social rung is well outside my wildest imaginings, even without your reminder, Adam. She could obviously have her pick—"

"You can say that again!" Wakefield cut in, punctuating his statement with a fist-slam on the table which triggered his own deep flushing. "She's rejected more eligible bachelors on the Eastern Seaboard than remain to be rejected."

'*Eligible.*' Wakefield recognized his own condescension. Wishing to avoid further insult of his truly missed laboratory companion, he apologized. "I am—I'm sorry, Randall. Forgive me. That didn't come out right. It's just I've known Elizabeth since childhood. I attended St. Paul's with her brother, Prescott. And despite our long, shared history, I would never dare—That is, I wouldn't have the courage—" Wakefield stopped himself. Despite intuiting his friend's deep disappointment, still he couldn't resist repeating, "Elizabeth Perrish? Really? I don't mean it to sound—"

"It's forgotten," Archer brusquely interjected. Overt markers of social standing had, after all, followed him around Harvard like dogs nipping at his heels. Archer masked his disillusionment at his 'friend's' reaction, determined to avoid a permanent wedge between himself and the man who, aside from Dole, could prove most useful to his career aspirations. *First things*

first, after all. The man's breakthrough microscope could cata-
pult Archer to the forefront of pathology. He needed Wakefield
far more than Wakefield would ever need him. Yet, still seething
inwardly, he swore, *Once I reach the pinnacle of my profession, I
will never again swallow such slights and insinuations.*

While disappointing and maddening for Archer, the
exchange was nearly choking an acutely embarrassed Wakefield. "Look, old boy, despite how it may have come across, my
reaction is really more about Elizabeth than you. She's been
unreachable, literally out-of-bounds, for as long as I've known
her. She's feisty, headstrong, and rebellious. No one seems to
know to what end, least of all her family. She's driven them to
distraction her entire life. Prescott often reported her volatility
had the whole household tiptoeing around her."

Wakefield snickered at another memory. "For example, her
adamant refusal to attend the finishing school her mother had
enrolled her unmarried daughter in following high school
graduation. Elizabeth argued vehemently to go to college. A
few of her friends were going to the likes of Vassar, Smith, and
Radcliffe, the obvious choices. But Mrs. Perrish was against it. I
overheard them arguing.

"Mrs. Perrish had said something to the effect of college girls
being so 'dreary and unattractive,' that men don't like smart
girls, so what was the point? 'You'll marry well—one hopes and
soon—raise a family, and devote your life to them,' pointing
out a proper wife was instrumental in her husband's and her
children's success. She emphasized that Elizabeth didn't need
a college degree for any of that, and that she'd only be wasting
more of her 'precious and limited time.' I'll not forget Mrs. Perrish's summation: 'You're marrying age *now*, Elizabeth dear. The
clock is ticking!'

"Elizabeth countered with the fact that it was no longer the
nineteenth century. She appealed to her father, with whom she
had always been especially close, to inform her mother that

women can and should do more in the modern world.

"But poor old Bradley Perrish simply could not stand up to his wife, Eleanor, nor publicly contradict her."

Wakefield grinned. "But I suppose Elizabeth got the last laugh. Still refusing finishing school, she insisted and won the argument, with her father's support, to earn a state teaching credential instead. Her rationale, for the sake of convincing her parents I suspect, was that said credential would be useful in raising her own children.

"After they'd extracted Elizabeth's clear understanding that any subsequent paying job of any sort would be out of the question—'unthinkably beneath your social station, dear'—her parents deemed a teaching credential relatively harmless, and relented."

Wakefield sat back, smiling and sniggering at the drama on view in his head. "Those were the same days she battled her mother every time she attempted to sneak out of Perrish House in the flapper costumes she'd adopted—insisting modern women were a generation unto themselves, far from the confines of their parents' times. Of course, Mrs. Perrish insisted such attire only made her look cheap and common. 'You have our name to uphold, Elizabeth, as well as your own!' she'd insisted, to no avail."

Finally noticing Archer was neither amused nor mollified, standing in wary attention before him, Wakefield changed tacks. "But of course, I know Elizabeth to be a great girl. I'm happy for you, Randall, truly. I hope you can keep it going. She'd be quite a catch for—"

"—the likes of me?" Archer completed his thought, hope for this friendship waning by the word.

"For *anyone*, Randall, and I mean it. Elizabeth would be hard to handle, independent in the extreme, although certainly exciting. Hats off, old man. Bravo!" Wakefield clapped politely. "But a word of caution," he added in seriousness. "Her family will not allow it. The Perrishes have very specific plans for their sole daughter, plans she has thus far defied. Understand that they have the will, the power, the wealth, and the influence to make any threat to those plans disappear. You, my friend, have been forewarned."

Wakefield could see Archer had been smitten beyond reason, and he'd be the last man to blame him. So once again, he reversed course. "What am I saying? Listen to me—Dr. Doom-and-Gloom. The two of you just met, you share, ah, something in common. Enjoy the moment while you may, Randall!"

Wakefield spoke as if to himself, "This news will break big amongst Boston society." He imagined the responses when word of Elizabeth Perrish stepping well outside expectations spread from her family's circle outward. *Randall Archer who? His family is from where?* Until Wakefield, himself a part of that circle, faced the ugly truth that such reactions mirrored his own.

"Look, Randall," Wakefield squirmed on the seat, swallowing hard, "we have a lot to catch up on. Allow me to fill you in on my progress these last weeks—which has been considerable despite the dearth of study slides."

He rose, nodding toward their locked study area, and Archer eventually followed. Once inside and seated beside the micro-scope, Archer sought clarification, "So, Adam, I have your blessing then? There's nothing between you two—"

"Of course!" Wakefield insisted. "However, do indulge my curiosity. Tell me how you pulled off this—this feat."

Cracks appeared in Archer's defensive walls, his reflections softening his hardened façade. "Honestly, Adam, no one could be more surprised than I am," he admitted.

"I had heard Elizabeth had been hospitalized," Wakefield said, "but I'd assumed she'd gone to St. E's, given her family's long association. Her condition must have been very grave indeed to have been taken to Mass General. Prescott had promised to let me know when she was ready for visitors, but he never did.

"So, well, Randall, tell me," Wakefield encouraged, sitting beside his partner, "you participated in her appendectomy. And then?"

§

The anesthesia had worn off slowly. A groggy, disoriented Elizabeth Perrish blinked open what proved to be dazzling deep-blue eyes to find a stranger sitting on her bed, holding her by the wrist.

Snatching her hand away, Elizabeth demanded, "W-Who—who are you? What are you doing?" She glanced around, befuddled and alarmed, before concentrating with apparent difficulty on the stranger. "Where am I?"

It was her expressive blue eyes that initially captured Archer's notice. He felt himself drowning in their depths until his patient, struggling to get away, moaned in pain. "Please, Miss Perrish," he tried to control her movements. "Please! Be still. I'm Dr. Archer. I assisted in your emergency appendectomy. In fact, I stitched you back up myself." Upon hearing this, Elizabeth stared down toward her stomach and moaned again, collapsing back on the bed. She glowered at Archer, seemingly confounded by him and the situation.

Her striking beauty, even after surgery, held him captive and rendered him speechless. *You could swim in those fathomless blue eyes,* he thought, startling himself with the unusual romantic notion.

"I want the real doctor," she commanded. "And my parents! Where are my parents?"

"The surgeon will be by on his rounds shortly, Miss Perrish. And I'll locate your parents for you. They were leaving your room when I arrived." The richly dressed couple had barely glanced at Archer as they passed at the doorway to Elizabeth's room. "But rest assured, your surgery went swimmingly." *Now, where did that word come from,* he wondered, forcing himself to look away from her eyes. "You're in Massachusetts General Hospital, and you've just come through major surgery. But we got your appendix out in the nick of time." He smiled at the memory. "It was a very fine surgery if I do—"

"It hurts everywhere. I want the real doctor! And my parents!"

Archer slid off the bed. "If you'll let me record your pulse, I'll go find both the 'real doctor' and your parents. I've already given you something for the pain, which will take effect momentarily. In the meantime, lie back and rest. That's all you have to do right now, Miss Perrish. Rest."

Elizabeth tried to resist, protesting this youthful imposter, insisting on 'a real doctor.' But her determination began to drain away, her confusion and fear diffusing as the pain medication sapped her of fight. Archer knew his very first patient in his surgical rotation would be asleep in minutes.

Uncertain that she'd hear, Archer promised her as well as himself, "I will find your parents, Miss Perrish. And I will be back to check on you myself."

§

Propped against pillows in her hospital bed, Elizabeth Perrish was riffling through *Harper's BAZAAR* when Archer ducked his head in the door. "Ah, Miss Perrish," he said, inching inside, "I see you're feeling much better. Your color's improved and your hair—" Sunlight glistened off her long, dark waves when her head jerked toward him.

She felt her thick mane. "My hair? Is what?"

Mesmerizing, the too-young-to-be-a-doctor thought, fighting a blush. "I mean to say you look much recovered. How are you feeling today?" He approached her bedside cautiously, then stood awkwardly beside it.

"I suppose you've come to examine my abdomen. *Again,*"

she said, taunting him as she pulled at her gown. The doctor bent over her, his tangle of dark curls thankfully obscuring heated embarrassment. While he traced the fine line of stitches he'd forever marked her with, she studied him up close. "Well, Doctor, will I live? I must say, my tummy never commanded such attention before."

Archer prolonged his examination until he'd regained a bit of self-possession. "Come on now," she teased, "you're not really a doctor? If you don't mind my saying, you look awfully young to be—"

"A medical resident, to be precise." He replaced her gown and stepped back. "Excellent work, if I do say so. You still don't recall our having met before, albeit briefly. Adam Wakefield introduced us one frozen night on campus not long ago."

Her brow bunched as she worked to recall. "Oh, yes! Prescott's birthday. It was freezing that night, I won't forget that. So, I presume I will live." She exaggerated a sigh of relief. "But a doctor in residency would be . . . closing in on thirty. Eight years of schooling after high school, then internship and residency. You can't possibly be thirty. I mean, are you?"

"Nearing thirty would be the norm, I grant you," Archer responded. "But I've been on an accelerated track since, well, in truth since high school."

"Just how accelerated was this track? And how old are you, may I ask?" She tossed aside the magazine, which fell open to an article entitled, 'Hoover's Trickle-Down Policies Fail to Staunch Economic Panic.'"

Elizabeth patted the bed. "Do sit, Dr. Archer. You're at an unfair advantage here. You clearly know *a lot* more about me than I you." She giggled at his discomfort. Sheer willpower enabled Archer to hold her teasing gaze and not let his attention shift toward the taut abdomen he'd been monitoring closely since her surgery. "Tell me about yourself, Doctor. Where are you from?"

Archer's blush spread as he edged onto her bed, secretly

thrilled as well as panicked that the beautiful patient he'd made numerous excuses to visit was at last noticing him. "Pennsylvania," he answered, disdain dripping from the word, "Pittsburgh area to be specific. But I haven't been back since I was sixteen, the year I graduated high school, and plan never to go back again."

"Sixteen? That is accelerated. You said your home state's name as if there aren't enough miles on earth to distance you from it. I have relatives in Philadelphia I always enjoyed visiting. The Main Line. Would you know the Clarks? No? Well, was Pennsylvania really so bad?"

The rotten-egg smell from the belching smokestacks of the steel mills transported Archer's senses to the place he'd forever left behind. The ceaseless spew fouled the air day and night with grit and smoke, grime sifting down like blighted snow. "More the situation than the state," he acknowledged, "but bad enough. Fortunately, Boston has been good to me. It's my home now."

Elizabeth's gaze narrowed as she scrutinized Archer more closely, including his unusual black-eyed stare. "So high school completed at sixteen, pre-med—"

"My pre-med track was completed in three years, not the usual four."

"Hmm," she huffed. "Pre-med track in three years, then medical school, I assume in the normal four?" When he nodded, she calculated, "An internship, then residency . . ." She threw up her hands. "Well, how old are you, anyway?"

"Twenty-five, but this baby-face has plagued me my whole life, especially challenging when the rest of my siblings took after my father, big brutes all, in more ways than size." He batted back his incorrigible waves. "I have another year of residency and then I intend to specialize in pathology—the study of disease. So in a few more years, you won't be able to send me out for the 'real doctor.'"

Elizabeth smiled at the jibe. "I was perfectly awful, I imagine. You forgive me?" She did not wait for an answer. "You're only

two years older than I am," she commented, looking apprecia-
tively at him, "and you've accomplished all that. How'd you get
to Boston from Pennsylvania at the age of sixteen?"

"Full scholarship with living stipend from Harvard, where I
plan to remain throughout my life and career. This is the first
place I've ever begun to feel at-home."

Elizabeth leaned toward him, touching his arm casually, her
hair tumbling forward in the process, both causing a surge in
Archer's pulse. "A full ride all these years? From Harvard. And
you've been on your own since sixteen! Extraordinary, Dr.
Archer," she said, approval glinting in the deep blue waters of
her eyes. "Inspirational."

§

Rushing into Elizabeth's hospital room, Archer nearly knocked
her off her feet before resuming a sedate, professional manner.

But Elizabeth was not fooled, not after all the time he'd made
for her, as though she was the only patient in the entire hospital.
"A train to catch, Dr. Archer? Oh please, don't be embarrassed.
I'm delighted you came by before my release." A small suitcase
was open and full on the bed. She slammed it shut and clicked
the locks before facing him directly. "As you see, I packed lightly
for my two-week stay."

After weeks in hospital gowns, the sight of her in civilian
clothes—a dress fitted to her slim figure—took his breath away.
"Doctor, would you help a poor invalid lady, who was recently
dissected and stitched back together by two very talented hands,
by carrying her valise to the entrance? My parents are sending
our driver to fetch me."

"Let me have the orderly bring you a wheelchair. It's policy
for patients—"

"Please!" she said, dismissing the idea. "I can walk. But you
can accompany me in case of any misstep." She indicated the

valise to him, but when Archer stepped in to retrieve it, she held it down on the bed. "Seriously, Randall," she said, staring straight into his naked and exposed soul, or so it felt. "Seriously, I'm happy they've kept me around long enough to get to know you." She released the luggage to him. "You're a remarkable and accomplished young man, directed by laudable ambition. And to think you've done it all without the help of a family or its name, without strings pulled or doors opened. I don't think you realize how truly remarkable that is, especially in today's failing economy."

She took a step toward him and said quietly, "I don't know anyone like you, Randall. And regardless of what my parents think, I find you and your story motivational. Could someone like me with so many advantages do something similar? I wonder. . .

"Perhaps it's not an appropriate question for a female to ask—which is what my parents would tell me. 'Look first for the pedigree, dear, then the money with which you'll be supported,' she mimicked. 'Your *job* is to marry well.' Alas, advice from Mother. It's as much as a woman in my position should expect.

"That's all that's expected of me, Randall." She stumbled backward onto the bed in brow-creasing contemplation, her loose locks settling around her shoulders. "Then what? After becoming a wife, a mother, a home manager, a volunteer, a club-joiner, and an entertaining accessory to the man I'm meant to support in all those ways, I'm to feel happy about it? Fulfilled?"

She looked up, noticing Archer listening intently, unconsciously hugging her valise to his chest. "What's wrong with me?" she asked. "Why does none of it sound gratifying, Randall? The men, boys really, my parents surround me with, are spoiled children compared to you and your drive and achievements. Perhaps like we women, those men struggle within their own social strictures. I really don't know. But I don't wish to be a part of it. In fact, I refuse!" she declared, coming to her feet. "I'm sorry, Randall. I didn't mean to run on like that. Shall we go?"

As Archer turned for the door, she stopped him, holding his arm until he pivoted back. Suddenly, all that divided them, including several inches in height, evaporated. She wrapped her arms around his neck and kissed him, inadvertently squeezing the suitcase into his chest. "Oh! You can't breathe. Sorry!" She stepped back. "Well then, let's go, Dr. Archer. My chariot awaits."

Now, it was Archer who held her back. "Elizabeth, I-I'd really like to see more of you. Would you, that is, would that be possible?"

"You mean see more than just my scarred abdomen?"

Archer nearly fainted with his up-swelling mortification.

Elizabeth laughed out loud. "I wondered when you'd ask. I should have kissed you a week ago." She waited, as if daring him.

He dropped her bag on the bed and encircled her in his arms. She did the same to him, teasing, "Be careful there, Doctor. We wouldn't want anything to mar your excellent needlework, would we—" His lips and body pressing against her stopped her mid-quip. They gave themselves over to an attraction which had been building to this very moment.

Archer broke off. In a rough whisper, he said, "I'd be severely reprimanded or worse if caught like this with a patient while on duty. Otherwise, I'd be tempted to lay you on that bed again for a more thorough examination."

She kissed him lightly and stepped away. "Let's not risk your grand scheme to the heights of the medical field—on an accelerated track, of course. Walk me out, Randall." She took his hand, but when they stepped into the hallway, crowded with people coming and going, they both let go.

Walking side by side, stealing glances, sharing guilty smiles, they approached the elevator. Finding the car empty, they launched into another passionate embrace as they traveled downward.

Archer could hardly take in what was happening. *She wants to see me again. She wants to see me!* Until the bell signaling the ground floor forced them to separate and stand apart. When the doors opened, Archer retrieved Elizabeth's bag, and they ventured into the chaotic hospital lobby. The crowd spontaneously parted for the couple like the Red Sea for the Israelites, something Archer realized Elizabeth Perrish was so accustomed to, she did not even notice.

A man in a gray uniform, black tie, and a cap he whisked off, called to them. "Here, Miss Elizabeth, let me take your suitcase." He pried it from Archer's grasp. "You're looking very well, Miss, I must say. A far cry from when I rushed you here."

"Thank you, Sean. I'm certainly glad to hear it."

He continued to eye the doctor suspiciously as Archer admired his double-row of shiny buttons. After an awkward pause, Elizabeth said, "This is Dr. Archer, Sean. You can thank him and his excellent care for any and all improvement you see. You go on ahead, Sean. We'll be right behind you."

With reluctance, the chauffeur replaced his black cap and moved through the crowd while Archer and Elizabeth straggled behind. Reaching a glittering Rolls Royce, also black and silver-gray, waiting to bear her away, the chauffeur held the door, impatient to separate his charge from the too-familiar doctor.

Elizabeth spun back so only Archer would hear. "Thank you, Randall. You may have saved my life—in more ways than one. This is my private telephone number." She pressed a small, folded paper into his hand, brushing his lips with hers before ducking in. The voluminous backseat swallowed her whole as the driver slammed the door with emphasis—Elizabeth safely on the inside, Archer on the outside, peering in.

The chauffeur openly scrutinized Archer as he rounded the vehicle. He straightened his cap and tie and slid in behind the steering wheel with a last meaningful glare at Archer. The engine rumbled to life, and they were gone. Archer stood, bolted to the ground, staring well after Boston's tangled streets had consumed the last gleam of the heavily chromed vehicle.

What was more overwhelming? he gauged. The private telephone number he held in his palm? The salty-sweet taste of Elizabeth Perrish on his lips? Her lingering scent? Or the ache each inspired in his groin?

Odd looks from passersby eventually penetrated Archer's daze. On the sidewalk before the hospital, he carefully unfolded the note Elizabeth had slipped him. A number and no more. He refolded and secured the treasure in his breast pocket, patting the spot repeatedly to make certain he hadn't imagined it all.

CHAPTER SIX

RIPPLE EFFECTS

1931

Everything about the day felt surreal. Archer, nattering nervously, created vapor clouds with his words streaming on the frigid winter air. He struggled to keep pace with Wakefield's long strides as they approached the Suffolk County Courthouse.

The young doctor fell silent as the pair scaled the stairs to the arched entry of the imposing stone structure. When they stepped into its grand atrium, Archer slowed to a stop. Wakefield took control and guided him through the vast hall and up a flight of stairs where signage indicated their ultimate destination. Wakefield held the door to encourage Archer inside the Justice of the Peace.

Elizabeth instantly drew both men's attention, standing out against the drab governmental décor in a crisp white wool dress, cinched at the waist over a loose, flowing skirt. She whispered and giggled with her best friend Betsey, their heads pressed together conspiratorially, until they spied the men in the outer chamber. Elizabeth rushed them, kissing and hugging Archer a bit more enthusiastically than was proper in public, if

Wakefield's pursed lips were any indication, and leaving Archer even more dazed when released.

"Don't you look handsome in that suit!" she enthused as Archer tugged at the unfamiliar collar, as uncomfortable to him as the setting. "We chose well, Randall. It becomes you. And that hat! Wherever did—"

"Adam gave it to me. A gift to mark the occasion. I'd admired his fedora, secretly I thought." Archer removed the warm hat when he realized Wakefield had done so with his. "It's vicuna."

She turned to greet Wakefield with a peck on the cheek. "Thank you for getting him here on time, Adam. I think we're up next." Excitement radiated off her. She sparkled with joy.

Betsey trailed Elizabeth, carrying a gift wrapped in silver paper and tied with a large white bow. She greeted both men and handed the package to Elizabeth, indicating with a nod at the wall clock that Elizabeth had best get on with it.

"Randall," Elizabeth gushed, passing him the box, "I've a present for you for our special day. Open it. Open it now. It's for the ceremony."

Uh-oh. Archer worried, glancing at Wakefield, *was I supposed to bring Elizabeth a gift?* With his hands already encumbered by coat, scarf, hat, and now a wrapped gift, Wakefield suggested he take a seat.

When the two scientists had convened earlier that afternoon in the medical lab, Wakefield had reacted with overt surprise to Archer's appearance. "You're looking positively dapper, old boy!"

Archer had replied, "Try not to sound so shocked, Adam." But then asked, "Do I look ridiculous in these clothes? Elizabeth insisted on shopping with me. You wouldn't believe how much money I spent for this one occasion. I'll have to work twenty-four hours a day for months in the lab to recover! And will I ever wear such things again? Likely only to my own funeral."

"Don't be silly, Randall. Today's the most important day of your life. I'm sure that in itself justifies the expense. Now, let's get a move on. I promised Elizabeth I'd get you to the courthouse on time." He then handed a large parcel to Archer, adding, "Oh, and I brought you something to mark the occasion that will top off your new look perfectly."

Wakefield now focused on Elizabeth as they sat in the anteroom to the justice of the peace who would marry her to his research collaborator and, increasingly, his friend. "You look stunning, Elizabeth, I've never seen you in pearls before. And those are especially lovely."

"I tend to avoid pearls. They've always felt like part of *the uniform*. But these," she fingered them lovingly, "these were my grandmother's. They seemed appropriate for today. I hope she's here in spirit—at least one of my relatives in attendance at my wedding."

Wakefield kissed her cheek. "The prospect of marriage clearly agrees with you. You know I wish you every happiness. Imagine, you and Randall. Aren't you two full of surprises after what, ten, eleven months?" Scanning the room, Elizabeth's last remark sunk in. "Where is everyone?"

"We are four, Adam. My parents warned me if I went through with this, I'd no longer be a Perrish. A civil wedding didn't lighten their mood either. Mother is undoubtedly consulting the Episcopal priest as we speak regarding annulment or excommunication or some such pious rigmarole." She giggled, unfazed, before sobering. "I wonder if Randall will ever meet my family, my former family?"

"I'm sorry to hear that, Elizabeth, and it is concerning. You know times are awfully rough out there, and you're hardly used to scrimping, to put it mildly. Have you thought about how you two will—"

"Please, Adam, you sound just like them. Don't rain on my parade, not on my wedding day."

"Right, of course, I apologize. But where's Prescott? Surely your brother would wish to witness his only sibling's wedding."

"He might have come, but Betsey's mother told me my parents threatened everyone, said they'd take it as a 'personal affront' should anyone attend this deplorably unfitting ceremony. I'm actually surprised Betsey crossed the line. And you as well, Adam, if you did so knowingly?" When he made no comment, she nodded. "And I deeply appreciate it, old friend."

"You're my nearest and dearest," he responded. "How could I have missed this? Besides, who would have stood for Randall?"

"You're a dear and a darling, and I shall never forget it." Elizabeth kissed him on both cheeks, then straightened his skewed bowtie, making an under-her-breath comment as she did so. "I had hoped you'd rub off on Randall, Adam, not the other way around." She smiled mischievously until she heard her name.

They turned together toward Archer, holding up his pant legs to show off gleaming black wingtip shoes. "They fit, Elizabeth, and smell new. Thank you. I'm sorry I didn't bring something for you—except the ring, of course. You still have the ring, don't you, Adam?"

Wakefield patted his pocket, mussing the pocket square peeking from within. Elizabeth straightened that as well with another meaningful glance.

"Archer-Perrish," the clerk rang out, announcing the time for the foursome to follow him into the inner chamber of the presiding justice. They assembled before the surprisingly young-looking man in somber black robes, rolling back and forth on large feet as they gathered before him.

Elizabeth reached for Archer's hand as the justice spoke of the seriousness of marital bonds. "In sickness and health. Till death do you part." Soon, he was inquiring after the rings, which were produced by Betsey and Wakefield and passed from them to the justice and onto the couple.

With rings slipped on shaky hands, Elizabeth grinned madly while Archer eked out an unsteady smile. The justice alluded to eternity symbolized by the rings' golden circles. Then, with

the powers granted him by the state of Massachusetts, he pronounced Randall Archer and Elizabeth Perrish husband and
wife. "Mr.—excuse me, *Dr.* and Mrs. Randall Archer."

Shell-shocked, Archer required prompting to "kiss your
bride." He barely brushed her lips, but Elizabeth would have
none of it. She embraced him, kissing him with fervor until Betsey's and Wakefield's clapping broke things up. The newlyweds
accepted congratulatory kisses, slaps on the back, and much
noisy joking from the two friends who'd braved the Perrishes'
wrath. Then the clerk brought it all to an abrupt halt, uncer-
emoniously shooing them out. "The justice has a schedule to
keep," he reprimanded them.

"So now what, you two?" Wakefield asked as they layered on
winter outerwear in preparation for returning to the freezing
afternoon.

"Well," Elizabeth said, smiling at her husband, "I think we
should have a celebratory something or two, don't you agree,
Randall? Let's go to our place. Our place," she repeated. "Hmm,
that has a ring to it.

"When I was moving out of Perrish House today," she continued, "with my parents warning me such a move would be
final and booting me out without a penny, I took what I could
and relocated it to Randall's apartment. It'll be a tight squeeze
for the foreseeable future, but we'll manage, won't we, darling?"

The vision of imposing Perrish House, stolen on his rigged
detour of Beacon Hill on a day his curiosity had gotten the best
of him, haunted Archer. It only exacerbated his concern for his
new wife and their new life in subsidized student housing.

But Elizabeth went on with her story. "Anyway, I happen to
know where Father hides his illegal alcohol, so I procured a
couple bottles of good champagne, vintage Veuve Clicquot! I
think this calls for nothing less. You do like champagne, Randall, don't you?"

They had descended to lobby level by elevator and waited

for the doors to open as Archer answered, "Champagne? Mmm, yes, I think so. I hope so." The telltale blushing he could never quite control caused all four friends to laugh out loud.

Elizabeth took her husband by the arm as they left the courthouse. The foursome bundled as best they could against the cold and braced for the biting wind, which forewarned of a long, hard winter.

§

Glasses clinked, toasting the newlyweds' long and happy life. Wakefield took a seat on the only chair available in the cramped one-room apartment. The newlyweds and Betsey crammed onto a small sofa which, given its obvious absence, Wakefield assumed would fold out into the couple's marital bed. The chair was quite close enough for him.

He tried to banish the unfavorable comparisons his visions of Perrish House presented as he surveyed the dreary flat Archer would now share with his wife. The few admirable items that Elizabeth had recognizably contributed stood out against the dreary, functional furnishings that had come with the place.

There was a Coromandel screen, providing some moveable privacy within the single room, now partially concealing the wash basin and door to the water closet. She'd hung a few favored oils of European scenes—harbors crammed with colorful boats, mist rising over Notre Dame de Paris—on limited wall space. She'd even managed on her move-in and wedding day to place a vase of fresh flowers on the Japanese tansu she'd installed, serving as a coffee table.

Wakefield pondered the number of times he had been greeted by uniformed doormen and serving people beneath the chandelier in the entry hall at Perrish House. How many fine hors d'oeuvres had he accepted off the blue-and-white Chinese export Mrs. Perrish collected? Or Bradley's fine champagne in delicate crystal coupes? Elizabeth Perrish would live *here*?

Clearing his throat, Wakefield decided he'd held onto his own news as long as he could. "Seems I have a bit of news myself."

Betsey and the Archers nodded. "Do go on, Adam," Elizabeth prompted when he hesitated. "Your news?"

"Not to take away from your wedding day, Randall, Elizabeth, but yes, I need to tell you of a decision I've reached." He appeared reluctant. "I've been thinking for a year, more or less, about spreading my wings. Despite my European tour and subsequent US travels, Boston is the only place I've ever lived and worked. And, well, I suddenly felt the need to—to broaden my horizons."

"'Broaden your horizons?' Are you saying you're moving, Adam?" Archer asked, incredulous. "Out of Boston? What about our—"

"Now, now, hear me out, please. I'd been toying with the idea, as I said, when Harvard delivered the deciding factor. Seems my post-doctoral position has been terminated, rather abruptly. With the economic realities plaguing the world, not to mention my family's drastic losses, finding a good, stable job became not only prudent but necessary."

When no one reacted, Wakefield explained, "I count myself amongst the lucky when I report to you that I found one, a good job—a professorship in Physics at the University of Los Angeles, where I'll also head its physics laboratory.

"All in all, the offer has gone a long way to ameliorate both Harvard's dismissal and my personal circumstances after rampant bank failures . . ." Wakefield grew thoughtful, speaking to Elizabeth. "It seems your forebears had the wiser notion for protecting capital. Don't invest in the banks, just own the land they sit upon." Wakefield shook his head. "I never thought about any of this before, had you, Elizabeth? I've taken so much for granted, determinedly avoiding all practical or disquieting notions on my privileged path of least resistance."

Elizabeth looked crestfallen as the old friends gazed at each other. "I wish there were something I could do, Adam, but at the moment—"

"Wait a minute!" Archer finally reacted. "Harvard terminated your post-doc position? When? And—and you're moving? Across country? To Los Angeles? Good God, man, *why* on all counts?"

"Dean Bainbridge claims it's a funding issue, though that's somewhat hard to believe, despite the ever-expanding ripple effects of the market crash. Is there a better-endowed university anywhere?

"As for Los Angeles," Wakefield added, "you both know it completely captivated me when I toured the United States after earning my PhD. And—and it seemed the perfect time for stimulation and out-of-the-box thinking. And doing."

"Ah, yes," Archer muttered, "the infamous 'second sabbatical.' But Adam, you'll be as far from Boston as you can be within the United States. Why? Why wouldn't you look closer to home if you needed to make a change? Plus, given the trajectory of our joint project, I question your need for added 'stimulation.'

"*All* the important schools are here," Archer asserted, "and prize-winning scientists in every field from whom every researcher benefits. What kind of stimulation will you find in Los Angeles?" he scoffed.

Elizabeth appeared too stunned to speak, staring at Wakefield until Betsey chose the moment to make an early retreat. "You'll all forgive me, but I really must go," she said rising to draw on her coat. "I want to get home before the storm breaks. Congratulations again, you two." She kissed each person goodbye and vanished.

Archer picked up the stalled conversation by lamenting, "Well, that's that for our research. Strange the timing of your firing by Harvard, though. New procedures have just been instituted in the medical lab that went into effect immediately.

There's to be a tightening of who's admitted to the lab, and when. If I read between the lines correctly, only Medical College personnel will be permitted, especially after hours and then, only with prior approval. People like you from other disciplines are to be restricted to regular daytime business hours, once cleared by the medical hierarchy.

"Just like that, Adam, these new rules made our secretive study impossible. Although, I have to admit, thwarting laboratory protocols as we've been doing had grown increasingly difficult for me." Archer dropped his voice. "Not to mention research that appears to be undermining nearly everything the Medical College teaches."

Archer studied his subdued wife and friend. "Completing my education and protecting my scholarship must be my priority, regardless of mind-boggling discoveries. I need a grant for my specialty fellowship covering an additional two years. I confess part of me will be relieved not to have to juggle our rule-breaking anymore.

"But," Archer concluded, his conflicts obvious, "there goes the project, Adam. I wonder if we will ever stumble upon an opportunity like it again?"

Before Wakefield could respond, Elizabeth came to life. "Adam, you're really moving to California? Leaving Boston, your family, and friends three thousand miles behind?"

"Elizabeth, as you well know, my family has been decimated financially, as have I. Both siblings gone, both parents now as well after their wrenching losses. My mother couldn't survive losing two of her three children and gave up years ago. And if you ask me," Wakefield's voice cracked, "Father simply chose not to struggle on after our wealth vanished.

"The move may seem precipitous, Elizabeth, but I've considered it carefully. Staying on would inevitably remind me of loss and more loss . . ." Wakefield recovered himself. "You recall how I loved California—its mountains, deserts, ocean, its spirit of reinvention and limitless opportunity, somehow all reflected in its diverse topography. Possibility literally informs the place."

"Ah yes, the call of the Wild West," Elizabeth replied with sarcasm. "I do remember how you inhaled Zane Grey in your youth. Was that why we always wore cowboy and Indian costumes at Halloween while everyone else we knew dressed as Pilgrims?"

Wakefield agreed. "Right you are. I loved Zane Grey."

But Archer was disconsolate. "I can't believe you've never mentioned this before, springing it on us like this. You must have been planning this for some time."

"I have, since—well for some time, as you say," Wakefield owned up. "But our research would have ended regardless, Randall. You just said as much. There's been some fallout between our respective deans or some such politics at the University. Dean Bainbridge wants my microscope returned to the physics lab posthaste."

The room fell into a sullen silence until Elizabeth's exaggerated sigh of acceptance broke the spell. "So when, Adam? When will you leave?"

"Soon. After tying up my affairs. I'm to start as quickly as possible." Guilty at his friends' dejection on their wedding day, Wakefield scrambled to restore the mood. "I'm sorry. I did bring clouds to your wedding day. Please forgive me. But California is not the end of the world. I'll be back from time to time. And perhaps you'll venture westward for a visit? It's only a three-day train ride nowadays! Imagine the countryside you'd travel through." Both Archers failed to react.

"Besides," Wakefield tried again, "you'll be up to your eyebrows, Randall, as you wind up your residency and begin your pathology specialization. You won't have time to miss me, either one of you. And maybe, old boy, those dark circles we were discussing earlier at the lab, marring that handsome face of yours, will disappear with sleep you've been neglecting due at least in part to our work. You really need to get more rest, old boy. Perhaps it's a good thing I've been booted from your lab."

Wakefield swallowed hard, unsuccessfully controlling an unsteady smile. "And you two will have the time necessary to become a solid couple. You have each other now." Wakefield stood, realized there was nowhere to go, and slumped back onto the chair. "How about more of your contraband champagne? We were celebrating your wedding day, were we not?"

Archer forced a grim smile, rising mechanically to retrieve the bottle from the kitchen sink he'd filled with ice. Mismatched glasses refilled, the threesome sat in close quarters, not knowing where to rest their eyes. In a final attempt to alleviate the gloom which now pervaded, Wakefield attempted another toast. "To Elizabeth Per—Archer and Doctor Randall Archer!"

"And to you, Adam," Archer rejoined, raising his glass half-heartedly. "A friend and collaborator who will be much missed as he seeks 'out-of-the-box thinking and doing' on the other side of the country. To your success and happiness as well, Adam."

"And yours," Wakefield responded, hiking his glass in the air toward the newlyweds before downing a long, slow swallow.

CHAPTER SEVEN

THE NEW DEAL

1933

The years earning his pathology certification flew by in a busy whirl. Archer's classroom and laboratory work were demanding and exciting, augmented by continuing tasks in the medical lab and performing special requests and private assignments for Dr. Dole. Now as Dean of the Medical College, Dole regularly extolled Archer's brilliant future at Harvard. Archer felt pride at his unique position, doing the dean's bidding. He chose to trust that the corners cut were in fact minor—'timing issues' as Dole often referred to them—rather than falsification of research data.

Archer's responsibilities forced lengthy separations between the newlyweds, countered by the forced proximity of their tight living quarters. Married life, too, was new and exciting as the Archers grew into a rhythm that worked for them. Instead of long absences becoming a problem for the couple, they inspired Elizabeth to carve out her own path, something she had longed to do.

Out of necessity, she wasted no time putting her state

teaching credential to use, landing a position at the primary school, the Ross Academy for Girls, which she herself, along with a long line of Perrish females, had attended. The teaching position came with the added advantage of being within walking distance of the Archers' apartment. Her rather meager earnings took on inordinate importance, helping support her doctor-in-training husband while greatly enhancing her sense of accomplishment.

Perhaps the biggest surprise in the evolving married life of the Archers was how Elizabeth took to the teaching of young girls. She was good at it, gaining enormous satisfaction from her work. The girls' minds were so open. They had not yet been carefully schooled in what was expected and what was not acceptable.

Near the end of the semester, Elizabeth burst into the Archers' apartment, hoisting a bottle of champagne on which she'd splurged, to announce, "Randall, we are celebrating!"

When he turned to face her, he asked, "Wherever did you find that?"

"The champagne? Amazing how quickly former contraband has reappeared since Prohibition ended. Finally." She then directed him, "Randall, take a seat and prepare to be amazed. Your wife has been named," she withdrew a framed certificate from her bag and held it aloft, "ta-da, as you read here, the Teacher of the Year! In my first full year of teaching!" She turned the plaque so she could reread it. "Wouldn't my parents be amazed?

"No," she sobered, "they'd be angry that I'd humiliated them even more by seeking and finding a job, 'like some lowly shop girl,'" she said, imitating her mother's staccato speech. "They'd take this honor as yet another personal affront." Her reflection drained her enthusiasm.

But Archer wouldn't let it drop. "Elizabeth, that is simply remarkable! Teacher of the Year? I'm so proud of you!" He rose to encircle her in a great congratulatory hug, taking the award to read carefully. "Astonishing! Aren't you full of wonders? You've adjusted to living in much-reduced circumstances, to hear Adam speak reverently about Perrish House, here in student housing," her eyes followed his around the small room, "like it was nothing. And now this. Flourishing in your first job, which certainly helps our finances. You amaze me, Lizbeth, truly."

"Thank you, Randall." She perked up again. "I've rather astounded myself. I wasn't sure I could handle any of it. But, to tell you the truth, I'm having the time of my life. When you're raised as I was, expectations slotting you into terrain you never chose, you begin to wonder if that's because it's all you're capable of. It eats at you, those doubts. Most girls like me never get the chance to see what they're made of, succumbing instead to others' expectations reinforced by everyone around them."

"Well," Archer whispered, placing her award safely out of reach before taking her in his arms again, "I'm glad we're both learning what you're made of." He kissed her long and searchingly until they were wrapped in a hungry embrace.

She broke away. "Randall, fold out the bed, would you. I'm finding after all the hard work it's taken to be honored for my teaching skills, I'm suddenly tired. I think we should lay down and nap. Or something."

But he was ahead of her, the bed folded out, pulling at her and her clothing and she at his.

§

It was nothing like the ceremony that had marked the end of medical school two years prior. A much smaller group of doctors who had completed their specialization in pathology were to be cheered and honored by families and friends following the final stage of their education and training, now fully Medical Doctors of Pathology.

Archer sat on the dais surveying the attendees, easily finding his beautiful wife, sitting erect and staring back at him with a proud grin on her face. But what a shock he had, finding Adam Wakefield seated beside her, their heads towering over the rest of the gathering.

Adam? He hadn't expected Adam! *Could he really have come across the continent for this? No, he probably had a reason for returning to Boston. But what a thrill to have him here again and for him to witness this long-in-coming final step.*

Archer had a hard time paying attention to Dr. Dole, exhorting those on the dais to be ever-mindful of the privilege and responsibility of the degrees they carried forward and the institution they would hereafter represent to the world, wherever they made their careers. Archer's mind wandered back to the handsome couple his wife and best friend made, their elegance dimming all others in the audience. *Adam is here!* He couldn't believe it.

When at last Dole finished his overused commencement comments, the doctors poured offstage toward the crowd as the attendees surged forward in applause. The milling mix offered kisses and words of pride and encouragement amongst new introductions and happy reunions.

After receiving a hug and kiss from his wife, Archer found himself surrounded by Wakefield's long arms. "Proud of you, old man," he said. "You made it."

"Adam! I had no idea you were in town. When did you get in? How long are you here? I'm so happy you could fit in my final advancement."

"Oh, it's no coincidence, Randall. Elizabeth wrote me about this day and I thought, I really must come see for myself that in fact you'd survived what, twelve years of a Harvard education? You've seen your dream to fruition. Good show, old man. My sincerest congratulations. I know how diligently you've toiled. Let's hope the hard part is behind you and your beautiful bride."

Wakefield squeezed Elizabeth's hand and patted Archer on the back. "Bravo, dear friends."

Just then, Dean Dole interrupted them to offer his own congratulations. He acknowledged Wakefield. "I recall meeting you briefly in the medical lab some years ago. I knew your family, Mr. Wakefield. Are you still over at Physics?"

Wakefield shook his head. "'Fraid not. I've been living in Los Angeles for the past two years. Still in physics though."

Dole turned his attention toward Elizabeth, looking strikingly feminine in a gauzy floral dress, flowing around her tall frame in the slight breeze. The blue hat with a mini-veil matched her blue gloves, all of which enhanced the mesmerizing deep blue of her eyes. Archer puffed up his chest over this gorgeous woman who belonged to him, especially seeing the way Dole, Wakefield, and those nearby admired her.

"So you're Elizabeth Perrish," Dole began. "Of course, I know your family well. I used to see Bradley and still see Prescott at the Harvard Club in New York from time to time. Pleased to make your acquaintance. I've heard much about you."

Elizabeth didn't miss a beat. She offered her gloved hand, saying, "It's Archer. Elizabeth Archer."

"Of course. Of course, slip of the tongue." Focusing on Archer again, Dole said, "I need to see you first thing tomorrow morning, say, eight? Come to my office. Charming to meet you all, but I must greet the others before the gathering breaks up. Tomorrow then, Archer." Dole turned to leave but was held up by a woman that looked somehow familiar to Archer. He found himself watching their interchange as Dole, obviously uncomfortable, glanced about nervously as though looking to escape. Until Archer's curiosity was diverted by his wife's question.

"What's that about, Randall?" Elizabeth was asking.

"The appointment with Dole?" Archer smiled, looking smug. "I'm pretty certain it's about fulfilling all the promises Dr. Dole has made me throughout these twelve long years you mentioned, Adam. Something about my brilliant future at Harvard. Don't be surprised if I come home tomorrow morning as Harvard Medical College's newest on-staff pathologist. Perhaps running the medical lab I've toiled in all this time. Perhaps a professorship. Or a post-doc position? The sky is the limit, my friends," he confessed with no attempt at modesty.

"Randy." The threesome turned toward the female voice belonging to a small, rather round woman, the very one who had appeared to discomfit Dole as he hurried away. "Randy, it's me, Della. Della Dolkowski, your high school counselor. You don't remember me?"

Archer just stared, taking in the much changed and aged woman he hadn't thought about for years, except in sexual dreams she'd inspired early on. No longer too young-looking to be a counselor, she was dressed in a coarse and loose-fitting garment and an old-fashioned hat partially covering her blonde hair, now faded to mousy—much like the rest of her.

An awkward silence stretched out. Elizabeth was the first to respond. She extended her hand and introduced herself. "Hello, I'm Elizabeth, Randall's wife. This is Dr. Wakefield, a longtime friend of ours. And you are Randall's counselor from back home?"

Staring wide-eyed at Elizabeth, Della Dolkowski seemed to shrink further into herself. But Elizabeth's firm handshake encouraged her. "I was Randy . . . Randall, is it now? I-I was his high school counselor. I've followed his success all these years from afar. My cousin, who helped arrange his scholarship to Harvard in the first place, kept me informed on occasion as Randy—Randall worked his way through to this day, brilliantly, of course," she added, turning back to address Archer. "And you did it! Just like I said you would. Somehow I couldn't miss seeing this. I hope you don't mind me barging in like this, Randy?"

Abashed by the striking comparisons between the life and

friends he'd made and the past that just would not stay buried, Archer stood mute and stunned. Here before him stood everything he had tried to outdistance. "But Miss Della," he finally managed. "I mean, *Della*—do y-you know Dr. Dole? I saw you two talking—"

"No, not really. We're related, but I don't know him. We've met only a few times. He rarely returns to Pittsburgh. But I did want to thank him personally for all he's done for you."

"*He* is your second cousin? Who made all this possible for me? He—he— He never said a word . . ." Archer couldn't organize the jumble this new information made of his thoughts. "Dole. Is that short for—"

"Dolkowski, yes. I suppose it is a lot easier than a long Polish name." She fell silent, glancing about nervously to avoid Archer's shocked stare.

Elizabeth covered for her husband. "You are quite a surprise, I can see, and how kind of you to follow Randall's long path and take it upon yourself to be here for him today. Right, Randall?" she added with emphasis.

"Yes, right. I mean, yes—yes, of course. Miss Della, you and your second cousin have caught me unawares. It's been so long. I couldn't be more surprised. Obviously. Thank you for coming all this way to congratulate me. Did you come all this way for that?"

When Archer's and his high school counselor's discomfort showed no signs of reversing, Wakefield stepped in. "Miss Dolkowski, we were just going to have an informal celebration of Randall's accomplishments. We'd be pleased to have you join us. A post-Prohibition beer or two. Would you—"

"Oh, no, I, no, I couldn't. I-I have plans. But I'm happy to have seen my most successful student ever reach his goal. Best of luck, Randy—Randall. I'm sure we'll hear big things from you wherever you go."

Both Elizabeth and Wakefield insisted that she come along. "Just a quick beer," they commented together. "After all the dry years, do join us—another thing to celebrate! And we'd love to hear about the 'Randy' you knew," Elizabeth added.

Archer paled at the thought but held onto a tight smile, nodding unconvincingly. "Of course, Miss Della, you must—"

But shaking her head, dull wisps flying, she declined. "No, you're very kind, but no. I really must go. Good luck, *Dr.* Archer. You've made your high school and your counselor very, very proud!"

As Miss Della disappeared into the diminishing crowd, Archer's pathology fellows pressed in, making excuses to be introduced to his wife. They eyed him with increased respect, their open admiration of Elizabeth reflecting nicely upon him. He basked in the wonder that was his wife as well as his colleagues' jealousy, instantly forgetting Miss Della all over again.

§

Archer regretted his restless night, tossing throughout on the small bed he shared with his wife.

Following their private celebration with Wakefield, as much about the latter's return to his friends and Boston as Archer completing his arduous education, Archer had been unable to suppress his exhilaration. *I'm done!* But his excitement warred with a niggling worry at entering the workforce in the throes of a devastating depression showing no signs of reversing. He, like the country collectively, held his breath that the recently elected president, Franklin Delano Roosevelt, could reverse the precipitous spiral that his predecessor's failed policies had not.

The more that Archer vacillated between hope and worry, the more he stirred. Elizabeth rolled one way, then the other, on the narrow fold-out. With weeks to go before the summer break at the Ross Academy, he knew she needed her rest.

Finally giving up on sleep, Archer rose and tried to brew coffee in silence. But, not knowing where the scoop was, he rustled through the drawer. Then he spilled coffee grounds on the linoleum and scraped them up. Next, with a clatter, he dropped the cup he was cleaning into their miniscule sink.

Tying her robe at the waist, Elizabeth stumbled around the screen currently partitioning the bed from the rest of the apartment and wordlessly took control. She wrested what she needed until the smell and thrum of percolating coffee filled the apartment with its delicious aroma and the pleasing sounds of a new day's beginning.

Only then did Elizabeth address her husband. "What's on your mind, Randall? You've just concluded *years* of education, and with flying colors I might add. What could possibly be worrying you now? Life is just beginning for you, for us! I'm bursting with pride and optimism, and you should be too."

"Yes, yes, of course. Just anticipating meeting with the dean, imagining all the possibilities lying in wait for my future."

"The dean's had his eye on you since before you entered medical school," Elizabeth reminded him. "So yes, I imagine there will be wondrous things from which to choose."

Archer again puzzled over the new information gleaned from Della Dolkowski the day before. Dole had had his eye on him long before medical school—evidently before he'd even arrived at Harvard. Still Archer didn't know what to make of it . . .

Elizabeth, intent on bolstering him before his big meeting, said, "I have every confidence that you will accomplish all you set your mind to, Randall. Hasn't life so far proven that point?" Archer cocked his head, smiling at the pleasant words that recalled Miss Della's from years ago. "But after all this time," Elizabeth added, "you'll finally begin earning a real living as well."

When the thrumming ceased, Elizabeth twisted her hair into a knot and poured two cups of black brew, unaware her comment about earning a living had touched a raw nerve in her husband, overly sensitive to the fact she'd been the 'breadwinner' throughout their marriage.

She handed him a cup, and they both sipped hot liquid, alone in their separate contemplations. "You know, Randall, making your own money, at least me making my own, supporting *us* as we began our life together, has meant so much more than I ever dreamed."

Archer glanced up from the small oven set to broil, where he'd placed two pieces of bread to toast. "I can only imagine," he sniped.

"It's made me feel I'm finally standing on my own two feet, solidly attached to the earth, no longer hitching a ride on the shoulders of the important men who've gone before. It makes me feel powerful and competent and . . . independent." She yawned suddenly, then smiled. "Am I making sense?"

Archer checked the toast before standing to answer, "Yes. As I've said before, Elizabeth, you're a wonder. Not just becoming a fine teacher, not just adapting to these tight quarters, and never complaining about my endless hours. Perhaps most impressive is Mrs. Brahmin's adjustment to the daunting reality of having to support her husband." He reined in his frustrations with effort, knowing they were about to end anyway. "Having never met them, all I can add is your family grossly underestimated you. Perhaps everyone did, including you." That he could say the same thing about himself and his own family struck him.

She thought about his words, and her smile widened. "You're right, Randall. *Everyone, including me.* Perhaps that's most gratifying of all, surprising myself. I'm quite certain my family would never believe me capable, even now, of holding a job, let alone being honored for my work in my first year. I pray my tutelage inspires my young students to remember they can shape their own lives too, no matter what anyone attempts to dictate."

She took a long sip. "That's the irony, isn't it, Randall, of family? They slot you into a position in their hierarchy, based on their beliefs, expectations, and needs. While growing up, you more or less have to make your slot work. But as you come to know yourself and perhaps wander off-script, the family resists any alteration to your assignment, at least without giving it a good fight."

Elizabeth poured more coffee, deep in thought. "It's as if any change, growth, or redirection diminishes *them*. Or does it interfere in your shared history—everyone staying in unmovable niches taking precedence over the individuals?" She huffed, "Or maybe parents perpetually believe they know what's best for their children, even when they are no longer children. Have you ever wondered about this, Randall?"

Ever wondered? Archer repeated to himself with an ironic chuckle. "Only since I could form thoughts, Elizabeth." A science award he'd won in elementary school, he couldn't remember for what, came to mind, along with the loud derision it had evoked. When he'd presented the award to his father, he'd questioned his son before his smirking brothers. 'What are you goin' to do with that? Decorate yer locker with it at the mill someday?' "Yes Elizabeth," Archer replied, "I have thought about it."

Archer put his cup down, then placed his wife's aside and pulled her to him, suddenly needing to assert his manhood in preparation for his pivotal meeting. "Who understands why the unavoidable process of growing up, growing less like your family, or never being like them to start with, is a threat, Lizbeth. Is it as simple as getting beyond their control? Or perhaps simpler yet, outshining them?"

But he was tired of this unsatisfying subject. He had a bright future to think about. He tightened his hold on his wife and kissed her. "You look beautiful in tangled hair, Mrs. Archer." Smiling at his praise, she returned his kisses with mounting passion.

Needing to find the bed again, they struggled apart. Archer gasped, "How much time have we got? I'm due on campus by eight." They glanced at the wall clock, then at each other with mutual urgency.

"Have we got ten minutes, Randall?" But he was already guiding her toward the rumpled bed. "And Dr. Archer," she whispered, lying back provocatively, "you can make up for our abbreviated morning tonight.

"Think of it," she brightened. "No more excuses for my husband to stay out day and night. Let's celebrate this newly-won freedom. Meet me at the Academy. I'll be done by three."

§

"You're perfect, Dr. Archer," Elizabeth pronounced, judging her husband's hurried grooming. He dashed from the apartment and arrived at the College of Medicine a few moments before his eight o'clock appointment with the dean. The dean's secretary was not at her post in the outer office when Archer entered. When she hadn't shown by ten minutes after the hour, he rerouted his pacing nearer to the inner office door. Hearing muffled voices within, he rapped lightly. With no response, he rapped harder.

The dean's secretary cracked the door, eyeing Archer coldly. "I have an appointment with Dr. Dole," he explained, "at eight." He nodded toward the wall clock displaying fifteen minutes after the hour.

With a withering glare the woman replied, "We are aware of your appointment, Dr. Archer. Please take a seat. The dean will be with you shortly." She shut the door in his face.

Archer sat. He picked up a copy of *The Journal of the United States Medical Doctors Association* and flipped through its numerous advertisements for medical equipment, drugs, and specialized facilities, skimming articles on diseases and approved treatments.

Something isn't right.

Archer made himself focus on an article delineating the many benefits of developing drug therapies that utilized synthetic or manmade chemicals, versus the naturally-occurring substances which had been used throughout the ages as curatives. The benefits of synthesized formulas, the article claimed, were that they were cheaper to develop, easier to assemble, and thus more readily available. They were producible on any scale in a laboratory setting, and the formulas were more easily studied and fine-tuned *vis-à-vis* patient interactions and possible secondary effects. Archer noticed that each synthesized drug under discussion was footnoted as 'patent pending.'

The article went on to list the three principal categories of disease based on their origins—viral, bacterial, and fungal—against which these formulas had proven effective.

At 8:40, Archer's apprehension evolved into annoyance. *What is going on in there? Why am I kept waiting, rudely, with no explanation?* This was part of the dean's grand scheme to keep him at Harvard 'at all costs'? His treatment seemed more ironic given the dean's stern emphasis on punctuality.

Archer's mind traveled to the memory of his wife's gorgeous body, which he'd left hurriedly and with difficulty. What he and Elizabeth could have done if they hadn't been short of time. Thinking of her long limbs and unbridled passions sent a heat wave surging through him as the inner sanctum door opened and the dean's secretary approached. The woman eyed him suspiciously, as though reading his randy thoughts, but said only, "Dean Dole is ready for you, Dr. Archer."

'Something isn't right' was the thought that chased from his mind his wife's taut stomach, scarred by the stitches he loved to trace with his fingers and tongue. Sitting behind his imposing desk, silver hair neatly plastered to his scalp, the frowning dean appeared to be studying columns of figures. When he glanced up, Archer noticed his unusual pallor. His sweating palm when he rose to shake hands increased Archer's sense of foreboding.

"Are you feeling well, Dean?" he asked, taking a seat facing him.

"Yes—yes, of course, I'm fine," Dole answered. "However, not everything is." He wiped his brow and launched into an explanation. "As you know, Archer, I've considered you my protégé for years, even as an undergraduate *before* you'd entered the Medical College, and throughout your tenure here."

"I've just come to understand the verity of that statement, Dr. Dole! You're Della Dolkowski's second cousin, the man I've owed a great debt to for—"

Dole cut him off. "There is some distant connection, yes, but I'd hardly call her a close relative. Back to the business at hand. Standing out as you have since pre-med is quite a feat here at Harvard, I must say. My personal intention has always been to keep you on until you assumed the role of esteemed medical faculty and attained a full-professorship in pathology."

"My personal plan as well, sir," Archer affirmed with audible relief, "since the very first lecture you gave the incoming freshmen. Actually, before. Harvard has been my only dream since I was old enough to recognize there was more to life than my family, home, and hometown."

"You've distinguished yourself without doubt. However—"

"'However,' sir?" Archer leaned forward, on the alert.

"I won't lie to you. There is a problem," the dean said, exhaling slowly. "Even Harvard is not impervious to the times we find ourselves in. The financial threat and ruin surrounding us is wreaking havoc. Perhaps for the first time in the University's long history, funding and expenditures have come under scrutiny. I'm afraid actual cutbacks may be required, even within the Medical College. Of course by extension, that means new projects and hires and concomitant funding will be strictly limited until, well, until we see our way through this."

Archer blinked as if he hadn't heard correctly. "What are you saying, Dr. Dole? I'm *not* here today to discuss an offer to stay on as a post-doc or in another role? You do *not* intend to keep me on at the College nor Harvard 'at all costs' as I've so often been assured—by you?"

"Look, I—"

"And the stock market crash happened nearly four years ago, Dean. The financial woes you allude to seem too convenient after your promises on this very subject—cost, literally, 'at all costs!' And," recalling Wakefield's question upon losing his post-doctoral position to the same spurious excuse, he added, "isn't Harvard the best-endowed university in the country, if not the world?"

Archer bolted to his feet, his body temperature spiking. Needing to process this unexpected turn, he paced before the dean's desk. "This is quite a different picture than the one you painted for us pathology fellows just yesterday, Dean Dole. You've been talking about the future of medicine and Harvard's rightful role at its forefront since we met. Your praise of me, your intention to keep me on at whatever cost, how do you balance such exhortations with what you're telling me now?"

"See here, Archer, this is not my choice! It comes from the very top. If you wish to know my best guess, you've made some mighty powerful and influential enemies."

Archer, brow wrinkled in confusion, stopped dead in his tracks to gape at Dole.

"As you're no doubt aware, Bradley Perrish and the Perrish name and family have been central to this University since its very inception. Your marrying Bradley's only daughter without his blessing has riled them all. Unofficially, mind you, I suspect he has let it be known he considers your presence an ongoing affront to the heritage of this institution and to him personally.

"Look at it this way, Archer. At least you were able to complete your education before this development. That's an enormous gift in itself."

Archer struggled for words. "He—Elizabeth's father, he has that much power?"

"I suspect so."

"But—but . . . you need me, Dr. Dole. Who else will do your bidding in the lab when drug test results must be sped along or slanted ever-so-slightly? I've taken risks for you, Dean! You owe me! I did everything I was supposed to do and everything without question that you asked of me."

"See here, young man!" Dole's voice ratcheted as his anger bled over his prior paleness. "You have served me and the institution well, of that there is no question. You'll be the first call I'll make, Archer, if and when things change. That's a promise, and the only one I can make to you right now."

Archer slammed back onto the seat. "But what will I do? Harvard's my life-dream, my only dream. I can't just . . ." Archer rose and paced again before halting suddenly. "Should I . . . divorce her?"

Dole's eyebrows shot up in surprise. His was a mirthless chuckle when he responded, "Further controversy surrounding the Perrish name would hardly win points for you, Archer. Excuse the language, but in their minds, a nobody from nowhere divorcing *the* Perrish daughter? You can safely assume that would not help your cause."

Archer slumped on the seat, head in hands, trying to contain rising panic and think. His wife's encouragements now mocked him: 'I have every confidence you will accomplish anything you set your mind to. Hasn't life so far proven that point?'

"I've prepared a detailed and laudatory letter of recommendation," Dole added, "which, signed as it is by the Dean of Harvard Medical, will carry real weight out there well beyond Harvard and Boston." The dean slid the letter across the desk toward Archer, reiterating, "If a way to bring you onboard opens up down the road, you'll hear from me, Archer. That I can promise.

"In the meantime, I'm certain you won't have long or far to look. If there's justice in the world, they'll be lining up to claim you, Archer. My recommendation, along with your education and achievements, plus the name of your alma mater, will serve you well in your job search."

Archer gulped down choking disappointment and rising panic. "I'm—I am speechless. Damn it, this comes out of the blue! Couldn't you have—was there no warning? And this, as the Depression worsens. After all the special favors I've done for you, not to mention my consistent outstanding performance. It all comes down to Elizabeth's father?"

"Unofficially, mind you, it appears it does. I'm sorry, Archer, truly. Do stay in communication, young man. Let us know where you land. You'll do Harvard proud wherever you go."

Right on cue, the intercom buzzed and the secretary's disembodied voice advised, "Your nine-fifteen call is on the line, Dr. Dole."

"Put him through, Mrs. Day." Palm covering the receiver, the dean added as his final dismissal, "Good luck."

§

Archer stumbled out of Dole's office and across the campus in a daze, the jeers of his lifelong detractors throbbing in his ears. 'I told ya you'd never fit in. Harvard? Who do ya think you are? Think you're too good for this family? The steel mills? Pittsburgh?'

A sudden thought stymied him where he stood. *Even the faithful Miss Della would be appalled at my failure after all she did to get me out and on my way. I've let her down too.*

He lurched ahead blindly, thoughts turning to Bradley Perrish, a man he'd never met and likely never would. Did he resemble that condescending Ansley, his scoffing ancestor on his bronze pedestal, scowling down on the campus? A man used to being in charge, expecting deference, and getting it. Even his bronze likeness exuded power and superiority.

He's won.

The thought struck Archer like a mortal blow to the gut.

Elizabeth's father has won. Adam had warned me but I believed my superior performance here amongst the elite would win the Perrishes over. What a fool I've been.

Long before Elizabeth would be forced to join me in the bread-lines or shelters, before selling apples on the street corner, before starvation, she'll leave me. Of course, she will. And Bradley Perrish will gallantly take her back, soundly chastened, and marry her off to a Rockefeller or someone equally suitable. In mere months, my name would not even be a memory, just a bad dream to be buried and never again mentioned.

Archer began to feel sick, lightheaded. He collapsed onto the closest support available, the raised stone base of— "Oh my God," he said, looking up at the statue above him of none other than Ansley Perrish.

"Well, Ansley," he stood to confront him aloud, "I've literally done everything I set out to do. Gained a prestigious education and multiple degrees. Finished at the top of my class throughout. Was mentored by the most powerful man in the College, gaining his loyalty when he needed 'insignificant adjustments' to laboratory test results and records. Yes, I went along, but who was he kidding? And none of it was good enough! No blue blood, no pedigree, no Elizabeth Perrish, no career at Harvard. Period."

Archer's indignation skyrocketed. His completed checklist had gotten him exactly nowhere. No job, prospects, money, or future.

It felt like going home again. Or worse, as if he'd never left.

Accusatory voices, past and present, warred in his mind, bringing tears. 'You're not near as smart as ya think y'are.' 'Imagine, someone from where again? Attempting to infiltrate our social order? Ridiculous. Outrageous!'

Archer covered his ears as a desperate decision took form in his mind. Before Bradley Perrish and all the Perrishes and their ilk amused themselves with his predictable failure, he should just end it. *I should end it now.*

He glanced up at the glaring statue and turned away. "End it now," he stated out loud, "before I have to witness their enjoyment at the spectacle of my downfall, like my own family would. I've lost it all anyway."

Yes, he thought, end it before Elizabeth walks out without a word, or worse, with biting words of disappointment, her patience lost with her husband and the futile promise she once saw in him.

§

Archer's plan evolved as he stumbled across campus with his thoughts churning. *The laboratory has plenty of medicinals I could use to do the job. I can make it quick and painless, even make it look like an accident to cheat those who would gloat. At least I'd never have to hear my family's taunts, nor ever think about Pittsburgh, the steel mills, social rank, success, failure, or money again. The deck has always been stacked against me,* for he admitted to himself. *How stupid to think I could find my way around that immutable fact.*

Archer became aware he'd been heading toward the medical lab. Far from routine, his path reflected the decision he'd reached on the only face-saving course of action open to him as everything slipped away. What better place in the world for him to end his life than in the Harvard Medical Laboratory, which had been like a home to him in Boston.

He entered the lab and surveyed the space for other occupants. Since it was a weekend, the laboratory was nearly empty. His mind turned to procuring a syringe and the solution with which he'd use to inject himself when a commotion at the entrance diverted his search. A blond man was attempting to push his way inside, arguing with someone blocking the door.

"Randall. Dr. Archer! It's me." He recognized Wakefield's voice, raised in irritation. "Tell this—this person to let me in.

For old times' sake."

Archer slammed the syringe in a drawer and reluctantly went to investigate. As he drew closer, eyeing Wakefield, a crashing insight washed over him. Wakefield had lost everything, his family, his money, his job. Yet here he was. He'd bounced back. Life hadn't mowed him down. He'd risen to meet its challenges, with grace and humor.

"Randall, please. Come speak with this—this security person," Wakefield cried.

And in the next moment Archer knew Elizabeth would do the same thing, rise to the challenge. It was simply her nature to carry on, to find a way. Archer, who had secretly denigrated them both as tragically out-of-touch—too removed and unable to comprehend the harsh underbelly of life with their silver spoons getting in their way—had to acknowledge in them both a resilience he could only envy. Shame overshadowed his despondency.

Archer spoke to the guard who had let him pass without so much as a question. "It's an old friend, Joe. He used to work here. I'm sure it's all right to let Dr. Wakefield pass."

Wakefield pushed by the guard. "Since when did the medical lab need a guard?" he asked before thanking Archer for vouching for him.

"What is this all about?" Archer asked the guard.

"He's supposed to have a special pass for weekend entrance into the lab, Dr. Archer. Everyone is," he added with emphasis. "Orders from above."

Having nothing left to lose, Archer said, "I'll take full responsibility."

The two scientists headed automatically to Archer's now-former work area. The locked space they once shared had long ago been abandoned. Wakefield commented, "Thought I'd find you here, old man. Old habits die hard."

"What are you doing here? What did you mean 'for old times' sake?'"

"I'm hoping for a glance at my first super-scope. I just stopped in at my old college. Said hello to Dean Bainbridge, who relayed the strangest story. I asked how the College of Physics was utilizing my first microscope, and he told me they'd never gotten it back from the Medical College. After repeated requests, your Dean Dole finally admitted they'd misplaced it, or it had been stolen. It was nowhere to be found at the medical facilities."

"What? That microscope of yours left this lab soon after you did. I assumed it had gone back to Physics. How does one lose a microscope, especially one so large and unwieldy? In fact, I asked about it several times during my pathology training, and was told it had been returned to Physics and could no longer be accessed."

"So it's not here then? And you have no idea where it might be? Strange indeed . . ." Wakefield gazed around the lab. "Not much has changed here otherwise. Are you still employed here part-time, even after your completion ceremony yesterday?"

"Uh no, I-I'm through." Tears suddenly pressured the back of his eyes. "I'm here attending to a few unfinished . . . odds and ends."

"Oh!" Wakefield stopped himself. "How did your meeting go with Dole this morning? You'll be running the Medical College soon, I assume?" he teased.

Tears threatened to overflow as Archer considered admitting his catastrophic disappointment. That would be difficult to do with anyone, but particularly to this old friend. He gulped down his emotion and cobbled a response. "Not exactly as expected, but look, Adam, I'm in a bit of a rush today. I'm due to meet Elizabeth at the Ross Academy." He checked the wall clock. "I don't have much time."

"All right. If you're leaving now, I'll walk out with you."

Archer gazed around the lab he might never again see, and made up his mind. "I guess I am leaving now." He fell into step with Wakefield. The moment to execute his hasty end-game had passed.

"My train leaves early in the morning for Los Angeles," Wakefield told him as they exited the building together. "I have a few things to do on campus, but I'd like to stop by tonight to say goodbye to you both."

§

Randall and Elizabeth Archer meandered along the banks of the Charles River hand-in-hand. Their plan had been to celebrate this unheard-of daylight opportunity to enjoy each other's company. The fresh scent of new grass and flowers promising to burst forth had also drawn rowers, walkers, and bikers outdoors in droves to enjoy the late spring weather.

But on closer inspection, the Archers wandered blindly, holding each other up more than romantically strolling. The springtime ambiance was lost on them both. Instead a heavy silence hung in the air between them. It masked the warming sunlight beneath which the rest of Boston gaily shook off the last remnants of a long winter.

Archer strained to read Elizabeth's expression, but her dark tresses tumbling around her downcast face foiled him. Yet dejection was plain to see in her rare slouch which had greeted him at the Ross Academy where she'd made her own stunning announcement. "Tell me again what they told you, Lizbeth. Word for word."

Glancing at him as if surprised to find him there, she shoved back her hair and cleared her throat. "'The continuing Depression requires the Academy to make difficult decisions to ensure its future serving young girls as it has for over a century. Unfortunately, the newest hire must, logically, be first to go. That's only fair.'"

"But—but you're the Teacher of the Year!"

"Last year. This year, the title apparently means nothing."

"There's been no hint or discussion that might have led you

to suspect—"

"There's been nothing, Randall. Nothing! Just last week, the principal praised my 'consistently outstanding work' with the girls." Elizabeth sighed, mist dulling her blue eyes. "It just doesn't add up. Something happened in the spring of 1933 to convert that pat-on-the-back to being *fired*? It's inexplicable ..." She trailed off in bewilderment.

'Inexplicable,' he sourly repeated to himself, identifying more closely than she could imagine with her shock and devastation. "I'm afraid our timing couldn't be worse, Elizabeth." She glanced at him. "Seems at the same time I've been severed from Harvard."

"'Severed from Harvard'? Randall, what are you talking about? Severed? When? This morning? You don't mean by Dr. Dole? After all he's promised you?"

"Hm-mm." Archer held back his disbelief and humiliation. "Apparently, Elizabeth, it's your father."

"What's my father?"

"The reason. Why I've been cut loose from Harvard." Her jaw dropped as she swung around to stare at him. Archer swallowed down bruising disgrace to explain. "Dole implied it was your father, Elizabeth, using his name and historic connection to the University to make certain I could not stay on." He walked on to avoid his wife's piercing gaze, battling to hold it together.

When he realized she hadn't budged, he stopped and turned back. "Under the circumstances, Dole advised me to leave Boston."

"My father," Elizabeth finally reacted. "More likely, my mother, behind the scenes. Of course." She caught up to him, and they again trudged along the riverbank, lost in their worries. "I take back the word 'inexplicable,'" Elizabeth announced. "It makes perfect sense. My family has an historic association with the Ross Academy as well as Harvard. My mother and I are among the many female Perrishes who've attended Ross. All the men attended Harvard."

She exhaled her bitterness. "They must have heard about my teaching. It's actually surprising it took this long. And it is so like them to use their money and influence to have us both tossed out on the street. I wonder if they're even aware what the streets are like right now? Not that it would have made a difference.

"They won't relent, Randall, not until I return to the Perrish fold under their terms and cease embarrassing them with my marriage and perhaps even worse, my wage-paying job."

Archer bristled at the reference to him. "I am an honored Harvard-educated medical doctor, Elizabeth. Perhaps that accomplishment might lighten their judgment?"

"You don't know my family, Randall. No, it wouldn't change a thing. Obviously." She changed the subject. "What of your colleagues, Randall? Have many of them found employment?"

Another bitter pill Archer labored to swallow. "Most, in fact, long before we finished up yesterday. But not foolish, trusting me, fully expecting my assured position delivered on a silver platter today."

"Was there nothing in writing," she asked, "no agreement you could point to?"

"You imply that I should have thought to get it in writing, that I'm ultimately responsible or at least I share in the blame? That I need more business acumen or social skills or contacts? How about an important family, which, save for you, Elizabeth, I simply do not have? Funny how that's come 'round to hurt me!"

"What?" Elizabeth countered. "Now you're blaming *me*?"

Archer snapped, "*You*, Miss Brahmin Perrish, only daughter of Bradley, certainly share in the blame." He stomped off but circled back. "Look, I'm well aware you've been supporting us financially throughout our marriage, and that you've done so without complaint. And that it is well past time I stepped up, that this is *not* at all what you signed on for—"

"Randall! What are you blubbering about?" she angrily interrupted. "Working, supporting you, finding success in the world I was never meant to enter—during the most difficult time in its history? It has been the adventure of my lifetime. I thought you knew that. I thought you were the one person in my life who understood *me*, the real me." Now she stomped ahead of him.

Archer hesitated a moment before chasing her down. "Elizabeth, I'm sorry. I'm just upset and . . . ashamed. After all I've done to assure my future, beyond just excellent performance and ambiguous 'favors' for Dr. Dole, to be blindsided by him and Harvard at the last possible moment." His voice quavered, "It is unbearable."

The couple walked on, side by side, no longer holding hands, drowning in uncertainties. Neither noticed a crewing race that burst into view on the Charles. In a last-ditch effort, the lagging crew caught and overtook the lead boat at the critical moment. One team collapsed in defeat, sinking with fatigue in their craft, while the other shouted and cheered, nearly tipping into the water in exultation.

Elizabeth walked faster and faster, her fists clenched. Archer jogged to keep up. "Oh, I'm so angry," she seethed.

"Me too. But what are we going to do, Elizabeth? Regardless who's behind it or why, our housing subsidy runs out at the end of the summer, we have no money to find another place to live and eat, and jointly we have no prospects—apparently not in this town. How will we survive? It's not as if there aren't *millions* just like us struggling with unemployment and in the soup lines."

Archer shivered at the images he could not squelch—the endless breadlines wrapping around city blocks, shanty towns mushrooming overnight with families displaced by massive foreclosures. The universal carnage was *gaining* momentum, not slowing. There were daily headlines of suicides even among the most affluent—formerly affluent—millionaires 'on paper' when stock prices flew through the roof. Those same 'millionaires' plummeted to destitution when 'margin calls' forced them to pay up on the stocks they'd bought on credit. Most couldn't and lost everything.

What is there to live for? Archer again found himself debating, defeat threatening to once more plunge him to the depths.

Roosevelt's 'bank holidays' had slowed runaway withdrawals, but people wanted their money. Now, they were to be deprived of what they'd struggled to save and for just such a rainy day? So much for the New Deal.

Archer gazed at the spring panorama. Nothing was as it seemed, nothing secure or securable, least of all the couple's future. *How much more can Elizabeth bear? Her drastically reduced living conditions are about to drastically worsen. What do I know about creating a happy home, let alone providing for one?*

"Randall!" Elizabeth blurted, the color rushing back to her cheeks, her eyes blazing into sharp focus. "They will not win. I will not let them win. I have a right to determine my own future. And I will!"

"But—"

"No. No buts. It's time we thought 'outside the box,' as Adam used to say. Hmm, Adam?" She paused. "He loves California, finds life there most agreeable. And he's thriving, according to everything he's told us. He certainly appeared content yesterday, and his letters have consistently glowed." Archer waited, fearing her implications. "Why can't *we* do that, Randall?"

"You don't mean leave Boston? Just leave . . . everything and move to California?"

"California, somewhere else, yes, precisely, and why not? Let's go somewhere, anywhere, my family can't manipulate us. Isn't that what your mentor advised? Why not follow Adam's example? It's working well for him. Hell, why not follow *him*?

California sounds fascinating. Imagine no more winter."

But 'buts' swamped Archer's veering emotions. "I-I've basically grown up in Boston," he whined. "I fully intended to spend my life here. Harvard was the only thing I ever wanted since I was old enough to know it existed." *Could I just leave? Should I?*

Archer observed his wife, pleased to see her feistiness returning, and unaware of how much her determination and optimism fueled him. *If Elizabeth Perrish can abandon her family's generational seat, surely I could do so? My decade in Boston doesn't compare to their generations and centuries.*

"What have we got to lose, Randall?" Elizabeth pressed. "Why not leave the box that is squeezing the life out of us, spread our wings, and find out what's outside that box, what the rest of the world has in store for us?"

Though infectious, Elizabeth's enthusiasm couldn't fully overcome her husband's dread, caution, and embarrassment. He gazed at the river in its ceaseless quest for the sea, asking himself again, what did he—what did the two of them—risk at this desperately low point in their lives?

If Elizabeth Perrish can walk away from her privileged upbringing in Boston and make a bold leap into the unknown, couldn't I? She is right, of course. We have nothing left to lose.

"Oh!" Archer remembered, "Adam. He's coming by before his early departure in the morning for California. We should hurry back if we don't want to miss him."

CHAPTER EIGHT

MASS MIGRATION

LATE 1933

Rumpled traveling suits broadcast the Archers' three straight days and nights of travel. When they stepped off the train into a strange new world at the far edge of the continent, their suits and the hats that poorly disguised rumpled hair, became oppressive. Especially Archer's vicuna fedora. They both stripped off the heavy gloves which spoke of the cold climes they'd left behind.

Disheveled and disoriented, the Archers found themselves amidst the clamor of the Los Angeles Rail Terminus. Air brakes screeched, steam roiled, and locomotives chuffed. They clung to each other in the scrabbling crowds until, as if under a spotlight, Wakefield's blond waves magically appeared, glistening under the light from the glass ceiling. Enclosing both Archers in a welcoming hug, Wakefield stood back to assess the friends he'd seen months before at the conclusion of Archer's specialization in pathology.

He'd left that couple, he recalled, as distraught as he hoped to ever see them. Elizabeth had just been fired from her teaching job, and Randall had been blindsided by not receiving his long-promised employment at Harvard. The financial ruin that loomed by summer's end had rendered Archer, in particular, embittered and hopeless. That the influential Perrish family had been behind it all proved the final straw. Though weary from their travels, the Archers looked a far cry better than they had at that memorable farewell meeting.

The Archers studied Wakefield in return, relieved that his healthy glow confirmed California did indeed agree with the Boston transplant. His hair had bleached a lighter shade of blond, while his pale skin had darkened slightly from the sunlight which caused both Archers to squint beneath their upheld shading hands.

"You look terrific," Wakefield pronounced, suddenly choked up at their presence and the full realization they were reunited and would be neighbors again.

"Don't you dare say that after three days and three thousand miles of train travel, Adam," Elizabeth warned.

"You do," he insisted, ambushed by just how much he had missed their closeness, blinking back the liquid gathering in his eyes.

Elizabeth patted back tears of joy herself. "We better watch ourselves, Adam. They'll lift our New England birthright at such publicly displayed emotion."

He controlled himself. "How was your crossing?"

The Archers spoke over each other, Elizabeth chiming in, "Incredible the contrasts one finds in this country of ours!"

"Long," sneered Archer at the same time, "but at least I caught up with my journals."

Wakefield glanced back and forth between them as the Archers stared at each other in disbelief. "*That's* what you have to say about it?" Elizabeth demanded of her husband. "Your journals? Not your first glimpse of the snow-capped Rockies from the vastness of the Great Plains? Not the crimson sunrise washing over the multi-hued Painted Desert? Not the orange groves guiding our last miles into Los Angeles?"

Chastened, Archer said no more.

Brow cocked, Wakefield commented to his old research partner, "From the sounds of it, my friend, you missed a lot. Who knows if you'll ever again have the opportunity?"

"Oh, I didn't miss everything," Archer snapped, "if that's what you both imply. I couldn't completely ignore the 'sights' of the Dust Bowl as we rumbled through Kansas and beyond. Mile after mile of total devastation—abandoned farms, equipment left to rust in barren fields, dead animals left to rot, deserted homes, all of it blackened by clouds of airborne earth our train passed in and out of, blinding us one moment only to clear and reveal more desolation.

"Nor will I forget," an indignant Archer worked himself through his own worst fears into outrage, "the people who'd lost everything. Clothed in rags, walking with their families and paltry possessions piled onto donkey carts, making their way to the promised land—thousands of miles *on foot* to California. Just like us, Elizabeth, minus the comfy private compartment with a window to keep out the grit—not that anything could entirely. Did you wonder when you saw them how many will make it all this way? Or what awaits them here if they do? Oh, what's the use," he added under his breath.

Startled by Archer's vehemence, Elizabeth and Wakefield stared at him until Archer's rising blush colored over his travel pallor. "We should be going?" he suggested contritely.

Elizabeth responded, "Yes, Randall, we were fortunate that your new employer enabled us to travel in that comfy compartment. It was appreciated more as each day passed. The desolation of the dust was frightening, of course I agree, Randall. I will never forget those hopeless faces." She shook her head to try.

"But we passed through astonishing beauty as well. Your listing of the worst aspects of our trip failed to include the Chicago stockyards, an affront to all one's senses." She squeezed her eyes shut against that vision. "I'm stunned that's all you've taken from our adventures crossing the continent. I found the United States in its entirety enthralling."

Archer was grouchy, he knew it, from the ceaseless rocking of the railcar, the clackety-clack of tracks rumbling beneath and reverberating through everything, including them. After three days and nights, the constant motion and rhythmic din dulled him like a drug. Then, arriving in this foreign, too warm, glaringly bright, sprawl of a town hardly allayed his misgivings. *This strange jumbled non-city is to be my new home?*

"Look, you two," Wakefield broke in, "you're understandably worn out after your journey. Let's collect your bags, and I'll drop you at your temporary quarters at the University."

How ironic, Archer considered as he fell into step behind Wakefield and his wife, that despite the distance traveled from Boston, once again he and Wakefield would be employed by the same university and working on the same campus, much like old times. Of course, he had Wakefield to thank for it all.

Once Wakefield had heard their sad tale of shocking dismissals and shared fears for the future, he'd had an idea Elizabeth readily embraced. "I didn't mention it before because I knew your heart has long been set on Harvard, Randall. Plus, you both were thriving in Boston. But there might be something for you at ULA if you'd consider it."

Elizabeth had looked like she'd burst. "Something in Los Angeles, Adam, near you?" She had jabbed her husband hard in the ribs with her elbow. "Like what?" Wakefield had explained a serious setback experienced by the fledgling Medical College at the University of Los Angeles, a failure in its medical lab that had endangered patients and lab workers and cost the College and the University as a whole a major misfortune in reputation.

"The doctor in charge was demoted," Wakefield had continued, "and the University is actively looking for a strong replacement to revamp the lab and rectify its procedures. It may not be what you've been dreaming about, Randall, but it would be an impressive first step in your career." Archer had simply gazed at Wakefield in silence.

But Elizabeth had proclaimed, "I think the outside of the box has just presented us the opportunity we were discussing, Randall!"

Wakefield now studied their faces, squinting against the bright sunshine. "Perhaps I should stop and get you both sunglasses," he said, snickering as they blinked beneath ineffective shading hands. "The sunshine is blindingly bright here every day. So, follow me. I'll point out what I can of Los Angeles on our way." Paying a porter to carry their luggage, Wakefield led them through the bustling terminus outdoors into even more glaring bright light.

"Will we take a cab, Adam?" Elizabeth asked.

"My carriage awaits, ma'am," Wakefield responded, drawing up beside his used 1932 Chevrolet and unlocking the trunk.

The Archers exchanged a glance. "You have an automobile, Adam?" Archer asked.

"It became a necessity. The distances here are too great, public transit almost nonexistent, no single city-center to service, all of which made cabs impractical." Wakefield fell into his familiar habit of digressing. "It's rumored that what was once, not long ago, a model public transit system—the Red Cars and the Yellow Cars—was undermined by a consortium of automobile manufacturers, gas and oil companies, and tire and rubber producers, conspiring to keep automobile prices low until the public transport went under. Now automobiles fill the streets. It is unmistakable, this is car country, but I've always wondered about that rumor. But then again, who believes in conspiracy theories?

"Here you go," he said, opening front and back doors, "hop in."

Elizabeth shared the cavernous backseat with a few small bags while the two men settled in front. "So how does it feel to finally be finished, Randall, and starting a whole new chapter?"

Archer shrugged, pursing his lips. "In the end, Harvard proved to be a disillusionment. Which explains why I'm sitting here." He gazed out the window as the car began to move, his recent scolding inspiring him to pay attention to the environment he was meant to inhabit.

Wakefield puzzled over his friend's foul mood, chalking it up to physical exhaustion and the enormous adjustments he knew would disconcert risk-averse Archer. Until he learned the ins and outs of his new circumstances and charted a successful course through it, he would obsess about the changes and risks every waking moment.

Wakefield redirected the subject. "I'll wager you'll love it here once you get used to it and its dazzling sunshine, Randall. I think Elizabeth will as well. She certainly appreciated the diversity of the country she just toured. In a way, California is a microcosm of such diversity."

Archer avoided that sore subject again. "Tell me about the University of Los Angeles, Adam. How's your work going?"

Before answering, Wakefield checked the rearview mirror to find Elizabeth absorbing all she could beyond the car windows as they drove westward. "I couldn't be happier," he answered, "not that it wasn't an enormous adjustment and a real comeuppance to face how essential my job and salary have become. But fortunately, I have a great amount of freedom in my duties and my lab. In fact, Randall, I've been waiting to tell you this in person once I knew you'd been offered and accepted the lab position and that you two were coming west. I've improved the microscope I developed back at Harvard, at least as far as distortion goes. I can't wait for you to try it.

"Your arrival is well timed from my perspective," Wakefield continued, glancing to-and-from the road. "I was about to go searching for a trusty medical partner such as yourself to supply me with fresh disease specimens like those we investigated back

East before the mysterious powers behind the scenes abruptly called a halt."

"You've completed another microscope, Adam?" Archer said as they picked up speed and left the rail terminus in the rearview mirrors. "That is great news. But I expect I'll have my hands more than full properly re-establishing ULA's medical laboratory. Given the failure of my predecessor, whomever he may be, and the unwelcome publicity he's generated for the young Medical College and University, I'll need to plant my feet securely on the ground before I let up for any reason.

"I must assure my future and fast," Archer concluded, "after learning how quickly, and without warning, it can all be snatched from beneath me. Our future, I should say." He glanced back at Elizabeth, too entranced by the scenery flashing by to have heard. "Lucky for me, someone's botched job created the opportunity. I was not faring well in my job search. Your introduction of me, Adam, along with the position's generous funding from a pharmaceutical company interested in partnering with ULA's medical lab for independent drug testing, may literally have saved our lives. I thank you again for your belief in me. You and Elizabeth, your encouragement, have meant everything." He quashed an ambush of emotion.

"I've made a promise to myself after the calamity that undid my entire life-plan, and I make it to you now. I will work without cease, nose to the grindstone, no shortcuts or easier paths, to make the most of this opportunity, this second chance for a life like yours, Adam. A life of integrity, I suppose, is the term. And pray the self-belief I see guiding you and Elizabeth is its by-product." *No more emulating that manipulative Dole,* he vowed to himself.

"Kind words, Randall, and you're most welcome. But knowing you, it won't take long to get the lab humming. I've experienced your work ethic. Just remember, my microscope and I are ready as soon as you are."

Wakefield double-checked Elizabeth via the back-facing mirror, seeking to draw her into the conversation. "How's Prescott, Elizabeth? Has his bank survived? Has he? Is he still in New York?" The stark change on Elizabeth's face was his answer, her bitter shrug, reinforcement. "So the climate hasn't thawed between any of the Perrishes and the Archers, obviously."

"Those flowers, Adam," Elizabeth pointed out the window, "the ones with the exaggerated stamen and brilliant petals? Could they be hibiscus?" When he nodded, she exclaimed, "But hibiscus is tropical. And Los Angeles is high desert or chaparral or some such climate, is it not?"

"You've been reading up on Los Angeles, Elizabeth. Good for you. You'll find just about everything grows here, though heaven knows why with so little precipitation."

"Beautiful," Elizabeth sighed, reverting to the passing display beyond the car windows. "I didn't expect it to look so green, so lush . . ." She leaned toward the front seat to tap her husband's shoulder. " . . . which I take as an omen, Randall. We shall flourish here like all this glorious vegetation surrounding us, wait and see."

§

Juggling both his concern for his passengers and the importance of their first impressions of their new home base, Wakefield drove west, resisting Archer's queries about his new microscope until he had convinced himself Elizabeth was more than content to concentrate on this new habitat. Once she'd set aside her hat to let the wind loosen her hair, Wakefield no longer held back.

The front seat filled with talk of powers of magnification and resolution, new laboratory procedures and practices Archer had honed during his pathology fellowship, and gossip about the University that would be their professional homes going forward as well as the one going back.

They journeyed along a curving road which, Wakefield pointed out, had recently been re-named 'Sunset Boulevard.' The unusual sight of a bridle path down the center of the boulevard, horses and riders ambling along with automobile traffic on either side, surprised them. "Beverly Hills," Wakefield said as if that explained everything. At a sharp swerve northward followed by a downhill curve westward, the sparkling waters of the Pacific Ocean suddenly winked into view. Undulating blue silk gleamed as far as the eye could see.

Except for Elizabeth's gasp at the sight from the backseat, the car fell into silence. "You've reached the end of your journey, my friends," Wakefield proclaimed, adding with a dramatic flourish, "behold the edge of the continent and the majestic Pacific that hedges it in." He allowed the Archers to absorb the vista that still caused his own heart to swell.

Brushing back the welling in her eyes, Elizabeth covered her reaction by sniping, "Let's hope it's more welcoming than the other ocean at the other end of the continent."

Archer looked back at her in surprise. All three dissolved in laughter, tension at last released. "I never paid much attention to the Atlantic back in Boston," Archer admitted, realizing it for the first time. "I mean it was there, everywhere one looked, until I guess I just stopped noticing."

Elizabeth arched her brow at the comment, but said only, "It's glorious, Adam. Don't you agree, Randall? Our temporary housing, Adam, is here at the beach?"

"I'm afraid not, Elizabeth. I took this little detour to show the two of you one of the more striking facets of your new hometown." As he spoke, he maneuvered his Chevy onto the coast highway, pulling onto the beachside shoulder to allow the Archers an unobstructed view of the coastline, stretching in both directions into the mists.

Elizabeth shoved bags aside and slid to the passenger side

of Wakefield's car. She rolled down the window and gulped in sea air as it tousled loose strands of her hair. Sunlight glinting off those wisps formed a dynamic halo. "Thank you, Adam," she said quietly. "A detour most appreciated."

She sat back, grinning from ear to ear. "We're going to be just fine here. I know it, Randall. We will be fine."

CHAPTER NINE

FEAR ITSELF

1934

Amongst Dr. Archer's least-desired professional duties was the formality of his introduction at a Medical College staff meeting. The meeting was held after the hubbub of a reorganization of the Medical College had occurred, and after the new semester had begun. By then, he'd informally met the doctors who regularly interacted with the lab. But still, he dreaded this formality.

At the dean's request, Archer rose to tepid applause from the doctors in attendance, noticing many of the white-jacketed men, who varied widely in age, staring at him in wide-eyed wonder. The blush infusing his boyish features and his short stature exacerbated his youthful, almost childish, first impression. Again he bemoaned his fate of resembling the diminutive mother whom he'd never known. Add to that his accelerated education, and Archer was in fact the youngest doctor in the room by years.

The whispers and guffaws that arose enraged Dean Culp of the Medical College. When Archer took his seat, working unsuccessfully to disguise his mortification, the dean stood,

waving a paper at the gathering. "I'd like to read to this assemblage of *professional gentlemen* a few of the achievements and
accolades this young doctor has amassed to date." He snapped
the paper sharply, bringing all to silent attention.

Unlike the rest of the faculty, Dean Culp was the sole doctor
in a three-piece suit. It matched the gray color of his thinning
hair and great, bushy brows. It reminded Archer of Dole, and he
wondered if all medical college deans dressed similarly.

Culp straightened his tie and put on his glasses to read.
Clearing his throat, he began, "First off, young Archer completed high school at the age of sixteen, *summa cum laude*,
which explains the full scholarship to Harvard he won. *Before*
he entered its Medical College, he completed Harvard's four-
year undergraduate pre-med program in only three. That would
make him nineteen upon entering medical school."

When Dean Culp paused to peer at the gathering, one of the
younger doctors glanced evasively away. "Yes, we've all a few
years on Dr. Archer, some more than others." A few bobs and
snickers thawed a bit of the chill.

"I should ask you, Dr. Archer," the dean went on, "did medical school at least require the normal four years to complete?"
When Archer nodded, the dean commented, "Good. That
should make the rest of us feel somewhat better."

The dean read on. "*Before* he was even one of them, while still
an undergraduate, young Archer was selected from amongst
competing medical students—still in pre-med himself, mind
you—for part-time work in the medical laboratory. It's something he continued throughout his years of schooling, training,
and even throughout his specialty in pathology, all of which
were earned at Harvard." Impressed glances flitted Archer's
way. "If what I remember about those years still holds," the dean
joked, "Dr. Archer apparently doesn't need much sleep."

To widespread chuckles, the dean continued. "He may have
another advantage over us mere medical-mortals. Archer

knew *before* medical school he would specialize in pathology and consciously built his career in the medical lab, which may explain his innumerable honors earned there." Dean Culp held out a listing as though those in attendance could read for themselves. "All were earned with the highest distinction. They are simply too numerous to delineate here, so I'll send around a synopsis CV which you can read at your leisure."

Archer repeated bitterly to himself. 'Young doctor.' 'Young Archer.' Would he never be allowed to grow up? But he did notice the formerly amused and doubtful expressions on his new colleagues' faces had sobered following the dean's summary. Archer appreciated Dean Culp's support but just once wished it weren't necessary. Like the underaged kid from Pittsburgh, would he always have to fight to prove himself?

More polite applause as the dean wound up his remarks and took his seat, moving onto other business. Furtive glances from fellow faculty skittered over Archer. He knew he had to create a stronger start somehow. At a pause in the proceedings, he motioned to the dean and stood. "If I may add? As you've all heard, gentlemen, I have a considerable number of years in the medical lab at Harvard—literally half my life. Basically, the lab is where I grew up. I've been privy to all aspects of laboratory work and procedure as well as cutting-edge research, including a human trial of a promising drug. But that was Harvard."

Archer knew he shouldn't keep name-dropping, the dean had done quite enough, but he couldn't help himself. "So if there's time today, now or perhaps afterward, I'd ask each of you who directly interfaces with the medical laboratory to be so kind as to summarize for me what it is you need most from my operation. What's most critical in its reestablishment to you. Help me prioritize and shape the new laboratory, which by the way I will have completed within the month."

To his last statement a chorus of disbelief ensued. "A month?" "Impossible!" "Really?" "You can do that?"

"It's an ongoing work-in-progress, of course. But I'd be happy to address individual concerns as we move towards perfection, which is the lofty goal I've set."

Archer sat down, hesitancy in the group palpable, until one doctor spoke up. "Assurance of non-contamination of important specimen and culture studies. A big problem previously which made test results unreliable and/or endlessly delayed. And we all know that often moments matter!"

With that the dam broke. The doctors present jockeyed to express their needs and frustrations in vehement terms until the dean stepped in to call a halt. "Well, that should be enough input for your first staff meeting, Dr. Archer. Do you have any comments on what you just heard before we really must move on to other business?"

Archer huffed dismissively, feigning a complete lack of concern. "I appreciate the input, gentlemen, and would be happy to respond case-by-case if you wish to meet one-on-one. Better yet, give me a few more weeks to finalize equipment, procedures, and especially manpower. Then I'd be pleased to have you stop by our newly laid-out lab where I will personally walk you through how I've addressed those concerns.

"I'm happy to say," Archer concluded, "none of what you mention are things I haven't seen or done before in my dozen years of experience in Harvard's Medical Laboratory."

The audience looked wary after Archer's performance, but the dean, well pleased. "May we move on now, *gentlemen*? I wish to discuss the monthly reporting all department heads owe me each month. You'll want to pay close attention, Dr. Archer, as this directly affects you going forward."

Archer sat back, holding in a sigh of relief while the dean conducted departmental business. He tallied the innumerable difficulties in reopening a tightly run lab in the short timeframe he'd promised. But he would do it. He intended to get well ahead of the inevitable departmental and University politics,

assuming ULA was similar to Harvard. By so doing, he hoped
to stymie those critics and detractors lying in wait. He had no
idea who had maneuvered for the position he'd won, not to
mention who'd lost it, but he knew they were out there as surely
as faculty tenure struggles and intradepartmental posturing
existed throughout the realms of higher learning.

How well Archer remembered the blatant, mean-spirited
rivalry he'd witnessed among Harvard's medical faculty. Now,
with his future, perhaps even his survival in this bankrupt world
on the line, he would resolutely stay well ahead in that game.

§

With reluctance, Elizabeth took time away from her first priority since relocating to Los Angeles—finding and establishing
the Archers' first real home. It was a task she found surprisingly creative and enjoyable, expanding beyond the cramped,
single-room student apartment the couple had shared for two
years. But a holiday tea given by the wife of Dean Culp in Elizabeth's honor was no less than a command performance. Besides, she hoped she might make a friend or two to populate a
new life in a new city, which, while concentrating on her home
search, she'd been unable to do.

She had chosen her outfit carefully, mindful of first impressions. A navy wool dress, cinched at the waist with covered
buttons down the front, was accented by a scarf, gloves, shoes,
and a hat in various shades of blue, complimentary both to her
dress and her cerulean eyes. She'd even considered her grandmother's pearls, last worn at her wedding, but at the last minute
deemed them 'trying too hard.'

Passing her own final inspection, Elizabeth entered a meeting
room in the Medical College reserved for the faculty wives' tea.

A smartly-dressed coterie of women of all ages—had she
been expecting Annie-Oakley-clad westerners? she giggled

inwardly—clustered around a beautifully-draped table laden with cookies and assorted sweets, teas, condiments, lace napkins, and a white flower centerpiece which scented the air with . . . jasmine? Elizabeth sniffed, making a mental note to plant spicy-smelling jasmine somewhere in her new garden.

Conversation ceased as Elizabeth made her way inside. The women appeared to range in age from close to Elizabeth's own twenty-seven years to well into their sixties. The eldest among them, her pure white hair exposed beneath an old-fashioned flowered *chapeau*, stepped forward. "Mrs. Archer, welcome. I'm Mrs. Culp, Claire, wife of the dean of the Medical College. And these lovely ladies," Elizabeth's eyes followed hers as they skimmed over the group, "comprise nearly all the faculty wives in our College. After hearing so much about your husband and his impressive background at Harvard along with tidbits we gleaned about you, we're so happy to make your acquaintance. Aren't we, ladies?" A twittering of smiles and welcomes ensued. "And may I say you have the most startling blue eyes!"

Under the firm guidance of Mrs. Culp, Elizabeth found herself squired around the room for individual introductions, which included, in addition to each woman's name, her husband's and his position at the College. Elizabeth smiled, shaking gloved hands, noting out of the corner of her eye one of the younger wives, nearer her own age, hanging back, overtly sizing Elizabeth up.

"Oh yes," Mrs. Culp announced upon reaching her at last, "this is Edna Black, the newest addition to our informal little women's club, until you of course, Elizabeth dear."

Elizabeth extended a gloved hand. "Pleased to make your acquaintance, Mrs. Black." The young woman half-heartedly accepted Elizabeth's hand but avoided eye contact.

"Edna's husband stayed on at our little College after earning his medical doctorate with its very first graduating class . . ." The dean's wife seemed to lose her train of thought. "That is, initially Dr. Black wore several hats at our fledgling College. An internist by training—internal medicine specialty, as you know, dear—he also lent his skills to establishing the medical laboratory. However, now that your husband has arrived, Elizabeth, Edna's husband can happily revert to internal medicine, both on the teaching staff and at University Hospital. You must be thrilled at the prospect of seeing more of Dr. Black, Edna, since the Archers' arrival."

Mrs. Black strained for a smile over determinedly blank features, her gaze faltering between Mrs. Culp and Elizabeth. Discomfort between the two was palpable but unexplained. "Of course I am, Mrs. Culp. Mrs. Archer," Edna forcibly gushed, "welcome to the Medical College and its occasional wives' social club."

"Elizabeth, please."

"Elizabeth," Edna repeated, failing to offer her own first name. "Have you and your husband found a place to settle yet? Los Angeles is so spread out, hundreds of square miles within its boundaries. I would imagine it could be daunting to a newcomer. I myself," Mrs. Black proclaimed, "am born *and* raised here—as is my husband!"

Edna Black's obvious pride in that statement confounded Elizabeth. Her darting eyes were as distracting as her endless primping—pulling at her gloves, patting down her skirt, pushing at her up-do. Though she appeared to be less than half Mrs. Culp's age, she wore an ill-fitting, outmoded dress that nearly outdid the dean's wife's dated appearance.

"I believe we have found our first home, Mrs. Black," Elizabeth replied. "Dr. Adam Wakefield of the College of Physics, an old friend of Randall's and mine from back East, referred a realtor who has been touring me through the urban sprawl. We've narrowed the landscape by deciding to stay close to campus and Randall's work. But actually, I've enjoyed getting to know Los Angeles in the process. And as I said, I think we've found the right thing. We'll soon know about the house."

"How do you find Los Angeles compared to Boston and Harvard and all that history and tradition back there?" Mrs. Culp asked.

"I like it here very much, thank you. History and tradition can cut two ways, I discovered. Perhaps that's why—"

"And your family?" interrupted Mrs. Black, adjusting the veil on her hat, calling attention to her dull hazel eyes. "Where will your children go to school, based on that 'right thing' you'll soon hear about?"

Mrs. Culp affirmed, "Like any city, Elizabeth, the right school district is critically important."

"I haven't paid much attention to that, I confess. Randall and I have no children nor immediate plans, and the anticipation of spreading out beyond the single-room apartment we shared since our marriage—"

"No children?" Edna Black exclaimed, straightening up to finally meet Elizabeth's gaze without flinching.

"Future plans, of course," Mrs. Culp presumed. "If you don't mind my asking, dear, how old are you, Elizabeth?"

"Twenty-seven," Elizabeth responded.

The two faculty wives gazed, wide-eyed, at each other. "You really mustn't wait much longer, dear, to start a family, if I may say so," advised the dean's wife. "Why, Edna's not quite your age, and she has three little ones at home, don't you, dear?"

Elizabeth grasped for control of this conversation. "You may be right, but once we're settled, I intend to pursue a teaching position. I discovered in Boston the enormous gratification of teaching young girls—"

"Surely you know jobs are hard to find these days!" Edna exclaimed as Claire Culp nodded agreement. "Wouldn't that be taking a job from a man who must support his family? Would that be fair, Mrs. Archer, when times are so trying? And with your husband stepping into a *directorship* at the lab, you obviously don't need the money. When so many others do. Desperately."

Elizabeth glanced around, suddenly aware she'd become the center of a ring of women listening curiously to Mrs. Black and Mrs. Culp advise the newest girl in the neighborhood. She found not one sympathetic expression in the circle. "I just loved teaching," she admitted, "and hope to do more of it. That's all."

Elizabeth pondered, *was it selfish to want to teach girls?* Was having children of one's own the only respectable thing a woman could do? Particularly one of such worrisome advancing years, whose husband could comfortably support them?

This is the kind of thinking that inspired Randall and me to leave Boston in the first place, she grumbled inwardly. But Elizabeth knew that wasn't the real story. They'd left Boston because of her family and their objection to her husband as well as to her holding a job. At least only the latter bias was being mirrored here. Scanning the gathering, Elizabeth questioned whether she'd stumbled upon a replacement 'family' quite prepared to take over where the old one had left off.

"Thank you for your advice and concern," Elizabeth managed to say. "But it's one step at a time for this newcomer. First, Randall and I need to get settled. Oh my, don't those scones look excellent?" she oozed. "I must try one. Please excuse me."

Taking as much time as she could at the refreshment table, she assembled a plate while quelling her anger—*everyone but me seems to know what it is I should do,* she fumed. When Elizabeth glanced up, an older woman she hadn't been introduced to met and held her gaze. Her powdery skin crinkled in a sympathetic smile, while her green eyes glistened with amusement.

The woman pointed out, "The clotted cream is the best thing on the table. Be certain to try it." She leaned in closer, her scent of violets preceding her. "And don't let these silly women, jockeying within the College hierarchy to outdo each other, ruffle you. Your husband's position means you're coming in at a lofty level, catapulting you over many of them, which they're small enough to take out on you. It's all so meaningless," she sighed, surveying the clustered wives with a shake of the tight gray bun on her head.

She turned her twinkling eyes back to Elizabeth. "I'm Jane Grove and I apologize for arriving late. I do try to avoid these affairs altogether. Perhaps you understand why? But I sincerely hope you craft a long and happy life here in Los Angeles and at the University. If there's anything I can do to assist you, I'd be honored, Mrs. Archer, truly." She put out her hand and Elizabeth accepted it gratefully.

"Elizabeth, please."

"Elizabeth. Jane. Tell me about the house you hope to occupy."

Elizabeth happily launched into her all-encompassing project. "Architecturally it's called 'Mediterranean Revival.' The Spanish influence is not only historic to this city's founding, but the style is utterly charming and warm. I love its less formal, rambling quality, completely the opposite to the Federal style I grew up with . . ."

§

More weeks elapsed before Archer made an unannounced appearance after-hours at Wakefield's physics lab. "Figured you'd be here," Archer said as he slouched into the chair facing the desk in Wakefield's office within his lab.

"Ye gods, Randall, you look like death warmed over. They're working you too hard over there?"

"Somewhat, but it's my fault, really. I made a promise I simply could not fail to keep, to have the medical lab up and running smoothly by month's end."

"Which I assume you'll do, but at no small expense to yourself. That also means Elizabeth has been left largely to her own devices in a strange city. How's she handling all the changes?"

"She's used to my irregular hours by now, and actually, she seems quite taken by the newness of Los Angeles as well as by our first home. Through her home search, she's seen more of Los Angeles than I likely ever will. She's excited about the one she found and is busy planning how to finish it, furnish it, and lay out its surrounding gardens. She's quite caught up in it all and thank heavens, since she doesn't have a lot of friends to share the lonely hours with yet."

"She'll have her hands full for some time, I'd guess, from the brief viewing I received once you'd purchased your new place. Well, now that you're here, Randall, let me show you my new scope. Follow me." Wakefield led him into the lab, to a high table with a familiar but even more complex microscope sitting atop. "There she is," he said with pride.

Archer silently circled the mechanism several times. He asked questions while continuing his examination. Wakefield followed him, happy to respond and point out improvements. At long last, Archer drew back a high stool from under the table and plunked heavily upon it. "So, where do you think this version stands in terms of magnification?"

"Still approximately sixty-some-thousand-times magnification. But this scope includes vast improvements in lighting and resolution."

"Well, let's see it in action, Adam. What slides might you have around here to view?"

"I have a few," he said, positioning one under the viewers. "Be my guest, old friend."

Archer peered into the viewing mechanism and made several adjustments to clarify the specimen.

Wakefield gave him a few moments before addressing his hunched figure. "You know what I'm going to ask next, I'm quite certain."

Archer's bloodshot eyes met Wakefield's. "Yes, I'm afraid I do." He sighed, rubbing back the fatigue. "It's a little a different now that the lab is mine, I suppose, but the same regulations and protocols apply. Fresh specimens are just as *verboten* here as they were there. And I made a pledge to myself—no more shortcuts or questionable acts. You and Elizabeth inspired me to the straight and narrow."

Wakefield snorted. "Thanks, but I must say again you medical researchers practice strange science. In that case, get the dean's sign-off? Or just make a few living slides to remind ourselves of what we were doing before we were shut down at Harvard. What could it harm, Randall?"

Now it was Archer's turn to huff. "I've just taken over a laboratory that imploded under many disregarded rules and procedures. I doubt the dean will be anxious to reintroduce extraordinary practices already, at least until he gets to know and trust me. And honestly, Adam, I'm far too busy to pick all that back up again."

Archer stood. "I'm sorry, but I've got to get some rest." He paused. "But I tell you what, Adam, when I work my way through the daily crises I'm handling, I'll see what I can do. Maybe a few living samples would be possible. It has been long enough that I question my memory, especially after my pathology fellowship confirmed unequivocally that what we thought we'd seen is 'medically impossible.'"

"Now where have I heard that before?"

"I know, I know. But I must see to my lab first. In the meantime, it's good to see you, Adam, and know you're close by again. When and if we get settled, Elizabeth and I will have you over to catch up and view our completed new place. But I don't expect that to be soon, given the state of the lab I found and listening to Elizabeth's elaborate plans. She's not one to do things halfway."

"Nor are you, old man," Wakefield added with a grin.

Archer paused again at the exit. "I like your new lab, Adam. And your new scope looks strange but equally interesting. I'll be back when I have more confidence in my lab's work quality

and consistency as well as in the establishment of a solid foun-
dation for my own reputation. Good night, old friend."

§

Not long after his late-night stop at Wakefield's lab on the opposite side of campus to his own, Archer found himself again
near the College of Physics. The temptation to drop in on his
old friend was more than he could resist. Still ferreting out
whom he could trust and who was maneuvering behind his
back in the politically-charged climate evidently common to
all universities, Archer suddenly found it imperative to see a
dependable friend. Politics and work challenges could wait.

Not finding Wakefield in his office or laboratory, Archer was
directed to a lecture hall in the building where Wakefield was
conducting a class on New Physics, whatever that was. Archer
stole into the rear of the hall to listen to his friend in mid-lecture.

"When in 1905 Einstein presented his now-famous equa-
tion, $E=mc\,2$—you all know that stands for 'energy equals mass
times velocity' squared—traditional physics or Newton's laws
came, if not under attack, under intense scrutiny.

"For the first time in scientific history, what humans perceive
as solid matter, or 'mass,' was related and equated to energy and
speed. Ultimately, the famous formula suggests that all three
are, at their most fundamental levels, aspects of the *same thing*.

"Are you all with me?" Wakefield addressed the classroom.

"So far, Professor. At least I think so," one emboldened student responded, to a chorus of guffaws.

Archer noted the students enraptured by their professor.
They, too, seemed to know from experience that Wakefield
could not be stopped until the insightful connections in his
mind were aired and considered from all angles.

"Good. Stay with me," he said. "We're exploring a profound
shift in understanding the universe in which we live. So then,

stated another way, mass and energy are differing forms of the same thing. Allow me to step back a moment," Wakefield again interrupted himself.

"Please!" another student called out to more laughter throughout the hall.

Wakefield shared in the laugh. "I never promised it would be easy or intuitive. But this is definitely worth the effort, especially for you physics majors.

"First, it is essential to bear in mind that even the most solid-appearing item to us and our senses, is, if one could peer deep into its *sub-microscopic* basis, formed by atoms and molecules in constant energetic motion. And to think," he slowed in contemplation, "it was not long ago—less than twenty years—that physicists unquestioningly accepted the atom as the smallest solid particle in the universe."

Wakefield gazed over his rapt audience with a broad smile. "Alas, here we witness that truth itself evolves! We will be meeting Niels Bohr in class at a future time, when we pursue his research into the numerous subatomic particles he uncovered inside the atom.

"But in the meantime . . . in the simplest terms," an exhilarated Wakefield explained, "what this all boils down to is that at the most basic level of existence throughout the universe—at the *sub*-microscopic level—everything we know or perceive is nothing but pure energy."

Archer so admired his friend in action, making the most difficult concepts more understandable. But judging from his students, he also managed to be entertaining, stimulating, and well-liked. He recognized Wakefield was only getting started and regretted he hadn't more time to monitor his physics lecture.

Reluctantly, Archer made his way back to his own reality, fraught with its own fundamental energy of a kind Wakefield hadn't referenced.

§

Archer entered the physics lab bearing a carrier in his hands which Wakefield dared hope held the fresh specimen slides he was so anxious to study under his newest microscope. Alluding to the elapsed time since they'd discussed studying fresh specimens, he said, "The challenges continued after all, I surmise."

Archer exhaled in exasperation, placing the container on the lab table where he'd found Wakefield beside his microscope. "Don't ask," Archer commanded. "I tried several evenings to get over here, but amongst my many challenges, transporting live specimens between our laboratories on opposite sides of campus presented a unique one. Luckily, I was able to rig a cool-storage container for specimen slides that keeps them separated, protected, and useable for a time."

Archer unzipped the top of the thickly-insulated container to retrieve what looked like a stack of padded trays from within. Each tray was subdivided into individual, numbered compartments, each holding a single slide. Archer unfolded a list from his breast pocket that identified, by matching a number to the slot, the hospital patient the specimen was sourced from, his or her disease, and the time and date of specimen extraction.

"I barely had time to create these few slides today, Adam, but it's a start. Once we've allowed the samples to come to room temperature, which won't take long, they'll be ready to demonstrate your new machine's potential."

"Right-o. Can't wait to see what we see, old boy! Hand over a slide and let's get started."

"These are *live* specimens, Adam, remember!" Archer barked. "First gloves and a mask, and we'll need to take the precaution of sterilizing the microscope and our work surfaces before we begin. Then we'll need to dispose of gloves and other used gear back at my lab, unless the physics laboratory has a protocol in place for disposing of harmful material?"

Wakefield shook his head no.

"As I thought. I brought disinfectant as well as a sealable container we can toss used paraphernalia into once finished."

Wakefield tugged on the stretchy safety gloves and tied the mask behind his head, briefly wondering if his own watered-down blue eyes took on any of the added intensity Archer's deep black pools did when half his face was covered. "You've thought of everything, Randall." As Archer opened the disinfectant, an acrid odor filled the air. "Don't you have anything we could use that doesn't smell so awful?"

Archer ignored the comment. He was satisfied only when the two of them were properly protected from contact with the samples as well as the other way around, and the entire area had been sterilized. "*Now* can we begin?" Wakefield whined.

Archer extracted one slide, having reached room temperature, and passed it to Wakefield. After placing it on the stage beneath the binocular viewer and making minimal adjustments, Wakefield stared down the scope in silence. He sat back, astonished. "Honestly, Randall, I'd forgotten how exciting, how hypnotic, these microbes were. And still are, my friend!"

Archer confessed, "I'd convinced myself we'd imagined them, since nothing in all of medicine even hints at such a phenomenon. They're there, Adam? Just as before?"

"See for yourself," Wakefield replied, a wide grin crinkling the skin around his eyes as he stood aside to offer the viewer.

After lengthy observation, Archer glanced somberly at Wakefield. "We weren't imagining . . . nor seeing things."

"No, we weren't hallucinating, old boy. The microbes cavort as before!"

Archer exhaled slowly. "You know, Adam, especially during my fellowship but even before, I exploited every opportunity to investigate what might explain this—this occurrence we've witnessed repeatedly. But I found nothing, not a hint during my specialization in the study of disease. In fact, modern medicine decrees that it is *impossible* for *all* diseases to display a similar viral-sized microbe, unless of course it's a viral disease.

"I was reminded by colleagues and professors alike, in no uncertain terms, that medicine has for decades categorized diseases based on their pathogenic source, either bacterial, fungal, or viral as well as a few less-common classifications. And viral is the *only one* which could display these tiny virus-sized microbes.

"My wondering aloud as to possible unwanted effects on the samples from commonly used slide-preparatory solutions was initially met with incomprehension. There is no choice in using the solutions to heighten visibility nor is there evidence of unwanted effects and never will be. Due to the much weaker magnification power of common microscopes, dependent upon those solutions.

"Until their powers of magnification are greatly improved to levels like you've achieved, Adam, there is no visible benefit in studying fresh, living samples. No point. Nothing would be detected by common scopes. And therefore, medicine judges that there is nothing to detect.

"I know you think I'm a stickler for rules," Archer said after further consideration, "although I've broken plenty of them. But one night in the lab, after you'd left Boston, I tried it. I assembled a fresh sample and put it under the most powerful microscope available. And guess what? It didn't look much different from the pre-treated ones frozen in place by chemicals. No dancing microbe evident under even the best of regular microscopes."

"Of course," Wakefield said. "The lesser magnification powers of common microscopes brought about the use of fixative solutions in the first place. Medicine doesn't know what it's missing."

Archer smirked at a memory. "I really stepped over the line in a pathology symposium, venturing a question as to whether one pathogen under certain conditions might transform or evolve into another type of pathogen. I was nearly laughed out of the room with comments like, 'Conditions such as poor laboratory procedures?' 'Contamination?' 'One's wild imagination running away with him?' 'Exhaustion and overwork perhaps?'

"That mere possibility was met with an outrage and denial that dismissed it and me as lunatic fancy. I was even taken aside by the head of my fellowship program and counseled to keep my 'crazy, unfounded ideas' to myself. Or I risked staining my 'exemplary' performance record.

"No, Adam," Archer shook his head, loosening a few black curls from their pomade, "orthodox medicine does not permit these similarly-sized and -acting microbes to exist in *every* disease we've ever tested. In all my years of study, education, training, and experience, the possibility simply does not exist in mainstream medicine."

"Well," Wakefield quipped, "with the help of my microscope, modern medicine will finally see for itself."

"Medicine had that opportunity at Harvard, don't forget. Your original microscope, did it ever turn up?"

"I don't think so. The strangest of mysteries."

"I told you I'd asked about the one we'd used during my internship," Archer repeated. "I sought to borrow it back from Physics for advanced pathology studies, but received the vaguest of responses and inexplicable delays. My request was never outright denied, but your 'scope, which might have opened a few closed minds, never reappeared. Nor was it mentioned until you relayed to me it had been *lost* by Harvard's Medical College."

"Hard to believe," Wakefield agreed. "Nevertheless, we again observe the sub-bacterial-sized microbe on this fresh slide, just as those before. So, Randall, what are we looking at, meaning which disease?"

"I brought only typhoid slides tonight. When I realized the hour, it was the handiest sample in my lab. Plus, I'll admit I needed reassurance that we hadn't been fantasizing back in Boston, or misremembering, before I spent too much of my scarce time on this. I assembled what I could to make it over here tonight."

"And?" Wakefield demanded, "are you reassured?"

Archer shook his head in disbelief. "I cannot deny what two pairs of eyes clearly see."

"Great. What I think we should do next—"

"Hold on there, Adam. We can't afford to make any assumptions about something that would surely put us at odds with the medical establishment, not to mention possibly shake it and my career to the very core.

"What we *have* to do next is sample a wide swath of diseases. We must confirm our original findings: that different diseases categorized by their different disease-pathogens—not necessarily only viral—present a similarly-sized and -active microbe, that is, when observed fresh and untreated. We must be certain we're on rock-solid ground here. This line of inquiry has far-reaching ramifications that will be controversial *at best*. We must bear in the forefront that this discovery could severely affect the entire medical field, not to mention the vast interconnected groups that depend upon and support it—all of whom already suffer in this Depression."

When Wakefield seemed too stunned to respond, Archer added, "I hesitate to remind you, Adam, given your demanding schedule, that producing more microscopes which can view this level of detail without preparatory solutions will be critical to moving our research forward onto solid footing."

Wakefield harrumphed. "Anticipated you there, old man. I've been aware of your fears and worries from the start as we strayed farther and farther from 'medical orthodoxy.' I've gotten Dean Grafton to arrange with the College of Engineering a streamlined production method for building these microscopes in quantity. We're still at the planning stages, but it could make a difference and hopefully soon."

"Excellent, Adam. If only the doctors I've worked with could see for themselves, perhaps they'd be less . . . what's the word? Defensive? Less inclined to suspect my intelligence, even my mental stability in their scramble to protect the status quo? I confess to you now, this new microbe is a subject I dread being associated with in medical circles."

Wakefield's disgust and disbelief showed in the frown lines on his brow. Biting his tongue, he said only, "I say again, it's very strange 'science' you medical types practice."

CHAPTER TEN

SOCIAL SECURITY

1935

Elizabeth sat at the desk in the library of the Archers' new home, daydreaming about finishing its backyard. Her view of the yard was framed by the French doors open before her. The multi-arched arcade running the length of the structure at its rear added further visual framing. An abundant garden was taking form in her head as she referenced possibilities in the glossy gardening book lying open on her lap.

"I always envisioned parterres for my first garden," she commented. "But then again, I never imagined owning a home like this." Archer's signing bonus and salary, aided by Elizabeth's inheritance from her grandmother, received when she turned the specified age of twenty-seven, had drastically changed the Archers' standard of living, seemingly overnight.

Their new 'Mediterranean Revival' stood on a large, unfinished lot not far from campus. The previous owners had not completed the inside, moved in, nor begun to landscape. Like too many others whose personal finances collapsed with the economy, the owners were forced into a quick sale of the home—the unfortunate circumstance which sadly assisted the Archers in its purchase.

Seated in his favorite green leather club chair in his favorite room in the house, the wood-paneled library, Archer glanced up from his reading. "What did you say, Elizabeth? 'Parterres?'"

"I don't know why I mentioned them. They'd be ridiculous with a Spanish Colonial home. No more prim, symmetrical Federal style for us, Randall! I mean to embrace all that's novel and unique in our new environment, as I've done with this home and now hope to do with its landscaping, especially the garden I'm conjuring."

Archer snapped his newspaper sharply and returned to his reading with an irritated scoff, "Parterres."

"Of course we'll have roses, lots of them. This climate should ensure a beautiful yield, year after year. I'm thinking about a gurgling fountain in the middle of the backyard," she said, staring at the spot behind the house, unaware her husband had tuned her out. She flipped a few pages of the book on her lap, pausing to dream aloud. "Lush plantings of lavender surrounding a fountain in Moorish tiles of purples, blues, yellows, and of course terracotta to match the terracing we'll install in the arcade. A pergola covered with weeping wisteria between the garage and house. And while I'm thinking shades of purple, I could fill in with hydrangea, ceanothus, irises, offsetting pink bougainvillea—or maybe white? And fruit trees—plums are purple. But we must have an orange tree. They're emblematic of our new city. And lemon . . ."

Elizabeth sighed with delight at the conjured image until the voice of her mother interrupted her daydreams. 'Gardening, Elizabeth? It's dirty and low, especially if one puts one's own hands in the dirt!' Elizabeth had always found it ironic that despite such opinions vigorously offered, Eleanor Perrish had been a proud founding member of the prestigious Beacon Hill Garden Club. *Mother liked her flowers far removed from their muddy roots*, she reflected.

Elizabeth, on the other hand, had been drawn to the glass conservatory behind Perrish House from an early age. So much light, color, and warmth. The Perrishes' ancient driver-gardener, Timmy, who came with the house when her parents inherited it upon her grandparents' passing, had encouraged her interest in the scents, sights, and balminess of the place.

Timmy had inspired her appreciation of all plant life. "All God's creatures grow to the light," he'd explained in his thick brogue, holding a watering can, a clump of fertile earth in the other hand, and looking skyward where installed lights supplemented Boston's weak winter sunshine. "Dirt, rain, sunlight. It's that simple, Miss Elizabeth. You'll be seein' soon enough," he'd added as he helped her plant her first seeds.

However, once Mrs. Perrish had discovered Elizabeth dirtying her hands in a most 'unladylike' fashion, she'd been banned from the conservatory. Clandestinely, Timmy, along with his wife, the Perrishes' cook, had supplied young Elizabeth with gardening gloves and an old smock Timmy's wife shortened to shield against mud-spatter and telltale dirt beneath her fingernails. They'd risked encouraging the lonely child whose mother was distant and whose father was often away. Luckily, Mrs. Perrish never entered the conservatory, so its warm, moist air had quickly become Elizabeth's favorite refuge from the family she never pleased, nor fit into. Timmy had been only too happy to nourish her and her interests on the sly.

"Still," Elizabeth spoke aloud, banishing the past and concentrating on her current project, "planting cacti goes a bit too far for me, at least at this point. No, I think I've assembled the rudiments of a beautiful plan."

She glanced over to find her husband had fallen asleep, papers scattered around him. She settled back, eyes on her fantasy garden spiraling outward from its fountain, almost able to hear its splashing and inhale its rose-scented breezes.

§

When Archer arrived at the physics lab for what had become their routine after-hours study, bearing the cool-carrier presumably filled with yet more specimen slides to examine, Wakefield groaned, "More? Have we not run the gamut of diseases to test and retest, given our months at it? What could you possibly transport in that carrier of yours that we haven't looked at dozens or even hundreds of times by this point?"

Archer stopped in his tracks to glare at Wakefield. "You refuse to understand what we're playing with here, Adam. There may not be a disease we've haven't observed before. But due to the explosive nature of what we've uncovered, with an entire industry under threat of collapse should our discoveries bear out, what does it hurt to be 100 percent certain of the prevalence of similar microbes in every disease?"

"'What does it hurt?'" Wakefield shot back, exhausted from his extracurricular projects, which besides investigating this new microbe, included overseeing the streamlined production plan for his microscope. Not to mention his normal lab and teaching responsibilities. "You mean outside of victims dying of these diseases who may have been saved by our uncovering the virulent form their malady had taken?"

"We are nowhere near using this knowledge to cure disease, Adam!" Archer's voice ratcheted sharply. "You must be mindful—"

"Will we ever be?" Wakefield lashed back. "Honestly, Randall, I can't help but suspect all this repeat testing amounts to no more than your foot-dragging. What are you afraid of?"

Archer sat the carrier down and lifted its contents out to warm to room temperature, the accompanying noxious odor spreading as he did. Archer passed protective gloves and a mask to Wakefield and slipped on his own. "I don't want to argue about a scientist's responsibility to seek and share truth, Adam, not again. Let's stay focused on the work and review these slides."

Once the samples were ready, Archer clipped one into position on the stage of the microscope and peered down. Puzzled by what he saw, he checked his list against the numbered compartment from which the specimen had been retrieved. Again he stared into the viewer.

Driven to his wit's end by these prolonged and redundant observations made late into the night after his daytime duties, Wakefield drummed his fingers with impatience. Gloves and mask donned, he waited for what seemed like forever, while a mute Archer switched out one slide for another.

In a dire tone, Archer at last whispered, "They're not here, Adam!" Archer was too alarmed to gloat over the fact that his excessive caution might have proven justified. "The microbes! They're not here!"

"Impossible, Randall. They've been seen consistently, night after night, month after month. Every damned disease, every damned slide, every damned night."

"See for yourself, Adam," Archer dared, stepping back from the scope.

Trying to control his testy mood, Wakefield made adjustments before peering in. He froze. At last he asked, "What's on this slide? A sample of what disease exactly?"

Archer double-checked his list and the slide's vacant slot in the tray. "Typhoid. You found no microbes as well, I take it?"

"Correct." Wakefield rubbed his fatigued eyes and looked again. "How can this be? We've viewed plenty of typhoid slides before—an unfortunate by-product of the unsanitary conditions in the tent cities mushrooming up around us. All those previous samples revealed the cavorting microbe." He dropped his head in thought. "I recalibrated the scope this morning so that cannot be a cause . . .

"Could something be interfering?" Wakefield at last questioned. "Something in my lab perhaps? Just tonight?" He slid off the stool and wandered off, willing his brain to stretch for an answer. He stumbled upon a post-doctoral fellow in the adjacent laboratory section. "Henry?" Wakefield exclaimed in surprise. "What are you doing at this hour?" He checked his pocket watch.

"Oh, Dr. Wakefield!" the young man startled. "I had no idea anyone else was here." The young man smiled. "You look like you just came out of surgery with that mask and gloves."

Wakefield slid the mask down around his neck. "Just taking extra precautions for a project I'm working on, Henry, the next sector over."

"Well as you see, Dr. Wakefield, I've been experimenting with the cathode ray tube," he indicated the device he held, which looked like an oversized light bulb with a narrow, elongated neck, "and doing so when I won't be interrupted. I'm studying wave properties at various frequencies as they travel outward from a source and—"

"I thought I heard voices." Archer rounded a solid, shelf-lined partition which divided the lab into sub-sections, much like his own laboratory setup.

"Henry, meet Dr. Archer, MD," Wakefield offered. "Randall, Henry, a gifted physics post-doc, who is studying—"

"Wave frequencies produced by the cathode ray tube. I heard," Archer paraphrased. "Meaning electromagnetic waves at specific rates of vibration, Henry?"

"Exactly, Dr. Archer. The cathode ray tube allows me to beam any frequency in any direction I wish, although I've been on one frequency for some time now."

Archer addressed Wakefield. "Weren't you just speculating about something in your lab interfering with our observations tonight, Adam?"

Wakefield nodded, his eyes slowly widening. "Do you suppose the frequency Henry is beaming?"

"These solid sectional walls could *not* stop such waves, could they?" Archer questioned.

"No! No, they could not," Wakefield replied, his imagination ramping quickly. "What frequency have you been testing, Henry? And for some time now, you say?"

"Seven hundred sixty kilo— Sorry, 760,000 hertz," Henry answered, "for about the last hour. I'm sorry if it interfered with your work, Dr. Wakefield. If you want, I'll shut down and come back another time."

"Don't change a thing, Henry!" Archer commanded the confused young man. "Do exactly what you've been doing until we return." Archer raced back to the Wakefield microscope, its inventor close behind. For a moment, Wakefield considered addressing Henry's bewildered expression until he realized he simply didn't know how.

§

Archer wasted no time selecting another slide to inspect with the microscope as Wakefield came up beside him, almost afraid to ask, "Are they there?"

Archer switched out another specimen slide and repeated the process. "No. Neither one of these two slides revealed the microbe. Take a look." Turning the scope over to its inventor, repositioning his mask, Archer wondered aloud, "The *only* four slides of the hundreds of live specimens we've examined by this point to show no vigorously moving life-form . . ."

Wakefield shook his head in disbelief. "My point precisely. Pass me another, old boy." Once the specimen was set on the stage, Wakefield peered in, reared back, and peered in again. "They're here! Randy, the microbes! They're back!" He checked again. "Whatever is happening tonight?"

Archer checked his list. "That last slide is a living pneumonia sample." He double-checked. "*All* the others we viewed, each with no microbe, were typhoid, Adam."

The scientists stared at each other, deductions and

implications carrying them still farther into hostile, unchar-
tered territory. Wakefield spoke first. "All right, Randall, first
let's have a look at *all* the slides you brought tonight, regardless
how long that might take. Perhaps, we'll detect a pattern or a
logical explanation will present itself."

Archer withdrew unexamined slides from their slots one by
one for Wakefield to observe, replacing each once he'd finished.
A highly motile microbe appeared in all others—save every
single typhoid specimen.

"Only typhoid . . ." Wakefield pondered. "*If* the frequency
Henry is currently directing affects only one disease in its living
state—as in this case with typhoid—might we hypothesize that
other wave frequencies, or vibrating electromagnetic energy,
might affect other diseases in the same way?"

"Possible," Archer said, dark eyes narrowed in concentration,
"though far-fetched. It could mean the typhoid sample was con-
taminated here or in my lab, in the hospital, or even en route.
Or it may relate to an abnormality in the donor-patient which
has been overlooked."

Wakefield tried another route. "I can't believe *I'm* the one
to suggest this, but why don't we reconvene tomorrow night
and attempt to recreate this phenomenon. I could get Henry to
beam the same frequency for us. You, Dr. Archer, bring as wide
a range of fresh disease samples, including as many typhoid
slides from as many different patients, as you can assemble."

§

With Henry recreating and directing with the cathode-ray-
tube the exact frequency of vibrating energy as the night before,
both Wakefield and Archer took turns observing a spectrum
of untreated specimens under the microscope. When the same
result was achieved—no motile microbe in evidence *only* on
the typhoid slides—Archer grew visibly disturbed. The typhoid

samples had been drawn from several University Hospital patients, and with consistency, none contained any frantic microbes. Thus, the anomaly was not due to a specific patient. Yet
all other diseases remained unaffected. In them, the microbes
danced on as before.

Archer personally had ensured procedures and protocols
were stringently adhered to at each step of the assembly process—from biopsy or fluid draw, to slide assembly, to transport,
and finally, to observation in Wakefield's carefully sterilized lab.
This led the scientists into hypothesizing a connection between
living typhoid and the specific frequency from Henry's ray-tube.

But even the hypothesis of a connection between a disease
and a frequency greatly agitated Archer. "There's nothing in
medical literature! *Nothing* in all my years in the classroom or
the lab that allows for this motile microbe we found in all living
diseases extracted from terminal patients. Let alone a possible
correlation to a wave of energy as Henry's been beaming.

"I-I'm baffled, Adam," he admitted in a small voice, "and
frankly frightened. The ground beneath the Harvard education I stand upon is quaking. I fear something is about to break
loose and threaten total collapse."

"Let's not overreact, old boy," Wakefield said to calm his
partner. "We've uncovered an apparent correlation between the
specific hertz Henry's recreated for us and typhoid. Let's simply
plan to test and eliminate as many possibilities as we're able.
That way we'll at least narrow down our questions."

"Right," Archer agreed, sucking in a breath to steady himself.
"Can you enlist Henry full-time after-hours to help us scroll
through the full spectrum of wave frequencies against as many
different disease specimens as I can procure?"

"Perfect! In other words," Wakefield rephrased the suggestion, "let's see if other electromagnetic vibrations have a similar
effect on other diseases, somehow eliminating the microbe as
Henry's original frequency appears to do to typhoid."

"Excellent next step. But," Archer reiterated, "it is essential we're both cautious and thorough."

"Yes, I've heard that somewhere before, Randall," Wakefield deadpanned.

Archer rushed on without detecting the jab. "We've already noted small variations in the microbe from disease to disease— differences in coloration and motion patterns. Perhaps those variations suggest other unique qualities we've yet to uncover."

"For example," Wakefield conjectured, "their own unique rates of vibration, or individual frequencies."

Wakefield's excitement soared. "We have just speculated that the microbe of each individual disease has a *signature* vibration rate!" Wakefield shook his head in awe. "Heady stuff, old man, I must say!"

§

Archer slowed at the driveway to his two-story home, which the lowering sun had tinted peach. He braked, incredulous at what his wife had created with an incomplete house on an un- finished lot. He had seen none of the possibilities Elizabeth had brought to glorious fruition.

Two large sycamore trees perfectly framed the butter-yellow stucco, their dappled trunks themselves Impressionist art. The terracotta walkway Elizabeth had installed highlighted the curved terracotta roof tiles. Knowing his wife adored the color purple, he appreciated how she'd masterfully utilized lavender plants to border and divide the front lawn while leading visitors to the entrance. The balance and proportion as well as the con- trasting purple-and-golden hues were, in Archer's admittedly inexpert opinion, genius.

Though he'd half-heard his wife talking about the day- workers she'd hired to install the fountain and the terracotta terraces in the front and back, he'd paid little mind. What he did recall now as he admired it was Elizabeth's distress over the sad fact that workers, even skilled ones, were too readily available during the so-called 'Great Depression.'

He'd simply been relieved she was happy and busy with her own projects, knowing it lessened the pressure on him while she spent most weeks and weekends alone in a strange city where she'd made no real friends. Something about the other doctors' wives? Archer couldn't remember, but something had prompted her to concentrate exclusively on the house and garden to avoid them.

Parking his almost-new Ford Brewster in the garage behind the house, he entered another magical realm at its rear. Viewed from the wisteria-dripping pergola between the garage and house, her garden spread joyously out from the bright Moorish-tiled fountain at its center. While the fountain splashed and plinked its water music, immature flowerbeds predominating in blues and purples circled outward toward the perimeter of the yard, where beds of roses promised extravagant blooms. Fruit trees dotted the furthest edges of the property, completing the promising wonderland.

Archer inhaled the air spiced with the night-blooming jasmine she'd worked in, wondering when and how she had accomplished it all. The garden in its infancy already impressed. He recalled Elizabeth stating, *'I intend my efforts with both this house and the garden to last our lifetime—hopefully longer!'*

He still marveled as he reached the back door. But upon entering it, he crash-landed in a diametrically opposed reality.

Frantically boiling pots on the kitchen stove filled the interior with a wall of heat and humidity. Elizabeth, hovering over maps strewn across the kitchen table, didn't notice his entrance.

When he sneaked up behind her to deliver a kiss to the top of her bent head, she screamed and reared back. "Oh ye gods, Randall! You scared the living daylights out of me!" She checked the clock on the wall, once, then twice. "What are you doing home? It's still daylight, though barely. Will the University stand without you?"

Archer overlooked her sarcasm. "Sorry I scared you, Elizabeth. Adam is away at a conference, and for once, nothing calamitous occurred in my lab today. I thought I'd come home to dine with you. That is, if you haven't eaten?"

"That would explain it," she said, standing to rub her neck muscles and stretch. "I'm trying a one-dish meal, a salad that contains pasta and chicken. Oh no! Which I forgot about! Damn it." She rushed to lift a lid off a pot, the smell of blackened meat rising. "The chicken is burned."

She pivoted to face him. "It was an easy-sounding recipe from this morning's newspaper, which I figured, being a salad, wouldn't matter how cold it became before you got home. And if the recipe failed, that is, if I failed at it, I could throw it out with no one the wiser." She checked the pasta boiling on the stove and switched off the flame. "Overcooked! Well, if you're hungry enough, perhaps you're game to try my latest culinary endeavor?"

Archer paused to think. "I am hungry. I don't think I had lunch today. I usually grab something at my desk but I guess I forgot. However, Lizbeth, let's enjoy the garden over cocktails before the light fails completely. I must admit that I never fully appreciated its magnificence, like the home it enhances. Your garden, in particular, Elizabeth, is, well, it's beyond words even in its early stage."

She eyed him suspiciously, her brows pinching. "If I didn't know better, Randall, I'd suspect something—a cute coed perhaps—prompting you to butter me up like this?" She laughed at her husband's horror as she released her hair constricted at the nape of her neck. "Joking, Randall. Honestly.

"Well," she added, looking skeptically at the food on the stove, "this will be a night to remember. The Archers dining at a normal time, together. Go freshen up, Randall. I'll stir up the

Manhattans and meet you in the garden in ten minutes. Hurry now before we lose the light completely."

§

Fifteen minutes later, showered and changed, his hair glistening in a wet and lumpy mass, Archer sat beside his wife on the wrought-iron garden bench near the bubbling fountain. He inhaled the warm, scented evening air. The dying light muted the world's harsh edges as Archer raised his glass. "To you, Elizabeth. We must do this more often. It's heavenly out here at this hour."

They clinked and drank. As the silence lengthened, it occurred to Archer that his wife seemed unusually quiet. "Magnificent job, all of this, Elizabeth. I'll never know how you figured it out so perfectly." When she only nodded, he asked, "You seem distracted, Lizbeth. When I surprised you tonight, were you studying maps of Los Angeles? What are you conjuring up now that you've all but finished our first home?"

Elizabeth's expression hardened when she met the admiration in his gaze. "As wonderful as our home has turned out, as fun and satisfying a project as it has been as has the garden, I should have been 'pounding the pavement' from the moment we arrived here, Randall."

She extricated her hand from his and leapt to her feet. "Los Angeles seemed such a boomtown, growing in every direction, I never dreamed finding a teaching post would prove so difficult." She paced the garden path, venting frustration.

"Yes, I was, Randall, examining maps of the city and county. I've placed all the schools, public and private, on the maps, then drew concentric circles farther and farther from our home."

Archer studied the indistinct image of his wife in the dying daylight. "Smart, Elizabeth. So you'll start applying for a position at the closest schools and work your way outward until you land one?"

"Oh darling, I am *well* past that. I've already covered every-thing nearby and have moved onto longer and longer driving distances. All my job applications have resulted in exactly nothing. 'We're not hiring.' 'We're laying off another round of staff.' 'No need to leave your CV. Were we to find ourselves in the position to hire again, we'd start with those we had to let go. It's only fair.' Now where have I heard that before?"

She slammed back onto the bench, jostling Archer's drink. "What does one say to that, Randall?"

He thought about Roosevelt's 'Second New Deal,' and all the misery it was meant to combat. Like the sprawling tent cities that, in California, swarmed with the added influx of millions of so-called 'Okies' fleeing the Dust Bowl, ravaging the center of the country. "It won't be easy, Elizabeth, I grant you, with the local economy under additional pressure. But you're a gifted and honored teacher. Something will turn up. You just have to keep at it."

She said nothing, staring at the water babbling cheerfully in the fountain before slowly coming to her feet. "Let me toss the salad, and we'll eat. If it's inedible, there's always my trusty standby—scrambled eggs and toast. Give me a moment. I'll call you when it's ready.

"And Randall," she paused on the pathway to the kitchen, "I'm glad you've discovered our garden. It's for us to enjoy for as long and as often as we are able."

CHAPTER ELEVEN

RENDEZVOUS WITH DESTINY

1936

It was early evening, the medical lab emptying out, Archer winding up his duties before heading over to the College of Physics to pursue his secretive research with Wakefield and his super-microscope. As he tidied his desk, jotting explicit instructions for his secretary to prepare his monthly report for the dean, Dean Culp himself walked in unannounced.

"Dr. Archer," he said, settling himself in the chair before the desk.

"Dean Culp! I-I wasn't expecting you. How—how nice of you to drop in," Archer stammered. With the dean gazing around his office and saying nothing further, Archer asked, "What can I do for you, Dean? It's rather late in the day, and I was just winding up before I, uh, leave."

The dean met Archer's eyes. "I see you're working on your monthly report. The statistics you've stacked up for this lab almost since inception have been impressive. Only rare retesting required due to your accuracy, no complaints of any note since the day you took over. Good work, Archer, very good indeed."

"Thank you, Dean Culp. I'd lie if I said it wasn't a challenge, and it still is, but to a lesser degree. It required almost an entire turnover of staff. But we're there, and things are running more smoothly, I'm relieved to report."

"Hmm, that's reflected in your report then, of course." The dean attempted to scan the upside-down draft Archer had prepared for typing and submission before the month-end deadline.

"Of course, Dean Culp." Archer leaned forward, effectively blocking the report from the dean to whom it would be addressed, not fully aware of why.

Like all department heads who submitted departmental summaries each month, the deans of each college then combined and synopsized their college's activities and accomplishments from the prior thirty days. Those reports were then sent up the line to the University President's office for final amalgamation of the entire University system. Archer hated the paperwork but had to admire the efficiency of the process for keeping the highest levels of bureaucracy informed about the University as a whole. Not to mention, he had no choice in the matter.

"I'll be heading home shortly myself," Dean Culp remarked. "Perhaps we could walk out together. Claire gets rather put-out when I cause dinner to go cold." He smiled. "And we don't want to aggravate our wives unnecessarily, do we, Doctor?"

Archer chuckled politely. "No, we do not. But uh, I was actually going to make a stop on campus before I drive home."

At that moment, the student manager of the nighttime laboratory barged into the office. "Dr. Archer, I have— Oops, sorry, I didn't know you were in conference. Excuse me. I'll just leave your specimen slides in the carrier here on your desk. The identifier list is in the pocket."

Archer's heart thumped as the risky subject of his clandestine research with Wakefield on living disease samples was placed beneath the nose of his boss. Preparing slides in anything but the age-old approved way of 'setting' with added dyes and washes required the dean's pre-approval.

Archer stalled, "Oh, Jesse, thank you. That'll be fine. Have you had the opportunity to meet the head of the College of Medicine? Dean Culp, meet Jesse, our night manager. Jesse, Dean Culp. I tell you, Dean, Jesse is one to watch. His work is of the highest quality. The Medical College is lucky to have a student of his talent and responsibility."

Jesse stepped forward awkwardly and extended his hand to the seated dean who shook it tepidly, saying, "Hello, young man. Keep up the good work."

Jesse seemed unsure what to do, so he eased toward the door and said, "Nice meeting you, Dean. I'll lock up as usual, Dr. Archer. Good night."

The dean resumed the conversation. "This stop you're making on campus, it wouldn't be at the College of Physics now, would it?"

Archer's heart nearly thudded to a stop, another reason he'd intended never to get caught up in subterfuge and cut corners again. "An old friend of mine from our Harvard days works over at Physics, Dean. And in fact, it is where I was heading. Wh-why do you ask?"

"Dean Grafton mentioned your frequent presence late into the night at the physics lab. It sparked my curiosity. So I flipped through your last several monthly reports and found no mention of any such collaboration with Physics."

The dean studied Archer closely, increasing his discomfort. *I should come clean,* he thought, but still he hesitated, torn between fantastical discovery and the blunting limitations of the status quo.

"Surely Dr. Archer, with a wife like yours, one is not merely socializing into all hours of the night? Risky business indeed. How is Elizabeth adapting to our university and city? Quite a change from her Boston, I'd imagine. Claire mentioned they don't see much of her at the faculty wives' events."

"She's fine. It's an adjustment, but Elizabeth is remarkably resilient. She's been very busy, first finding and establishing our home. Next she's created a garden that could be award-winning. But currently she's embroiled in finding a teaching position, and for some time now actually. The Depression is certainly causing problems there."

"Yes, one can understand. Well, do give her our hellos and encourage her to get out more with the other wives. If I were you, I wouldn't let a beautiful young woman of her background spend too much time on her own. It's not good for the psyche, nor might I add, for a marriage."

Archer only had time to wonder at the unsolicited marital advice when the dean abruptly changed the subject. "So, what is it you do over at Physics every night that has yet to show up in your reports?"

"Well, Dean, my old friend and former collaborator at Harvard, Dr. Adam Wakefield, has been developing a unique, high powered microscope that I've been helping him assess and fine-tune. Ultimately, my extracurricular activities there should greatly benefit our college, Dean, and of course, this lab in particular."

"Hmm, I see. The specimens your Jesse dropped off, they're for that assessment?" The dean reached for the carrier sitting between them on Archer's desk, but Archer slid it out of reach. They were live samples, after all.

"Yes," he said, patting the carrier protectively. "Yes, routine disease-sample study slides help analyze the powers of Dr. Wakefield's microscope."

"Well, perhaps you could summarize the assistance the Medical College is *donating* to Physics in your next monthly, Archer. I'd be interested to read about this special microscope and exactly what makes it so special."

"Of course, sir, yes, in my next month's report for certain." In the silence that followed, Archer finally suggested, "So shall I walk out with you, Dean?"

"No—no, you finish up. I'll see myself out, Archer. And I'll have my eye on your next month's report. Keep up the good work, son. But take some time for yourself and your wife. Relocation cross-country could be jolting in so many ways, as can the process of reestablishing yourselves here, as a couple as well as individually."

§

"Someone is talking," Archer accused as he entered the subsection of the physics lab staked out for their study. Wakefield and Henry looked up in surprise. "Henry, we asked you for complete confidentiality while we work our way through to understanding what it is we've uncovered here, along with what it might mean. You're not spreading the word out there, are you?"

"Of course not, Dr. Archer. Honest, Dr. Wakefield. You asked me to keep this research to myself for the time being, and I have." Henry's indignant expression faltered. "Oh. Well, there was a friend of mine from the Medical College that I might have mentioned it to. I'm sorry, I really am. It was a slip, and nothing of importance, I promise."

"What's happened, Randall?" Wakefield asked, alarmed at the case of nerves Archer exhibited.

Archer ignored him. "Henry, we must have your word that no further slips will be forthcoming. Can you absolutely guarantee us that?"

Henry blanched and nodded furiously. "I'm sorry. It was a slip. It will be the first and last, I promise."

Wakefield said, "Look, it's been a long day, Henry. You've worked hard and well. We couldn't do this without you. Why don't you take the night off? Dr. Archer and I have summary paperwork to review. You needn't stay for that. Take the night.

You deserve it. Go." A shamed Henry couldn't vacate the lab fast enough with another apology and rushed goodbyes.

"What's this?" Wakefield turned on Archer. "Henry has been invaluable. What will we do if you run him off? Although, by this time, our list of diseases and their individually correlated frequencies is probably as complete as it will ever be."

Archer slammed onto the stool. "Perhaps I'm overreacting. I'm sorry, Adam. I'll apologize to Henry tomorrow. It's just Dean Culp dropped into my office moments ago, and, it seemed, was fishing as if he'd heard or suspected something. You know I'm not permitted to create and handle live specimens without reams of special pre-approvals and documented procedures in place. This outside-of-protocol study of ours is both personally and professionally risky."

Archer sat, struggling to settle down. "I've seen firsthand how medicine fights to uphold the status quo during the best of times, which these times definitely are not. The possibility of our discoveries upending the entire field . . ."

Archer slumped over the table with a sigh, cradling his head in his hands. "I find myself wondering who in my lab might be keeping Dean Culp informed of laboratory goings-on like Dr. Dole had me do back at Harvard. The dean went so far as to imply I need to make time for myself and my marriage, that leaving my 'beautiful' wife on her own invites another kind of trouble."

"He said that? The nerve!"

"Wasn't it? What does he know of me or my marriage or my wife? But when Jesse interrupted us and sat the filled cold-carrier down between us, I nearly fainted. I snatched it away when he reached for it. Imagine what might have happened if he'd opened it. He could have been exposed to all sorts of killer diseases! Though, admittedly, their chilled state makes them less dangerous." Archer's weary sigh deflated him. "If not, I could be jailed for murder or reckless behavior, definitely back on the streets looking for a job."

"Your Jesse," Wakefield responded, "he's helped prepare the live specimens, correct? Have you accused him as you just did Henry of talking? He'd be more fully aware of the, what's the term you've used, 'unorthodox procedures' we've employed."

"I have instructed him on the importance of strict confidentiality, of course. And I trust him to observe our agreement."

"As I do Henry, despite his admission of a slip. Perhaps we both need a bit of time and distance to regain perspective. Take your dean's advice, Randall. Go home to your wife."

§

Months later, Archer turned into his driveway after dark. Unlike approaching his home in gauzy afternoon sunlight, the house after nightfall took on an ominous countenance. Dark windows stared like vacant eyes, peeking through the trees. The darkness within meant Elizabeth was in bed, something Archer himself desperately needed and as quickly as possible—if sleep would come. But after another truly shocking turn in his collaboration with Wakefield, he doubted it.

As the research tallied up the hours, only his worries outpaced them. Doubts and fears weighed more heavily each day. Additional months of study had proven their cobbled-in-a-moment hypothesis verified with consistency. What had struck Archer as unlikely *at best*—he had labeled it 'farfetched,' even ridiculous—proved almost harder to accept after verifications too-numerous to deny. The sub-bacterial-sized microbe found in all disease specimens when observed alive under the super-scope did in fact possess a signature vibration rate unique to each specific disease. No exceptions.

Compounding his trepidations was the fact that it made no difference whether the source-illness had been medically categorized as bacterial, fungal, viral, or of another pathogenic origin. *All* advanced-stage living disease specimens contained a similar microbe, and those microbes possessed a unique vibration rate associated only with that one particular disease. Period.

Archer parked his Ford in the garage behind the house, rubbed exhaustion from his eyes, and headed for the back door, oblivious to his surroundings while questions plagued him: what did it all mean—the microbes, their frenzied activity, and that the frenzy stopped upon exposure to its correlated frequency?

Though answers eluded him, he was acutely aware that the discoveries laid bare by Wakefield's powerful scope could provide the breakthrough of which he had long dreamed, thrusting him to the forefront of medical science. But they could also implode not only his career, but much of the field of medicine with an entirely new understanding of health and disease.

He stepped into the dark kitchen, flipped on the light, and was met with a scene of shocking disarray. His preoccupations fled before the uncovered pots on the stove, food congealing within. The open oven door revealed a pot roast gone cold, and a glance into the dining room revealed two place settings and an open bottle of wine untouched. He was initially disgusted by such waste given the hunger rampant in the world, but then it dawned on him.

He and Elizabeth had agreed to reserve one night during the week to dine together and stay current with each other's lives. His deplorable ignorance about her job-search struggles provided the initial impetus. And this had been the night. But as usual, his after-hours research had carried him off to another world altogether, and he'd forgotten completely.

Archer tiptoed through the darkened house and up the stairs. Before opening the bedroom door, he silently prayed Elizabeth would be sound asleep. He was simply too tired, too distracted, and too conflicted over where his research was carrying him to argue or beg forgiveness tonight.

He would grovel in the morning, and make a peace offering
to Elizabeth with an idea he'd had to ease her job pursuit. He
would offer to arrange an introduction to the dean of ULA's
College of Education, a man of good repute. Certainly the dean
could offer ideas to speed her hunt.

Easing into the bedroom, a relieved Archer found his wife
asleep in bed, her back to the door. He crept into the bathroom
and prepared for the night as quickly and quietly as he could,
then slipped delicately into bed.

As soon as his head hit the pillow, Archer plunged into the
deep sleep of the truly exhausted. He never knew Elizabeth rose
immediately and left the room, nor did he hear the commotion
she created, banging pots and pans in the kitchen, venting her
anger on the mess she'd left behind.

§

"The latest literature may cast light upon what we've been seeing in living diseases," Wakefield was saying as Archer entered
their area of the physics lab, the space containing the only
Wakefield microscope known to exist as well as Henry's fre-
quency-generating device. Records were kept in files along the
perimeter as well as piled on the shelving enclosing two high
lab tables.

Wakefield rested on a stool before his scope. "After we discovered the first typhoid slides *devoid* of the microbe, our study
veered onto a new trajectory. Once Henry first beamed the frequency onto the typhoid microbe that, we soon discovered,
matched its innate rate of vibration, we watched the microbe's
frenzied motion cease.

"Then we moved on to prove that other frequencies worked
similarly on the microbes found in other diseases when correctly matched. They too were deactivated after Henry's exposure in each case. Thus we were able to observe the microbe's

life cycle, or its evolution, in response to the initial and continued effect of frequency-exposure."

Wakefield glanced at Archer. "Agreed?" Archer nodded wearily. "Pull up a seat, old man. I've got a lot to discuss tonight." Wakefield's excitement blinded him to his partner's dull compliance. "Now," Wakefield pressed onward, "once we realized each disease microbe has its own signature frequency, we observed that by recreating that exact vibration, we triggered three distinct, evolutionary stages.

"First, the frenzied motion of the life-form increases upon initial stimulation by its exactly-matched frequency. Second, as beaming of that frequency continues, the speeding microbes change again, beginning to glow or fluoresce. Third, under prolonged exposure to its own frequency, all motion on the slide suddenly ceases, and the microbes can no longer be detected."

Tending toward the verbose, more exaggerated when excited, Wakefield's exhilaration prevented him noticing Archer had said not a word, slumping on a stool, head propped by his hands, working to concentrate on his partner's animated recap. Archer sensed Wakefield was warming to a full-on physics lecture.

"And to think, Randall," Wakefield gushed, "it was your comments about upending all of medicine. What was it you said? 'There's nothing in the field of traditional Western medicine that infers a connection between diseases and energy fields. *Nothing!*' And if we're drifting into a whole new way of understanding and treating disease, you then reminded me to think of the multitudes who could be displaced. That's close to what you said, no?" Wakefield finally noticed Archer's non-responsiveness.

"And your retort was," Archer replied flatly, "this I clearly remember: 'What about the multitudes whose lives might be saved?'"

"Right old boy, it did seem the obvious point. But, as I've thought about it further, I realized that medicine is perhaps about to undergo a radical shift similar to what physics has undergone in this century, and is still undergoing, in fact. A paradigm shift."

Wakefield cocked an eyebrow at his despondent partner. "Unlike you, Randall, *I* find it thrilling to ride a new wave of discovery into the future." He didn't allow time for a response. "Now where was I? Oh yes, paradigm shifts. Stay with me here . . ."

Wakefield sat, lost in thought, before picking up his lecture. "I've continued to read about Einstein as well as Bohr, who discovered an array of substructures *within* the atom," he paused for an aside, "and in so doing, demolished the long-accepted belief that the atom was the smallest, *indivisible* building-block of all solid matter throughout the universe. Well, I've pondered how all this might relate to energy affecting our microbial pathogens. From our repeated observations, a specific correlated frequency appears ultimately to kill them. At least, we know all activity stops."

Wakefield rose to pace between the tables. "We can assume that prolonged exposure to its perfectly-matched vibration would cause a transfer of energy, intensifying the microbe's vibration and speeding its activity as we've seen.

"There's a term we physicists use that applies here, Randall. 'Resonance.' It boils down to two similarly vibrating energy sources mutually intensifying each other. However, eventually that intensification overwhelms the microbe's cells, causing their innate charge to change. And in turn, that causes the cell's shape and pattern to change. Until finally cell function is compromised, and breakdown occurs."

Wakefield rushed to conclude, "Remember, old boy, everything in the universe is, at its essence, energy. Therefore, disease must also be an energetic form. Nothing is 'solid.' It's all, *we're all,* at our most rudimentary levels, widely varying concentrations of energy that is in constant motion."

Archer's head now pounded. Wakefield stopped his circling, noticing Archer's beleaguered slump as he massaged his temples, and the unusual dullness in his eyes. "I do run on, Randall. Forgive me. Are you all right tonight?"

"Sorry, Adam, having a hard time concentrating." Wakefield waited for elaboration. "It's Elizabeth. She was gone by the time I got up this morning, no idea where. No note. Unusual to say the least. And . . . and I'm afraid I've committed a few massive mistakes of late that have left her greatly angered." Wakefield pulled a stool around, sitting face-to-face with Archer to encourage him.

"At first, crafting our living spaces—damn fine job she did too—took all of her energy and attention. But eventually, with the task completed, she's met with total failure in her search for a teaching position. No one is hiring in this unstable economy."

"Even the Teacher of the Year in her very first year of teaching?" Wakefield remarked. "At a prestigious private school, no less?"

"Our sentiments exactly, Adam. But her thorough search at increasing distances from home has left her demoralized and depressed. And I wasn't even aware of it for far too long, with my unwavering focus on my own position, and then of course, our project.

"That disconnect prompted us to agree to dine together at minimum once a week to stay up to date with each other's lives. And the first such dinner was last night, Adam, which you may recall given I was here, I forgot." Archer relived the kitchen scene which had assaulted him the night before. "She'd left our entire meal in the pots she'd cooked it in, on the stove, in the oven, abandoning it all when I failed to show."

Wakefield shook his head sadly. "What kind of a friend have I been to either one of you? Truthfully, I hadn't allowed myself— I mean I haven't given Elizabeth much thought, not that either of us has had free time for undirected thought, Randall. But

suddenly I'm imagining her alone in a new home in a new city
with no old friends, finding her own way around while the two
of us absorbed ourselves in shocking discoveries, late into the
night, night after night.

"Look, let's call it a day, shall we?" Wakefield suggested. "Do
go home to your wife, old man. And beg her forgiveness for
the both of us. You look like you could use a good night's rest
anyway. I'm going to fold it up myself after reviewing ideas from
Engineering on streamlined production of my microscope.
With that behind us, other scientists will be able to replicate
and verify our findings. There will be no more excuses for not
announcing our initial discoveries to the world."

Archer struggled to his feet, biting back any number of reasons for not releasing their game-changing conclusions on a
suffering world. Instead, he left Wakefield in silence, saving his
energy for whatever awaited him at home.

But what did he fear? he pondered as he exited campus. In
the bright sunlight, ULA looked alive and invigorating, rather
than mottled by threatening shadows at his usual departure
hour. He feared where their research was pointing, which was
as far from mainstream, accepted medical practice imaginable.
That was all.

He considered his specialization in pathology, which initially focused on categorizing diseases by pathogen—viral, bacterial, fungal, and so forth. Next, it focused on the established
methods of treatment—surgery, radiation, and, increasingly,
drug therapies, used alone or in combination to combat those
diseases, with widely varying degrees of success and too often
with debilitating side effects.

Since Harvard and the utilization of Wakefield's novel microscope had enabled him to observe living specimens—something that began as mere curiosity and speculation—Archer
had been borne worlds away from his medical training. And
that was before he'd entered his study of pathology, during

which he'd remained alert to any and all possible explanations.

But any suggestion or comment based upon what he'd witnessed had been met with blatant derision. 'Lousy lab procedure' seemed to explain everything for his fellows. Having no way to demonstrate his point amongst the most gifted pathology specialists in the world, Archer learned to keep silent. Desperate to embrace the mainstream path of his chosen field, Archer found few, if any, other medical practitioners who considered the patient's inner state as key to its microbial ecosystem. Shaking his head, Archer longed to be among them.

But as his work with Wakefield continued, he'd reluctantly begun to intuit that disease appeared to evolve into a more virulent form as it progressed within a victim's increasingly toxic body. Did he dare utter such a thing to his non-believing and resistant field? He hadn't even shared these thoughts with Wakefield.

As Archer drove up the driveway toward the back of his house, the intriguing possibilities Wakefield's 'new paradigm' inspired prompted another thought. If everything in the universe is fundamentally energy, including disease, then surely energy must have an effect.

CHAPTER TWELVE

SHIFTING PARADIGMS

1937

The next planned dinner between husband and wife was finally set after Archer had done as Wakefield advised: begged multiple times for forgiveness and another try.

Archer arrived home before the agreed-upon time for the now and forever sacrosanct weekly dinner with his wife. Through the French doors opening onto the covered arcade, he glanced into the dining room. The table, set for two, was completed by a dazzling bouquet fresh from Elizabeth's garden. Thank heavens he'd not just remembered, he'd shown up early!

Elizabeth was testing something in the oven when he entered. She stood as he moved to greet her with a kiss. "You did it, Randall, I've got to hand it to you. Unless your presence at this hour is coincidence? Or your partner is out of town again?" She smiled at his crestfallen look and kissed his cheek. "Thank you. I know it was an effort, and I appreciate it. Cocktails in the garden at 7:45 sharp! Better get a move on. My Manhattans wait for no man."

At 7:45 'sharp,' Archer joined his wife at the small garden table holding their frosted-over cocktail glasses. His wife's beauty in a shimmering dark blue silk blouse and flowing pants enhanced the entire scene, amazing Archer anew. He breathed it all in and raised his chilled glass. "To my wife, the creator of this Eden for me to come home to."

Elizabeth paused, the plinking of the fountain surging into prominence. She took a long sip but sarcasm got the best of her. "What might I add to make it *more* attractive, Randall, and draw you home *more* often to enjoy it?"

Archer was stymied. He opened his mouth but no response came out. "I-I . . . I just meant to say you've done an admirable job, and—and it's delightful to be here with you."

"I know, I know," she relented. "Forgive me, Randall. I'm just testy. Cheers." They clinked glasses. "And how was your day, dear?"

It sounded so rote, it actually caught Archer's attention. "Elizabeth, what's wrong?"

She studied him, drink held in both hands before her face, hiding all but the storm in her eyes. "Several things, actually," she said, sitting her drink aside. "It boils down to having more time on my hands than ever before. And in that time, I've come to realize how far we've both come from Boston, Randall. Not just thousands of miles, but us, you and me, our relationship. Our roles."

Archer repeated her words internally before venturing, "I'm not understanding, Elizabeth. 'Our roles'?"

After another long drink and an exaggerated exhale, she again put her cocktail aside. "You know, Randall, Mother would be thrilled at all this—me, married to a doctor, no longer at risk of becoming an old maid, lovely home, glorious garden even if I do fiddle in it with my own hands. But most appropriately, *not* employed and *not* accepting money for said employment. Of course, you weren't the ideal marital candidate for Mother, but here we are."

"She's never met me!" Archer rejoined. "One might assume,

as closely aligned as the Perrishes are to Harvard, that my Harvard medical degree with honors might begin to counteract my numerous shortcomings." His indignation brought the conversation to a halt, Elizabeth looking startled. But he didn't wish to veer into touchy territory so early in this important evening. "You were saying, Elizabeth, that you're not happy. I can see that. I hear it. What would you like me to do about it?"

"Nothing, Randall! This is not about you," she snapped. "I-I just never imagined myself running as fast and as far as I have to end up exactly where I started!" She pushed away from the table as if to bolt, but she appeared to have second thoughts. "It's not your fault, Randall. Somehow," the anger drained from her tone, "it must be mine . . ."

"The job market? Is that what's aggravating you?"

"Yes. And no." She studied the fountain, unconsciously tapping a finger in time to its splashing tempo. "I've realized only now in retrospect how empowering it was, when we first married, to be the sole breadwinner. While you completed your education, we were partners, equals, in a world that decries such things between men and women. At least, that's how I felt. For the first time, I was succeeding beyond everyone's expectations of me."

"I'm well aware of what I owe you, Elizabeth. And I intend—"

"And now, Randall," she spoke over him, "like it or not, I'm just a doctor's wife, completely defined by you and your status. And not a very fruitful doctor's wife, if you agree with the other doctors' wives, having failed to supply you with a tribe of children."

"That is none of their business!" he exclaimed, lamenting the poor start to the evening. Rightly or wrongly, Archer felt as if she blamed him and he was damned tired of it. Why was everything, ultimately, his fault, he asked himself petulantly.

But upon taking a deep breath, he knew he needed to hear her out or it would be one long, difficult meal. "Listen, Elizabeth, you'll never be 'just a doctor's wife,' although you could do worse." The minute he said that last, he regretted it. He tried to smooth it over. "You are a strong and independent woman who happens to have a real gift for teaching children. And," he gazed around the garden, "apparently a gift for décor and gardening and whatever else you set your mind to."

"And yet, Randall," she responded, "the world stubbornly refuses to recognize my gifts. I've applied or tried to apply to every school in Southern California it seems, and here I sit, unemployed and frankly lonely and bored. There's no end in sight to this so-called 'Great Depression,' and there's no hope while it drags on. That's the sad state of affairs as I'm experiencing it.

"I know I should be grateful," she was quick to add. "I have you and your work ethic to support me in this comfortable style, and I am, truly. It sure beats student housing," she quipped, but her smile faded quickly. "Yet somehow during the longest, quietest hours of the day or night, I hear my mother reminding me, 'You're not so clever. Know your place, Elizabeth, and make it work.'"

Elizabeth's mimicry hit Archer like a low blow. How many times had his own work-hardened family taunted him about the very same thing, not being 'near as smart' as he thought? And when particularly frustrated with their little brother 'sittin' on his high horse,' refusing to 'pull his own weight' at the steel mills like them, brute force punctuated their messages. At least he'd gotten through high school before they could make him quit.

The only person in his life who'd encouraged him, Miss Della, stole into his recollections. She not only cheered his dreams on, she found a way to make them happen. She'd even given herself in the most intimate of ways. Her belief and adoration and her welcoming body had engendered very little sleep the night he'd spent with her. But once he'd boarded the bus to Harvard, he'd barely thought of her again . . .

Still he wasn't a complete failure, no matter what the Perrishes thought. He reminded himself of all he had accomplished.

Running a university medical lab at his age as well as providing the home and grounds he admired. And despite their unreachable social position, he was sitting across from their only daughter, a Boston Brahmin herself. Well beyond his reach, true, yet here she was! Ha.

Elizabeth, tears in her eyes, voice cracking, brought him back to the moment. "I'm slipping backwards, Randall, despite my best efforts. What if there is no escaping my expected role as a Perrish?" She quickly brushed back a trickling tear. "What if you can run but can never truly escape expectations?"

Archer mulled her words, asking himself, what if at the end of the day he was still just an Archer, like his family, with little use for education and willing to accept a bottom rung on the ladder to success, in fact, expecting little else? Did they, on some level, feel that was what they deserved? He shook his head to clear it. "Elizabeth, let's leave our families out of this. They only beat us both down. Good riddance to them all.

"Your resilience and determination have done nothing but surprise me since we met," Archer reiterated. "Given what you walked away from, your independence is perhaps the most striking of all. Adam, who has known you your whole life, seems even more impressed for the knowing. Don't sell yourself short. We've left our families behind, exactly where they belong. Now it's up to us to make the life we want."

Seeing Elizabeth's quivering smile, he added, "I've been so busy that I've forgotten multiple times, but I've wanted to suggest something to you. I should have done so long ago, and I apologize. I wasn't aware of how unhappy you'd become. But—but," he rushed to cover that statement, "all the department heads and deans regularly offer assistance to the families of fellow faculty throughout the University. I want to set you up with the Dean of the College of Education. He, like his College, has an excellent reputation. The primary school run by his College is reputed to be on the cutting edge in philosophy and teaching techniques. At minimum, he might shed light on your search, perhaps even offer an insider's tip or two."

Elizabeth looked taken aback and glanced away. When she gazed up again it was with the most tender expression he'd seen in months. "I'm so sorry, Randall. I've never been quite so alone nor frustrated. I'd be thrilled to meet with the Dean of Education and I'd appreciate your arranging it. And Randall, I'm sorry my mother will never be distant enough to cease haunting me. It's the last thing I wish to lay at your feet."

Archer chuckled bitterly. "Lizbeth, that version of family I completely understand."

She stood, bending down to kiss him. "Thank you, Randall. I'll see about dinner, with of course my standard disclaimer: such as dinner may be. Give me five minutes."

As he finished his drink, enjoying the garden's splashing sounds and spicy scents, he reminded himself how critical these conversations could be for their marriage. And even though his marriage would never be of primary importance to him, he vowed he would do his best to continue the weekly ritual. His talented wife was a real prize worth hanging on to.

Elizabeth deserved it. They both deserved the fruits of a well-tended marriage.

§

Archer received word that Wakefield would meet him in the medical lab after hours. With his microscope located at the College of Physics, it was unusual, but Archer felt relief. He needed extra time to finish the onerous monthly report for Dean Culp. The dean had insisted upon him including information on his shared research with Wakefield at the physics lab that he'd somehow learned about, a subject Archer wished to handle delicately.

So involved had Archer become in that and the standard

reporting of laboratory statistics for the last month—data on the number of patients and doctors his laboratory had served, diagnoses offered and used, drug efficacy tests, successes or retesting derived therefrom—he did not once check the time. Until a commotion arose.

He glanced through his office window into the lab, where he spied several students he didn't recognize. They were questioning the student night manager while hauling behind them a large, covered dolly. He rose to investigate just as the night manager reached his door. "What's going on out there, Jesse? Who are those boys? What have they brought?"

Before Jesse could respond, Archer observed Wakefield trailing in. The two men hurried toward each other. "I come bearing gifts, old boy, and not just any ol' gift, mind you. Look what I've brought you, Randall." Wakefield instructed the young men rolling in the cart to carefully remove the covering to reveal the second Wakefield Microscope. "Where do you want her?" he asked a stupefied Archer.

"You finished another scope!" Archer exclaimed. "Why, that's almost unbelievable with all the hours we've been putting in."

Wakefield confessed, "It wasn't easy, but the joint project with the College of Engineering is paying off. The students assigned to mechanize assembly to the extent possible were first-rate. This is just the prototype, so don't expect Wakefield Scopes to populate labs everywhere *just yet*. We still have a few refinements to make before we begin production.

"As I told you," Wakefield continued, "I've done some tweaks on this newer model, but basically it replicates the machine we've been sharing for far too long." He stood back, gazing at his newest creation before remembering to ask again, "So where do you want her, Dr. Archer?"

Archer's mind raced. The large, strange-looking apparatus sitting out in the open would surely invite questions and scrutiny. He was reluctant to discuss his controversial research with medical professionals, at least until he knew more about it *and* its likely effects on the field. Observable late-night sessions in concert with Wakefield would only intensify notice of the living specimens under study.

The medical laboratory was, much like Wakefield's, sectioned off by metal wall dividers-cum-shelving. If necessary, those areas could be closed off and secured from public view. "In there, boys," Archer directed, pointing to the empty section closest to his office.

"Careful now," Wakefield cautioned, following his creation as it was delicately moved to its new home. Archer followed them into the space, looking around to see who was in his lab at this hour, grateful it was just a few students.

After setting the microscope in place, Wakefield announced, "I'll need to do a bit of fine-tuning and testing before we can begin again right here tomorrow night. I'll arrange for a cathode ray tube to be lent from Physics and for Henry to train someone here to use it. At long last," he sighed, "this second scope should speed our progress by separately replicating each other's findings." Wakefield noted a flash of anger darken Archer's expression at what he correctly interpreted to be another jab at the doctor's slow process. But Archer suppressed it just as quickly. "Sorry, old chap," Wakefield added, "I just can't shake my own frustrations. But let's not rehash all that just now."

Wakefield noticed Archer's reserve. "What is it? You seem neither surprised nor excited to have such a scope at your fingertips, nearer the source of our studies as well as all others taking place in this lab."

Their experiments put him personally in danger of receiving the dean's wrath, Archer thought but left unsaid. "I—I am thrilled, Adam. Good work. It couldn't have been easy. I'm just a bit distracted tonight by a few loose ends I'm attending in my office. While you 'fine-tune' as you say, I'll finish and be prepared to get back at it tomorrow night." He turned to go. "Oh, and let Jesse know if there's anything you need. I'm going to try to get home to my wife for a change—twice in one week. I promised myself to never again forget her," he added, immediately regretting the slip of private information.

"Oh?" Wakefield searched Archer's face for meaning. "How is Elizabeth? I haven't seen her since she dove into the interior renovations of your house and the plotting out of a grand garden."

"Oh, she's all but done with all of that. She tells me she's telephoned you any number of times but never gets an answer at your home. But she's fine. You must come see her results now that the house is complete and the garden is maturing. It's truly remarkable."

"I'd expect nothing less," Wakefield replied. "And I'd love to see it. And her. Tell Elizabeth hello from me, would you please. Instead of telephoning my home, maybe she should communicate through you as *you* are whom I'm spending all my off-hours with as you know, here on campus."

"Yes—yes, of course, I'll suggest that. I'll see you tomorrow then, in my lab." But before exiting, Archer remembered. "And thank you, Adam. It's quite an accomplishment."

As soon as he'd returned to the open area of the medical lab, Archer called Jesse over. "Jesse, I'll be leaving shortly. My monthly report is on the secretary's desk to type come morning. And Jesse, I want that lab section with Dr. Wakefield's experimental microscope locked up as soon as the men leave. You understand? Initially, only I will assist him in determining its powers and usefulness."

"Sure, Dr. Archer. If you're not in when I leave in the morning, I'll put that key in your upper desk drawer, okay?"

"Yes, fine. You've got a key to my office. Be certain you lock it as well."

§

"It's indisputable," Wakefield exclaimed as another semester was winding down, sitting across from Archer in his office. "You and your assistant corroborated the frequencies and their correlated diseases. *Again*. We've both described the nuanced differences in the microbe from disease to disease in nearly the exact words. We've repeatedly observed the microbe's three-stage evolution before its intensifying vibration appears to destroy it. It's rare in research, but you and I, Randall, seem to be in lock-step agreement over shared and *consistent* findings.

"But what does it mean, these stilled viruses?" Wakefield asked. "And why can't we call them viruses, Randall, as at their size, what else could they be?"

"Because," Archer barked, "if we refrain from naming the microbe a virus, we'll give the medical establishment one less thing to take exception to. However, given our specimens are drawn from terminal patients, one can assume we're observing disease in its most virulent form. Which appears to be viral ..."

He thought before adding, "It does seem the energy transfer you previously mentioned, overwhelming normal cell function under prolonged frequency exposure, may in effect electrocute the microbe. However," Archer was quick to add, "whether the stilled microbes are dead and no longer able to transmit disease, or whether they're simply dazed or dormant, remains to be proven."

Wakefield sniped, "Exactly the point, Randall!"

Archer hesitated before venturing into a touchy subject. "Look, Adam, all these strange connections and discoveries we're making are undeniably exciting, but I need to ask something of you. I want you to be certain our study materials and records are always kept locked and secured."

"What's this?" demanded Wakefield irritably. "Secured? From whom?"

"Listen to me, Adam. I hadn't locked away your second super-scope from prying eyes in this lab for a day when questions began from doctors and even the dean about what we're working on. I've sensed for some time someone keeping tabs on us. Strange noises in the lab when it appears no one is here. Papers moved on my desk in my locked office. Even late at night as I cross campus, I feel someone watching and following, though I've never caught anyone. Movement just beyond my sight. All my imagination?"

"Or an attack of paranoia?" Wakefield offered but was ignored.

"I put off the dean's and others' questions, saying simply that my lab and I personally are assessing your new scope's capabilities. But the level of interest is without precedent, as if someone is speculating about our research on living diseases."

"Well, so what," came Wakefield's retort. "We've been through this before. 'It's outside laboratory protocol,' I clearly remember. Perhaps it's time, given what we're seeing, to question protocol itself, not only what we're finding."

Archer sucked down his frustrations. "Adam, you continue to take every opportunity to belittle my repetitive processes—"

"Is that what you call the repeated batteries of tests we've done—'repetitive processes'? After so much time, it feels more like foot-dragging, Randall, but I'm baffled as to why. You told me at our very first meeting years ago back East that you intended to be *the premier research doctor* in the world. And need I point out, my microscope might provide a way to accomplish that very thing? A never-before-seen microbe? Its reaction to a carefully matched electromagnetic vibration? *Both* discoveries are earthshattering!" Wakefield, vehemently insisting, slammed his fist on the desk. "So this reluctance of yours . . . it doesn't add up. I ask again, what is the real problem, Randall?"

"The problem—" Archer shouted before catching himself. He rose, closed his office door, and returned to his seat, tightly reining himself in. "The real problem, Adam, is that what we're finding and documenting flies in the face of my entire medical education and my years of specialized training in the field. It

veers well outside the sacrosanct Germ Theory of Disease put
forth by Louis Pasteur himself—a god in medicine. His theory
remains the accepted gospel to this day."

"Wasn't that theory offered a few *hundred* years ago?" Wakefield countered. "Does medicine intend to hold us and itself to
old paradigms forever?"

"The mid-1800s, but that's not the point. I'm saying since
we don't really understand what it is we've come upon, nor yet
know the end result of 'electrocuting' the microbe if that's what
we're doing, we need to be cautious about all we are about to
challenge—the very basis upon which modern medicine has
been built and practiced for a century. Our logic and proof
must be airtight, and thoughtfully timed."

"'Almost a century…'" Wakefield shook his head in revulsion.
"I'm beginning to comprehend why modern medicine was the
first profession to license and tightly regulate its practitioners
throughout their careers. A handy method to keep everyone
aligned within orthodoxy."

Archer bit his lip, holding himself back with difficulty. "I'm
advising caution, Adam, that's all. And a high degree of certainty before we go up against entrenched beliefs and regulated
practices. Do you really feel the two of us are ready to take on
the entire medical establishment at this point in our search?
And now, amidst widespread economic devastation?"

"I'm just a simple physicist," Wakefield bemoaned. "I don't
think about science the way you do. *I* think of it as a sacred duty
to search for truth wherever it may take me and share that truth
with others who may carry it even farther toward solving the
mysteries of the universe. And maybe, just maybe, *Dr.* Archer,
in the process save and improve lives on this planet."

Anger blotched Archer's skin as he struggled for control,
torn in so many different directions, he literally felt he could
implode. "I agree with you, Adam!" he asserted, grasping the
arms of his chair until his knuckles turned white. "Finding truth

is our sacred duty. But I'm asking for time for further trials to reach at least a preliminary understanding of what the final effect of the frequencies might be, before we square off against all of medicine and the innumerable interconnected interests which feed off it."

Archer forced calm. "And again, Adam, I point out that until other scientists have the ability to see the living microbes with the clarity we do via your unparalleled microscope, our research cannot be *independently* verified or replicated. Given our shared history, you and I replicating each other's work will not stand up to scrutiny.

"Say," Archer seized on a redirection toward safer ground, "how's the mechanized production of your microscope coming along?"

Wakefield gritted his teeth, his whole body stiffening. Controlling his tone, he confessed, "Funding has been abruptly pulled. Shades of our Harvard days, Randall? Seems promising research can no longer be afforded. Yet does anyone ask whether we can afford *not* to do these searches?"

"Pulled? Really?" Archer was shocked. "Damn. Is it always the same issue? Or perhaps the same excuse?" A chill passed through him. "Every time we get close. . . . Will it always be this damnable Depression that's blamed, which may never end? And where does that leave us in our conundrum?" he muttered under his breath.

But Wakefield heard him and reacted with another harsh remark. "Safe from all the small minds you're afraid to stand up to with likely the most significant discovery you will ever have the privilege of being a part of. Don't bother getting up, Randall," Wakefield snarled as he rose. "I will gladly show myself out."

§

Inexplicable delays, which only exacerbated his wife's desperation, caused Archer to question the willingness of the dean at the College of Education to consult on Elizabeth's return to teaching. But as both standard practice and professional courtesy amongst University faculty demanded, at last an appointment was set and kept.

Her thick tresses pulled back in a matronly bun, Elizabeth arrived early at the dean's office in the College of Education. Dressed in a dark fitted skirt and a simple white blouse meant to emphasize her seriousness, Elizabeth felt ready. She reread a copy of her CV as she waited at his secretary's direction in the anteroom.

Elizabeth silently practiced a few phrases to fill in details she expected to be quizzed on. However, each time she glanced up, she found the dean's secretary surreptitiously studying her.

Elizabeth patted her hair—which felt to be under control. Next time she caught the secretary staring, she checked her blouse—yes, fully buttoned. Her skirt—it covered her knees. A smear on her skin perhaps—she wiped her cheeks but found nothing. Maybe something in her teeth? Elizabeth asked the woman whether she had time to use the ladies' room, only to confirm therein that all appeared to be in order.

Returning to the outer office, Elizabeth found the secretary waiting to show her inside. "The dean is ready," she announced, stealing one last glance at Elizabeth before reaching for the door. "I'm sorry, Mrs. Archer. I've been staring at you, actually at your hair. I've never seen such a healthy head of hair, glistening every time you move. How do you do it?"

Elizabeth checked the heavy bun at the nape of her neck reflexively, noticing for the first time the mousy straggles over the secretary's skull. "Just lucky, I suppose," she replied. The woman sighed, shoving the door wide for Elizabeth, then shutting her inside with the dean.

Elizabeth took in the large space as well as the small man

behind its oversized desk. Half rising, the wizened little dean, with scant, graying hair and dull eyes of indeterminate color, strained a smile in her direction. With a tight nod, he indicated the chair facing him.

Elizabeth sat and smiled at him as he waited silently. "Dean Lucian, I cannot tell you how much I appreciate you seeing me today. My husband has spoken highly of your work—"

"Your husband asked that I spend a few moments discussing your interest in the teaching profession," the dean cut in. "It's nothing really, a professional courtesy extended to faculty throughout the University's colleges. Now, what is it I can do for you today, Mrs. Archer?" He checked the time on his pocket watch conspicuously.

"Oh! Oh yes, I realize how busy you must be," Elizabeth responded, her nerves ratcheting at his brusqueness. "I, well, it's just that I'm having such difficulty finding a teaching position, which was unexpected. Both Randall and I, mistakenly we've since learned, assumed that given the size and growth of this city, there would be opportunities, if not at every turn, at least somewhere within reach. But as I've been canvassing—"

"There is a rather serious economic depression going on, Mrs. Archer, in its seventh year now. And that is *not* taking into account the disastrous crop failures riddling the middle of the country that pre-date the so-called Great Depression. It alone drove millions of desperate people to our state. Which means regardless of the position offered, there are dozens if not hundreds of qualified applicants, even thousands for certain jobs. Was it really so different back in Boston?"

Elizabeth blinked several times, weighing the man's tone along with his words. Was he deliberately speaking down to her? No, she finally decided. Why would he? "I didn't realize you knew we'd emigrated from Boston, but of course the Depression is—"

"I'm quite sure everyone at this University is aware of you and your husband and his Harvard credentials, which perhaps explains such a young and inexperienced man landing a highly visible position. Unless perchance, as does sometimes happen, someone pulled strings for him."

Elizabeth's mouth fell open before she clamped it shut. "I'm not sure I understand what you are driving at, Dean Lucian. But more to the point, I brought my CV for you to see my teaching experience." She watched the paper slide across the desk and come to a stop on its own. "And to express to you my intense desire to find a way back to teaching. I found young women particularly rewarding to work with. It seems so important to open minds before—"

"Yes, the Ross Academy," he spoke over her, scanning her history without touching the sheet she'd offered. "Impressive. Perhaps someone pulled a string or two for you as well? But never mind. The fact of the matter is that you have no teaching credential for California, nor an excess of on-the-job experience. My best advice would be to start there. Get your state credential and see where that might take you. At least it would demonstrate your serious intention to return to teaching."

Elizabeth stared. "I assure you, Dean Lucian, my intentions are serious. But I—my husband and I—were hoping you would share your insider's knowledge and insights into the schools in the area, public or private, and perhaps possible ways I might approach them."

"First things first, Mrs. Archer. My secretary can provide information on the state's credentialing process on your way out. But I will admonish you, the influx of people from all over the country and world contributes to the general atmosphere in California. Here in a freer society, people are more apt to reinvent themselves, make their own opportunities, create their own chances. Most can't and don't wait for things to be handed to them. The word 'meritocracy' comes to mind."

"Dean Lucian!" she cried, indignant. "If you're implying that I'm waiting for—"

The dean abruptly stood. "I am sorry to say, Mrs. Archer, that I have an important presentation to complete for the State Board of Education. I've been asked to chair a committee analyzing the educational needs of the vast inflow of people from around the globe and the critical need to educate their children—instead of their young picking strawberries and sleeping in ditches in order for the family to survive." The little man shook his head sadly, adding, "Real people with real problems."

"Dean Lucian!" She could barely harness her anger. "Have I done something to offend you? You seem to have made up your mind about me before I even sat down."

The dean smiled pityingly. "It doesn't require critical analysis to assume you don't need the money teaching might provide, given your husband's position and salary here at the University. Perhaps you don't even need that? Anyway, speak to Annabelle on your way out."

Elizabeth rose slowly. The dean, smoothing his jacket, stood waiting at the door. Befuddled by their abridged meeting and her immediate dismissal, she stumbled through the door he held to encourage her ouster, asking herself, *What just happened? The man's curtness was borderline rude. But why?*

She paused before the secretary, trying to think of a reason to thank her. What had the dean given her—ten minutes maybe? No privileged and useful information. And certainly no 'professional courtesy'!

Elizabeth harrumphed, turning on her heel to stomp out, head held high.

§

Unfamiliar with the side of campus opposite the medical facilities, Elizabeth quizzed numerous passersby for directions to the Medical College. She and her husband planned to lunch

together after her meeting with Dean Lucian to discuss the exchange. Glancing at her watch, she realized despite the brief
time spent with the dean, she'd barely be on time, having been
kept waiting and then circling and retracing her footsteps on
her convoluted cross-campus route.

She arrived at the Medical College and Laboratory, her feet
and head hurting, only to find her husband's office vacant.
The first lab worker she encountered admitted he had no idea
where Dr. Archer had gone, but suggested she try Dr. Wakefield
over at Physics. "He's likely there," the assistant assured her, "or
someone there might know more."

That her husband had forgotten their lunch didn't completely surprise Elizabeth. A midday break was far too frivo-
lous a disruption of her husband's important work. But after the
dean had been, at best, brusque, it added further insult to injury.
Worse, she discovered she'd have to backtrack across campus
to where she'd begun. The College of Education, she learned,
stood next door to the College of Physics.

§

Upon reaching the latter, she climbed the three stories to
Wakefield's physics laboratory, where his office was pointed
out. She knocked on his door and heard a gruff, "It's open,"
before entering.

Seated behind his desk, Wakefield reviewed a stack of papers
without looking up.

"Oh no, Adam," she exclaimed to her childhood friend upon
entering, "You're alone!"

The minute he saw who his visitor was, Wakefield jumped
from his seat, tossing papers aside, and rushed around the desk
to embrace her. Drawing back, he exclaimed, "Elizabeth! This is
a surprise! A welcome one at that. Look at you. You look rather
serious. New hairdo—a schoolmarm bun?" The old friends

hugged again before Wakefield held her at arm's length for further inspection.

She replied dryly. "This," she patted the heavy bun, "was meant to impress Dean Lucian at Education with my professionalism, which by the way, failed miserably." She tugged the bun loose. "Where's Randall? I was told he'd likely be here."

"That's more like it," Wakefield commented as her waves settled around her shoulders. "Haven't seen him today, but it's still early. Please sit down, Elizabeth. Tell me what you're doing on campus. In fact, tell me everything. How's your house, your ambitious garden, life in Los Angeles? Goodness, it's been far too long. I know you've been busy settling in."

"Not as busy as you, it would appear. Aren't you ever at home? I've called too many times to remember. I wanted you to come see my work, at least have coffee if you don't have time to fit in dinner, even on the weekends, much like Randall."

"I don't seem to have a single spare minute ever," he whined, exhaustion suddenly overwhelming him. "But Elizabeth, tell me why you're on campus today. It is so wonderful to see you!"

They sat on opposite sides of the desk, Elizabeth sliding off her shoes beneath it. "First of all, my husband stood me up for lunch today—the first such meal ever planned. News flash, Adam, people know the two of you keep late-night and weekend hours together. I was told in his lab he'd 'most likely' be here." Elizabeth giggled at Wakefield's drop-jaw response to her innuendo. "Still so prudish, Adam. I'm kidding, sort of."

Wakefield relaxed, enjoying her penchant to tease. "Good that you showed your face in the medical lab then, Elizabeth. Your husband's co-workers certainly saw for themselves no one could compete with you."

"Oh Adam. I've missed you! Why haven't we seen more of you? Oh that's right—one of us has. This project you and Randall are working on has literally eaten up all his time and energy, since, yes, almost since we arrived in California."

Wakefield sighed, disturbed by the hours Elizabeth had spent alone while he worked late into the night with her husband. "How thoughtless of us. But it's been one bombshell discovery after another, Elizabeth. Which, though it is no excuse, has been hard to ignore despite all our other demands. I apologize for my part in stealing your husband's free time and attention. Forgive me? Yet truthfully, Elizabeth, what we're working on is a once-in-a-lifetime opportunity. I'm sure he's told you as much."

"Something like that," she responded vaguely. "But there is no excuse, Adam. I could have insisted Randall make time to have you over for a visit. Or gone ahead on my own if he couldn't risk wasting his time. Time, it seems, got away from all of us. I'm sorry."

"Thanks," he muttered, strangely moved. "So Randall stood you up today?"

"And I am hungry, Adam. Are you? You are allowed lunch, aren't you, since apparently neither of you is allowed dinner?"

"I'm famished, now that you mention it," Wakefield said, coming to his feet and tugging on his jacket, then hat. "Let me buy you a bite at ULA's finest. It's just a campus café but it's close and will do. We can catch up there."

§

After ordering sandwiches at the counter, the pair claimed a small table as far from the din of the crowded café as possible. Their order was soon plunked haphazardly between them by a student employee who clearly wasn't enjoying his work. "Anyone with a job in today's world should be happier about it than that surly young man," Wakefield said as the waiter strode off without a word.

"Let's not talk about the Depression, Adam, please. I have enough on my mind." She thought it through as they unwrapped their sandwiches. While Wakefield greedily dug in, she pushed her plate aside and mumbled to herself, "It was as if the dean hated me, though I hadn't met him before."

"Who? Oh, the Dean of Education, right? Sumner Lucian? I've met him a few times. He's got an excellent reputation. Why? What happened?"

"I don't really know, Adam. He kept me waiting far longer than the time I spent with him, and was rude and interruptive from the start. He kept cutting me off mid-sentence, then rushed me out with only the most perfunctory information on teaching. Oh, he did seem familiar with the Ross Academy, though he barely glanced at my CV.

"And," she went on while Wakefield chewed, "he made a comment about Randall's position, even mine at Ross, seeming to suggest strings had been pulled for us both. Then the man lectured me on the Depression as if I couldn't comprehend its detrimental effects."

"Strange," Wakefield said, swallowing. "Did he mention he's from Boston as well?"

She slammed back in her chair. "What?"

"Well, he is. From Boston. And . . . oh goodness, hold on a moment. He knows your brother. When Lucian and I first met and discovered our shared Bostonian roots, he asked where I'd gone to school. Upon disclosing St. Paul's then Harvard, he looked at me more intently, asking if I'd run into Prescott Perrish at either place. When I answered yes, at both in fact, and that Prescott and I had been close our entire lives, Lucian's expression went from curious to studiously blank. No mistaking it, the subject of your brother hit a sour note with him, but he clammed up. I have no idea what transpired between them."

Elizabeth stared at Wakefield while examining this insight against the dean's comments, which began to make sense. "It *was* like he knew me. He disliked Randall and me both. The man thought I was a Perrish! 'Strings pulled. Real people with real problems. A freer society,' implying no class-stratification here. 'Making opportunities for oneself. Not waiting for things to be handed to one ...'"

Wakefield, not entirely following her disjointed phrases, downed his sandwich as he watched her piece together meaning. She shoved back from the table, waving the sullen waiter over to ask that her sandwich be wrapped for her to take with her. She turned back to Wakefield. "Oh Adam, I can't thank you enough!" She planted a wet kiss on his lips in her excitement. "You've explained the inexplicable. That man assumed I'm still a Perrish. That both Randall's and my former employment in this dismal economy could only be explained by my family's influence. I can only imagine his run-in with Prescott, whom we both know can be quite a snob. Whatever it was, it clearly left something foul in the man's mouth for all the Perrishes."

Another of the dean's statements stopped her cold. "'Perhaps we didn't even need Randall's income ...' He actually speculated that, Adam!"

The waiter bore her wrapped and bagged sandwich to the table, and Elizabeth stuffed it in her bag.

"Hold on. What are you doing?" Wakefield asked, realizing Elizabeth was leaving before they'd had a chance to talk.

"I'm going to set Dean Lucian straight about who I am. And about who Randall is as well." She pulled herself up to full height. "I'm going to camp in his office until he has to see me, whether it takes the entire day. He'll have to come out of his inner sanctum sooner or later.

"Adam," she averred, "I am about to 'make my own opportunities' with no one 'handing me a thing.' I, better than most, know what's attached to such handouts."

With another brief kiss on the cheek, Elizabeth paused to thank Wakefield for the sandwich and for standing in for her husband. "You must come around, soon and more often. We both need to see you much, much more. Dinner Saturday night?" she offered.

Recalling his last conversation with Archer, not to mention their ratcheting disagreements, Wakefield hesitated.

Elizabeth read his hesitancy. "What is it, Adam?"

"Nothing." He swallowed back the bile. "Just a lot of long hours, and a difference in how we perceive the responsibilities of scientific discovery."

"Not completely surprising, given the amount of time you two spend together into all hours of the nights and weekends." She covered her blurted resentment with an unconvincing smile. "Look, you are our only old friend here, and we need you, Adam. *I* need you! Whatever your differences, let's lay them on the dinner table and work through them like adults. Adults can disagree, even frequently. Let's not let different opinions come between us. Saturday night? Seven?"

And he needed them both, Wakefield realized, wishing to hold onto Elizabeth after so much time had passed between them that could never be recaptured. "Seven it is then, Saturday. Thank you, I will look forward to it. But be certain you fore-warn Randall."

She leaned down and brushed his lips once again with hers, promising 'news' when next they met, then swept from the café like a Santa Ana blast—hot, strong, and ready to ignite what-ever stood in the way.

Brace yourself, Dean Lucian, Wakefield smiled, staring after Elizabeth and her locks swinging behind her. Her taste on his lips lingered—lipstick, a trace of coffee, even a note of toothpaste. Her scent lingered as well, and Wakefield sat back, breathing it in.

§

Despite or perhaps because of Elizabeth's extravagant welcome of Wakefield at the front door, the evening began awkwardly. He caught sight of Archer hanging back as he stepped inside.

Wakefield focused on Elizabeth and the house from its foyer, glimpsing the main rooms all the way through to the garden behind. "My goodness, Elizabeth. If I hadn't seen this place before you two began work on it, I couldn't begin to appreciate what you've done." He circled slowly, whistling his praises as he pivoted. "Hats off, you two!" he said to include Archer. "Simply wonderful!"

Wakefield approached Archer and placed a bottle of wine in his hands. Pointing out a few specifics of the post-Prohibition wineries developing in the Napa Valley eased the two into conversation.

"We'll have cocktails in the garden before we go in for dinner," Elizabeth suggested. "Randall, if you wouldn't mind? Three Manhattans, I believe?" When everyone concurred, Archer headed off to fetch drinks while Elizabeth toured their guest through the public rooms on their way to the fountain-side garden seating.

When Wakefield stopped abruptly in the middle of the living room, apparently stunned by the green Chinese upholstery fabric with its cavorting monkeys that continually made Archer cringe, Archer himself stopped, waiting to hear Wakefield's adverse reaction. *Monkeys? Now finally it's coming!*

But Archer was sorely disappointed by Wakefield's assessment. "Elizabeth, that green fabric sets off this entire room, and draws in the garden beyond, blending all your interior colors with just a bit of tongue-in-cheek. Wonderful choice."

Archer was floored. As Elizabeth and Wakefield proceeded toward the garden, he recalled his mission—three Manhattans—lamenting to himself, *if that is high-society decorating, then there really is no explaining taste!*

Wakefield's praises continued as Archer placed chilled glasses of reddish-brown liquid, tinkling ice cubes and a cherry bobbing in each one, before them on the garden table and took a seat. The splashing of the fountain provided a backdrop for

Wakefield's somewhat continuous oohs and ahhs. "Can you believe this place?" he asked Archer. "How did you ever conceive it, Elizabeth? What you've created is the polar opposite of Colonial—at least, American Colonial."

"So you approve, Adam. I'm glad. It's been a labor of love, my first attempt to cover an entire canvas, so to speak. No arguing with my mother about what was 'appropriate.' I just embraced what's different and unique that greeted us here in Los Angeles, stealing when I could from my travel memories, especially the Mediterranean countries which inspired this home's architecture in the first place."

"Could you offer me some pointers for my Spanish bungalow?" Wakefield asked.

Archer, feeling quite left out of the hubbub a few design choices inspired, interrupted. "Cheers to you all," he sang. "And welcome, Adam. Thank you for coming."

After they'd toasted, Wakefield was first to speak. "Cheers to the both of you for creating this magical space and for adapting to your new environment with diligence and panache. Fragrant flowers only add." They sipped again until Wakefield added, "I can see you were very busy, Elizabeth, while Randall and I have been all but ignoring you. Only when I saw you briefly the other day did I fully realize how alone you must have felt in an unfamiliar environment through all the—my God, could it be years—that I've monopolized him. I want you to know I am truly sorry."

The Archers spoke over each other. "Thank you for thinking about my problems, Adam."

"'Saw you briefly the other day?'" Archer repeated, looking quizzically from his wife to his partner. "Neither of you mentioned that. What did I miss?"

Elizabeth and Wakefield shared an indulgent smile. "Me," was her response. "Remember the lunch we planned after my meeting with Dean Lucian? No, I see you still don't. Alas, when

you stood me up, your lab assistant directed me to Adam's office
where he thought I'd find you. I have to tell you my feet not to
mention my head ached, doubling back over the campus. And
when you weren't there also, Adam gallantly stepped in and
bought me lunch."

"A sandwich you didn't even eat," Wakefield pointed out.

"Not right away, true. But it served me well during the hours
I waited to see Dean Lucian again."

"And did you?" Wakefield asked as Archer's head swiveled
from one to the other.

"Yes. I outwaited him as I told you I would."

"Well," Wakefield pressed, "what happened? I was thinking
to suggest that you start as a volunteer if possible, in order to
get your feet on the ground. I know it's not ideal, but perhaps
it would be better than biding your time alone day and night.
From the looks of it, you're more than finished with this spectacular project." He gazed around the garden and into the back
of the house, warmly lit from within.

"Interesting idea, Adam," she responded with a grin. "Look,
I have some news but first I have a meal to get on. Excuse me,
gentlemen. Enjoy your cocktails."

Both men followed her with their eyes from the garden into
the arched loggia until she disappeared inside the house. They
toyed with their drinks as they prepared to face each other.
Then both began talking at once. "Look old boy, I can imagine
the pressure you're feeling as incomprehensible discoveries
move the solid ground of medicine beneath you."

Archer spoke over him. "Adam, I know I've been slowing our
progress, but it's essential I know exactly—"

They both stopped and laughed. "You first, Adam. You are
our guest."

That laughter eased the way. "We've been friends a long time,
Randall, and we have shared the unexpected for years. That's
a lot to throw away to frustration as in my case, or to deep

concern as in yours. Surely we can find a way to stand in each other's shoes—"

"I'm sure we can, Adam. I want to. You're the best friend I've ever had. And one hell of a research partner. I've been privileged to be a small part of your microscope development. And because of it, I've seen things others simply cannot imagine. Or perhaps don't wish to imagine." They fell silent.

Elizabeth returned to the outdoor table, where she found the men sitting mutely. "Please, you two!" she cried, misinterpreting their silence, "you're meant to recover common ground here. Our friendship depends on it."

Archer rushed to explain. "We have! We've recognized that our relationship and mutual work interests are far too important to allow anything to interfere, Elizabeth. We shook on it."

"I'll drink to that," she said, lofting her glass from the ring of moisture it had left on the table during her absence. "Pleased to hear it. Thank you."

"Thank you," they both chimed in.

"So gentlemen, shall we go in? 'Dinner,' please note I use the term loosely, is served."

§

Both men noticed Elizabeth was especially upbeat during the meal, nearly giddy, grinning somewhat foolishly with little provocation until Wakefield pushed away his plate to focus in on her. "Okay, Elizabeth, what exactly happened when you went back to confront the Dean of Education after he so impolitely pushed you aside?"

A blazing grin preceded her announcement. "I was going to wait until I broke out the champagne with dessert, but I cannot keep this to myself any longer." She straightened in her seat, tossing her dark waves over her shoulders, and declared, "Gentlemen, I not only educated the Dean of Education about who

I am, I enlisted *and* procured his help in finding suitable work."

"Bravo Elizabeth!" Archer replied. "Is this the distraction that's had you in its grip this week?"

"You noticed!" Elizabeth exclaimed, quickly regretting her slip before company, even if it was just Adam. Embarrassed, she looked from one to the other seated man, and added quickly, "And I thought I was hiding everything perfectly. But yes, it's big news, at least to me." Both men waited.

"The nourishment from that sandwich you bought me, Adam, came in handy as I waited and waited for the dean in his anteroom. Every time the intercom squawked, I looked to his secretary expectantly, only to be disappointed and allowed to sit and wait. Finally, in the late afternoon, the squawk resulted in my new friend, Annabelle, rising to show me in for the second time that day.

"'Dean Lucian,' I began upon entering, 'I believe we got off on the wrong foot earlier today.' I then explained not only the circumstances which caused Randall and me to move west, but the 'humiliation' my proud family felt with my choice of husband, no matter he finished top of his class at Harvard Medical. And their further embarrassment at my seeking employment for which, horror of horrors, I'd accepted money. In their eyes, both greatly intensified their personal public shaming. But what's a girl to do when her family disowns her?"

Wakefield shook his head, almost hearing Mrs. Perrish's pared tones reminding Elizabeth that men did not like women they even suspected were smarter than they, let alone as independent and hard to control as she had always been. He snickered at the memory of the two of them, constantly at odds, before tuning back in.

"'I believe,' I told the dean," Elizabeth was saying, "'you assumed I was a Perrish still, and that their influence had eased my way and that of my husband. But it is not at all the case. In fact, it is the opposite. I have been completely disavowed. After my successes at Ross and his doctorate completed with highest honors, my husband and I found ourselves mysteriously and suspiciously unemployed and unemployable.

"'We are making our own way,' I assured the dean. 'But what I discovered in all this is that I have a gift and a passion for teaching. And that, Dean Lucian, is why I've spent the day on your doorstep. I heard any number of times during my attempts to find work that University Primary School under your auspices is the most forward-thinking, advanced institution of its kind in Southern California.

"'To that end, Dean,' I rushed on, afraid of being summarily dismissed a second time, 'I would gladly start in any position you might have, even as a volunteer, hoping of course it might one day lead to employment.'

"With that," she told her enthralled audience, "I once again sent my CV skittering across the desk to him. This time he picked it up and studied it carefully, so carefully in fact I began to suspect he was stalling. I braced myself. But as I had committed to rising above his rudeness no matter what, I held his gaze with a confidence I didn't feel each time he glanced at me."

As Elizabeth caught her breath, Archer wondered, *Volunteering. Why hadn't I thought of that?*

"'Fine,' the dean said after an inordinate amount of time spent pondering. 'I'll start you in a rotation through the grades and classrooms at University Primary, and should that go well, we'll mutually settle on a more permanent volunteer position.'"

"That—why, that's wonderful news," both men declared, Archer praying it would ease the friction his endless work hours added to his wife's dissatisfactions.

"Thank you. Indeed it is!" she gushed. "I've been at the school every morning this week since this all came about Monday. But that's not all, gentlemen. There is more."

Elizabeth waited for silence. "As I prepared to leave, thanking him profusely for the opportunity and assuring him he would not regret it, the dean remarked, 'Someone in your position might wish to take full advantage of the University while she awaits permanent employment.'

"'What do you mean, Dean Lucian?' I of course asked.

"'As spouse of faculty, you can access any degree program for which you qualify. In your case, a degree in education perhaps?'

"'You mean a bachelor's degree?' I asked him.

"'That is my meaning, yes,' he responded. 'The semester is underway, but you could begin by monitoring classes which hold interest for you and start in earnest at the new semester.'"

Wakefield came to his feet, clapping. "Excellent, Elizabeth. Well done."

Archer looked as if he wasn't sure he'd followed. "Are you saying you're going for a college degree in education? *And* volunteering at University Primary? All at the same time?"

"Truthfully, that's why I haven't said a word until now," Elizabeth admitted. "I had to be certain I could handle it. I spent the rest of the week volunteering at the school each morning, and loving every moment back in the classroom. Then each afternoon, I sat in on a class or two at the College, which was nothing short of inspirational. I'm mostly convinced I can do both, but I required reassurance before I spoke. You understand."

"Brilliant," Wakefield reiterated. "Brava!"

Archer stood and joined in the clapping as Elizabeth basked in their admiration. "You'll never stop surprising me," he said, genuine pride shining in his dark eyes. It was another reminder of the inner strength he had once discounted in both his dinner partners.

"Thank you," she mumbled humbly as their clapping continued. "All right now, thank you, but that's enough. Let me clear a few things and bring the champagne with me to the garden for an after-dinner toast. You two go on ahead."

While she shuttled food from the dining room to the kitchen, she hummed a tune both men recognized—*I've Got the World on a String.*

§

Following their companionable meal, the lasting glow from Elizabeth's surprises enveloped the two men in the garden, much like its heady scents. Neither spoke at first, lulled by feelings of satiation on multiple levels.

Wakefield at last leaned forward. "You've spoken of your fears of a cataclysmic shift in the medical industry, should all we've uncovered prove out."

"We're still a long way from that, Adam, but yes. It's troubling that nightly our observations and verifications seem to undo more and more of my medical education. Consider it as I have. If something as cheap as not much more than an electrical charge can effectively combat lethal disease, many doctors and nurses will go wanting—not to mention medical schools, hospitals, and offices of all sorts. Then consider the deep secondary layers—equipment manufacturers, suppliers of everything from aspirin to X-ray machines, facility builders, personnel. You see how the web expands—and at such a terrible time economically."

"But let's not get ahead of ourselves," Archer said, reversing course. "We have yet to obtain corroboration from several levels of testing—from our original study of specimen slides, we'll move into Petri dish cultures, then onto animal testing. Should all those stages show consistent results, we'd still have one final and major hurdle. The human trial."

Archer paused, anticipating a snipe from Wakefield about the redundancies he had already insisted upon, prepared to defend their necessity given what was at stake, for himself, yes, but also for the world at large. But when no derogatory comment was forthcoming, Archer picked up where he'd left off. "Particularly the animal and human trials will prove one way or the other whether residue from the stilled microbe remains harmful or whether the pathogen has truly been destroyed and is no longer capable of transmitting disease."

Wakefield responded thoughtfully. "I do appreciate your concerns, Randall. All this affects your many years of education, not to mention your cohorts and, as you point out, many far beyond the field of medicine. And I grant you, our timing is not good—" A crash from within the house halted their conversation. Both men gazed at each other, stood, then rushed toward the noise.

They came upon Elizabeth in the kitchen, standing in the midst of broken dishes and splattered food, some of which dripped from her blouse and skirt. All three stood gaping at the mess until, in concert, laughter broke out. "Have I mentioned," she gasped, "that I don't know if I'm entirely cut out for domesticity?"

When the men bent down to assist in the cleanup, she ordered, "Leave it, you two. I'll get the worst of it up, and the rest will most assuredly wait. Once I've changed my clothes, I'm coming out to have that champagne toast before it gets too late. I'm not done celebrating!"

Archer and Wakefield returned to the garden to finish the last of the wine. Wishing to extend the serenity, Wakefield began tentatively, "I've been reading more about Einstein. For the last three decades since his Relativity Theory in '05, he's been pursuing something that might shed more light on our work. He's attempting to generate another simple mathematical formula that describes no less than the entire universe. He's dubbed it the 'Unified Field Theory.'

"Einstein hopes to prove mathematically that the universe is one vast, interconnected atomic field held together by electromagnetic forces. In other words, flung wide throughout the universe are varying concentrations of energy in an infinite variety of forms and densities. One such form is mass—what we humans perceive as solid matter, like this table," which Wakefield tapped with his glass. "Like the moon," he added, gazing heavenward.

"Fascinating, Adam, I cannot deny it. To think that we, like everything, are made up of concentrations of atoms, which combine to form molecules, which combine into ever greater structures. Yet all of it, at its fundamental level, is ceaselessly pulsating energy. It *may* help explain the effect energy has on the disease form we've been observing. However—"

"I'm not interrupting, am I?" Elizabeth asked, materializing out of the ether. Both men, immersed in the macro- and micro-cosmic realms, startled at her voice.

Wakefield returned to Earth first. "No, no, of course not, Elizabeth."

She eyed them suspiciously as she dispensed champagne glasses and popped the cork off the bottle with a healthy bang. She poured the bubbling wine and waited. "Ahem?"

"Oh, right," Wakefield said, standing. "To Elizabeth and her new bachelor's program. And the return at long last to the classroom of the Teacher of the Year!" They laughed and sipped before he returned to his seat. "What classes have you audited? Have any piqued your interest?"

With Elizabeth enthusiastically responding, Archer at once grasped that the expansion of Elizabeth's world could lessen, slow, or perhaps even reverse the couple's growing, though mostly unspoken, discord over his hours, filled with work, and her hours, empty and alone. He sat up at full attention as his wife described her exhilarating new ventures, only then releasing a long sigh of relief.

CHAPTER THIRTEEN

APPEASEMENT

1938

At the new semester, with Elizabeth officially enrolled in her bachelor's degree program and continuing to volunteer at the primary school, the research scientists pushed ahead with more speed, using both Wakefield microscopes in their respective laboratories. In both labs, the microscopes and their study records and materials were kept securely locked away from curious eyes and unhelpful speculation, something they both hoped would not be necessary for much longer.

The testing of microbial cultures in Petri dishes exactly duplicated the results the researchers had achieved with the initial study slides. Upon exposure to their own innate frequency reproduced by the cathode ray tubes, the microbes passed through the evolutionary stages previously tracked to either dormancy or death. And the best way to prove definitively which—dormancy or death—called for moving onto the next stage—animal testing.

Archer's lab was the obvious place to locate this penultimate stage of their investigation. Wakefield, with his physics assistant, Henry, became a secondary test site as the trial turned to the harvesting of diseases from terminal patients at University Hospital as before, then injecting specimens into rats sorted into several test and control groups.

The highly respected double-blind-study format was strictly adhered to. The identity of the different groups was unknown to the assistants and a closely held secret by Archer himself. Harvested diseases were injected into rats and allowed to develop. While rats in the control group received either no treatment or a treatment of a randomly-selected frequency, the test group rats received frequency treatments properly correlated to their individual diseases.

Results again proved breathtakingly predictable. Control group rats which had not been injected with a disease lived on normally. Those which had been infected with a virulent illness but received no or an incorrect frequency treatment became sick and most died soon thereafter. The few hardy untreated animals able to struggle through their illness to survival proved a rarity.

Test group rats treated by the correct frequencies for their diseases recovered to live normal life expectancies, apparently illness free. And, both surprisingly and encouragingly, those recovered rats exhibited no signs of discomfort, sickness, weakness, nor detectable side effects of any kind, both during and after treatment.

The scientists put aside the duplicated reports of their findings that Archer had carried over to Wakefield's lab. Staring into space, both men reflected on their journey of discovery, more like a wild ride. They sensed they'd reached the pivotal place—the point of no return.

Wakefield at last summed it up. "Phenomenal."

Archer sighed. "Almost unbelievable. Such consistency at each and every step of our study is well outside the norm for laboratory research. Well outside my own experience."

Wakefield nodded agreement, again stating, "Phenomenal."

"So . . . there's only one hurdle left to leap, and it is a rather high one."

"The human trial," both men exclaimed at the same time, as though overwhelmed by the weight of those words.

"That will change everything, Adam," Archer warned, "like Einstein's and Bohr's work on both the macro- and microcosm. This will blow the cover sky-high off our secret research."

Wakefield laughed out loud at the analogy. "You'll make a good physicist yet, old boy! Rather lofty comparisons."

"I'm not exaggerating. No matter how I try to control a trial with humans, should frequency treatment again prove effective on terminal participants, hospital personnel will notice. Going from death's door to health again will be hard to hide, and harder to explain. Spontaneous remission? Over and over again?" Archer rubbed his eyes, trying to erase a vision of the field of medicine as he'd known it, decimated . . . by his own hand.

How had he come to this? he pondered. Medicine was all he had ever wanted—to be a medical doctor and researcher. Yet, here he was, poised to undermine it all.

He heaved another long exhale of resignation. "I've roughed out a plan on how to begin, Adam. I will select a small sample from the terminal patients in the hospital, varying to the widest degree possible their diseases, ages, and sexes. Along with their closest loved ones, each will be required to read and sign a strict confidentiality agreement covering treatments and condition changes, with all related conversations restricted to me or my designated assistants. Regardless, Adam, positive results will be readily observable."

Wakefield couldn't help pointing out, "You're on the cusp of a potentially momentous discovery, one which could save millions of lives at little expense and with no debilitating side effects." He held up his hands in surrender. "I know, I know, *only if* this final trial is successful. Still, you should be dancing on the lab tables, Randall."

Archer summed it up. "I don't expect successful human-trial results to be welcomed with open arms. Those with a vested interest in medicine as it's taught and practiced today will come after us with fierce resistance and aggressive scrutiny. Prepare for personal attacks to destroy our professional reputations if that's all they can come up with.

"You know, Adam, neither you nor Elizabeth has experienced how poverty, even just its threat, can affect people," Archer charged. "Despite your losses in the stock market, Adam, neither of you has ever known anything close to hopeless, starving poverty. Trust me when I tell you that cornered people are capable of the unspeakable, especially when scrambling to provide for themselves and their families. Or simply to hang onto what they've got, be it wealth, power, or control. It's a side of humanity I don't care to revisit, nor for either you or Elizabeth to become acquainted with."

Wakefield contemplated his friend. "You're really scared, Randall. What has you so spook—"

The door to Wakefield's office burst open. There, panting and grimy, stood Archer's lab assistant, white lab coat smeared black, wheezing and breathless. "Jesse!" Archer cried, "what are you—"

"Dr.—Dr. Archer," the young man gasped, sucking in air, "come quick! The lab—"

"My lab? What about my lab?" Archer demanded, pushing past Jesse, already on the run.

"Fire! A fire," Jesse rasped, unable to catch his breath. "There's been a fire—"

But Archer was already out the door, Wakefield in close pursuit, leaving the winded lab assistant to catch up as he could.

§

Fire trucks and police vehicles clustered at the entrance to the Medical College, red lights strobing the midnight campus and a gathering crowd in lurid runnels.

Archer raced to the entry, where a large police officer blocked the way. "Hold on there," the man barked, adjusting his large frame to fully obstruct access. "Step back! The scene has not been secured. No one's allowed in. You're interfering with a serious police operation here!"

"I'm Dr. Randall Archer of the College of Medicine, this College!" Archer shouted at the officer. "It's my laboratory in jeopardy inside. I insist you let me by. And my associates here," he indicated Wakefield and Jesse pulling up behind him.

"Sorry," the big man replied, unimpressed. "No one goes in. Orders."

Wakefield stepped forward, eyeing the man's badge. "Excuse me, Officer . . . Officer D'Angelo. I'm Dr. Adam Wakefield of the College of Physics here at ULA. You've met my fellow faculty, Dr. Randall Archer of the College of Medicine. As he mentioned, he's the doctor in charge of its medical laboratory. And this is his assistant, Jesse. We have highly sensitive research housed in the lab which we understand may have suffered in the fire. It is essential, Officer D'Angelo, that we save whatever we can of our original research.

"Or," Wakefield continued, staring the policeman down evenly, "that I take your name as the person who allowed it all to be destroyed when we explain to University officials what became of our important, long-term, and expensive study. Why it was allowed to burn to cinders when any part that could have been saved would have proven invaluable to medical research and potentially to millions of lives around the globe."

Only the cop's eyebrows moved, his bulk firmly embedded as before. When he finally shifted, it was to withdraw a notepad from his breast pocket and a pencil from behind his ear. "Dr. Archer," he repeated, "head of the medical lab, site of the fire. Dr.

Wakefield you said, Physics? And the young one?"

"Jesse," he shouted helpfully from behind the two doctors.

"And Jesse, also of the medical lab." The officer shouted over his shoulder, "O'Connor, over here." Another large policeman approached, to whom D'Angelo commanded, "Take these three back to the site of the fire and make sure they don't interfere with the scene until the fire chief gives the all clear. Hear me?" He turned back to the anxious threesome and demanded, "Don't touch a thing, ya hear? And stay with this officer until—"

But Archer, squeezing through the doorway first, ran down the hallway, Wakefield and Jesse racing behind, with lumbering Officer O'Connor struggling to catch up.

§

Against clattering footsteps that sounded like a panicked herd, the irregular plink of dripping water intensified as the men approached the lab.

Archer's first glance inside caused his heart to plummet to his feet. He braced himself against the doorjamb, knees threatening to buckle.

What had been a pristine and sterile laboratory had been replaced by soot-blackened walls and a ceiling where tiles went missing. In their place, disgorged wires, pipes, and assorted innards were exposed in gnarled, blackened tangles. Water rained and puddled throughout the room.

Amidst it all stood a fireman in full regalia, slick black jacket, large-brimmed hardhat, a bullhorn raised to his lips as he shouted orders. "Sam, that debris pile over there, check it again for hotspots."

Archer approached the man, who took no notice of him until Archer choked out, "What—what happened here?"

The chief swung around to him, eyes wide. "You are not allowed in here! You can see this is still an active scene, can't you? Get out and let us do our job!" He then directed his bull-horn at another member of his crew.

But Archer didn't budge. The chief glanced back, obviously surprised to find him still there. "This is *my* lab," Archer stated firmly. "I'm responsible for saving whatever work is possible. What can you tell me about this accident? What could have started it?"

The chief circled the room with his eyes before they turned back on Archer. "Some kind of explosion burned real hot. It quickly engulfed most of the room. What chemicals do you use over in that corner?" he asked, pointing to the area Archer had secured for the frequency research and animal testing.

Archer stared at the area. "None," he answered, facing the fire chief. "There were no chemical agents in that part of my lab. In fact, all flammables and volatile chemicals are stored in fireproof lockers when not in use—or we'd all be inhaling toxic poison."

"Strange." The man's brow, reddened from heat, crimped low over alert brown eyes. "All signs point to a sizable explosion there, spreading through the room. We'll have to sift the scene more thoroughly, of course, once all hotspots are put down. But that'd be my initial take from the evidence so far."

Archer again gaped at the subsection, realizing all the animals, any documentation that hadn't yet been duplicated for Wakefield, and all the equipment were a total loss. A total loss? Including Wakefield's microscope!

Going white, Archer pivoted to Wakefield. "Adam! Your scope …" Archer barely breathed the words. "Did you lock your lab when we left it just now?"

But Wakefield was already sprinting back toward the garishly lit night-campus, desperate to get to the physics lab and the only known Wakefield microscope in existence.

§

Archer slumped before Wakefield's desk, head in his hands, fingers combing his stubborn black waves loose from their heavy pomade, not that the gel ever completely controlled his tight coils. "Since the laboratory fire, in addition to the monthly reporting which takes way too much of my time, I must now account in detail to Dean Culp on all conditions in my lab— safeguards in place for any eventuality, our standard practices, all projects, and special studies.

"He also demanded I tally what was lost in excruciating detail, beginning with the section of my lab the Fire Department determined was the epicenter of that inexplicable explosion. Which of course led to many more questions about what we were testing on the lost rats and the entire course of study which had brought us to this place. All of which led to his harsh reprimand of me, given it had been done without his prior knowledge or his *required* consent.

"You told me you were helping Dr. Wakefield test the capabilities of his newest microscope, Archer," the dean had accused him. "This dubious project sounds significantly more than that! What scientific basis was there for taking such a risky and drastic deviation from standard protocols and practices? Sub-bacterial microbes never before seen? Reactive to electrical stimulation? Never mind," the dean had concluded in disgust, demanding a report on his desk first thing Monday. He reminded Archer to spare no detail of this 'reckless diversion.'

Archer then added, "The dean warned me he'd determine if there was blame to be placed for the losses. But he stated emphatically, 'I need my lab up and running, now! Do what you must to revive it immediately. I cannot run my Medical College without it!'"

"Sorry, old chap," Wakefield commiserated. "That is unfortunate. But look, there is a brighter side. Most of our work was duplicated in both our labs, meaning we still have all my copies and test results. We lost the rats, but I have those comprehensive test results also. And thank heavens," Wakefield's relief was audible, "we still have one of my microscopes."

Wakefield confirmed, "I've tightened security at the physics lab after that accident ... or incident. We should duplicate results again and, in an abundance of caution, keep an extra copy at a safe distance. But in the meantime, none of these unfortunate events changes the consistent results we've achieved through all three stages of testing. All stages have pointed to our obvious, next, and final step."

Archer angrily raked his fingers through his hair, having abandoned all hope of control over it while glaring at Wakefield. "Don't talk to me about the human trial now, Adam. Don't you understand my very livelihood is at risk here?"

Wakefield minimized his concerns. "It won't come to that, old boy, I'm sure. You'll explain your professional research standards in your report which *require* you to follow discoveries wherever they may lead, regardless of 'orthodoxy.' Orthodoxy," he repeated the word. "Is it not an extraordinary concern for Dean Culp, who aims for ULA's Medical School to break into the ranks of top research institutions?

"Randall, remind the dean it's called 'good science.' Surely he'll appreciate that such remarkable revelations on his watch could be career-elevating for the both of you."

"I don't know, Adam. With findings that fly in the face of entrenched medical doctrine and threaten to unhinge the whole field, with no way of telling how it would ultimately shake out . . . I don't sense Dean Culp would readily associate himself with that kind of gamble. If I were him, I wouldn't—"

Shoving his chair backward with a jarring scrape, Wakefield leaned in. "We've been through this too many times. We agreed that once we had thoroughly tested and verified our findings, it would be our duty and responsibility to make those findings known. You're not preparing to renege now, are you, when certainty gained through a human trial is within our grasp?"

Archer rubbed his hands over his face before meeting Wakefield's fierce glare. "No, I'm not going to renege, God help me. I already selected and recruited the initial group of terminals for our first human trial." Archer's mind flashed to the young woman who had stood by hopelessly as her husband faded away with cancer. Her tears had gushed when she thanked the doctor for the second chance he had just offered them both via inclusion in the trial. "No, no reneging. Be aware that we'll have to do all the final testing here in your lab, a difficulty we can likely overcome. But also, be aware this project may be halted at any time by Dean Culp or other higher-ups."

"A risk we'll have to take. Perhaps if a successful human trial literally pulls lives back from the grave, your Dean will choose to expand our study. Who could resist such a persuasive argument? Certainly not the head of a medical school."

"If," Archer stressed. "*If* we save lives."

§

Worrying about his partner and how his state of mind might hamper the final step in their study, Wakefield exited the College of Physics in a fog, barely aware of faculty and students flowing by. Until his eyes and chattering mind were arrested by a vision, bathed in a heavenly glow from above, appearing to float above human commotion.

The mesmerizing vision momentarily banished his worries until it came to an abrupt halt in front of him and spoke. "Hello, Adam. Adam? It's me."

Flushing with mortification, Wakefield remembered himself. "Elizabeth! I was . . . you looked so . . . that is, I was struck by how, uh, how happy and confident you look. College apparently agrees with you."

Studying him curiously through narrowed eyes, she eventually responded, "Yes, it does agree. I love my mornings with the

children and my afternoons with fellow students and professors, finding them both challenging and engaging. I am happy,
Adam. How about you?"

The directness of her question out of the blue embarrassed
him further. He stammered, "Of course. Of course I'm—"

"It's just that you appeared, oh I don't know exactly, lost in
space? Caught in a glorious daydream? A million miles from
here? Is everything all right?" she asked. "Your project with my
husband hasn't taken another bad turn?"

"Aside from the fire in his lab, you mean? No. It has slowed us
some." Archer's continued struggles to minimize the phenomenal early outcomes in the human trial, trying to rationalize or
minimize those results to better fit medical convention, sped
through his mind.

Elizabeth glanced at her wristwatch. "I've got some time
before class. Buy a girl a coffee?"

"Sure," he answered, glancing at his own pocket watch,
unable to recall the source of his former hurry. "Right this way."

§

Across the table from each other, Elizabeth's direct gaze un-
settled Wakefield. He dove into a deflecting subject. "Tell me
about your volunteer work at the primary school." The noise
level in the coffee shop was such that he had to repeat himself.
They leaned toward each other until she heard.

"Oh," Elizabeth's face broke into a broad smile. "I've just had
the most heart-warming experience," she replied, her breath
tickling his ear. "There was a little girl none of the other kids
accepted, a special case, admitted on a sort of scholarship as her
family cannot pay. It's one of the things I love about University
Primary, Adam. The kids are actually from every walk of life.
That in itself is so broadening.

"Anyway, she's from an immigrant family people call 'Okies,' though I think she's from Kansas. She shows up daily with matted hair and the same dirty clothes, keeping silently to herself. I think the other kids were scared of her.

"I asked the teacher if I could take her under my wing. She agreed as long as I gained consent from the child's parents. I appealed to them to let me meet her before class in the girls' locker room, where I helped her clean up and dress in the few clean garments I brought for her. Adam, you wouldn't believe the transformation a little soap and a hairbrush made. There was a cute little blonde girl beneath the tangle and dirt.

"Once the other children overcame their surprise, curiosity took over. They began to show interest in her at about the time the mass migration spawned by the Dust Bowl became the topic of our current events discussion. I shared my own story of crossing the entire country by train and my personal experience with the black clouds of topsoil driven by the wind that our train passed in and out of. Even with the window tightly shut, grit filtered into the compartment. I asked her if she'd care to share some part of her westward journey with the class.

"Hesitantly and so softly we strained to hear, she described riding in a mule-drawn wagon with her entire family, her cat, and dogs, and what few belongings they could carry. She talked about the cold nights when they huddled together for warmth on the wind-whipped plains . . ."

Elizabeth grew pensive. "There's something so forlorn in the ceaseless howling of the wind across the flatlands." She shook her head to clear away the disturbing sound.

"My students grew excited at her description of the Rocky Mountains seen from a distance, growing steadily into huge, towering peaks, iced with snow. Warming to the subject, she next described the scorching days of travel through the desert. She and her family crowded under the wagon for relief from the relentless sun, traveling both early and late to minimize the heat.

"But then the shy young girl described Indian settlements with herds of brown and white ponies in the distance, horsemen with muskets out on the plains, the endless ribs of train tracks forging their way westward. Until, as with Randall and me, the scent of endless orange groves perfumed her approach to her final destination." Elizabeth looked torn between her student's and her own overlapping memories from their cross-country journeys.

"When she finished, sitting down self-consciously, the other kids riddled her with questions. 'Wild Indians? Cowboys?' They shivered at the imagined dangers she'd survived. And in that moment, everything for her changed.

"So this morning, the child brought me a gift." Elizabeth gulped down emotion, extricating herself from their huddled closeness to reach into her bag and draw out a perfect orange. "She told me her father and brothers pick them, and they chose the best one for me."

Elizabeth's eyes watered. "These people, Adam, have nothing. They're barely able to feed themselves—not even a solid roof over their heads. But still they sacrificed to show me gratitude. I am so touched." She flicked away a tear, smiled tremulously, and positioned her coffee cup to partially hide her emotion.

Wakefield instinctively produced his handkerchief, dabbing at her wet cheek until she allowed her head to drop onto his shoulder. He breathed in her scent and, without thinking, began to stroke her hair.

Elizabeth raised back, taking the handkerchief to dry her tears, and apologized. "I'm sorry, Adam. I'm overreacting. It's just heartening to see an ugly-duckling-to-swan transformation and be reminded of the joy and hope we're all capable of finding."

"Truly touching, Elizabeth," Wakefield agreed, trying to reinstate proper space between them despite the noise level. "How fulfilling to watch someone's potential develop before your eyes, especially in such a child. I'm proud of you, Elizabeth. You're making a difference." He hugged her briefly before drawing back.

She returned Wakefield's handkerchief while continuing her off-putting examination of him. He concentrated on folding and putting it away, fearing she could read his muddled emotions, perhaps better than he himself. Instead, she introduced a surprising topic. "Adam, we've never discussed what you think about that laboratory fire. My husband has been haunted and jittery since. It was just a freak accident, wasn't it?"

"I think so," he replied. "Although it was a chemical fire where no chemicals were used. They simply weren't part of the research we were doing in that section of Randall's lab. But as I reminded him, someone could have mishandled a flammable, been sneaking a smoke in the lab though it's forbidden. I'm sure there is an explanation other than the one Randall endlessly dwells on—that we're being spied upon, and someone is trying to disrupt or destroy our work. It strikes me as too farfetched. Besides, what choice have we now? We're scientists who search for truth and must follow it where it leads, regardless of costs, convenience, or political expediency. Truth is truth, and it will find its way out into the world."

Elizabeth asked, "Who does he think would do such a thing? Spy? Destroy your work?"

"Exactly. Indeed, our studies could undermine widely accepted medical beliefs and practices. But these are health professionals we're talking about, the last people likely to resist a simple, effective, and cheap approach to curing disease."

"I should think you're right," Elizabeth concurred, glancing at her watch. "Oops, I've got to go! My professor frowns on tardiness." She stood, placing her cup on the table. "Thank you, Adam. I'm glad I ran into you today. Now that we're in neighboring colleges, I hope to see more of you."

After a kiss to both cheeks, Elizabeth lingered a moment

to again scan Wakefield's face. Discomfited, he glanced down. When he looked up, Elizabeth had been spirited away by the milling crowds. Much like the way she had appeared.

§

The all-but-dead young man whose wife had sobbed her thanks to Dr. Archer for the 'second chance' his admission to the human trial represented was released from University Hospital amid a buzz of suppositions about 'Dr. Archer's secret research.' Archer knew the buzzing would only increase when more positive results followed, and they were bound to. Each of the sixteen terminal patients in the human trial displayed varying degrees of remission following their frequency treatments, from conspicuous improvements in health to apparent cure.

"It's unheard of, old man," Wakefield repeated, sitting across from Archer in his laboratory office. "One of the terminals has already been cured and released? It's only been a month!"

"'Cured' is not a word we use, Adam! *Initial results* appear favorable," Archer corrected, unconsciously lowering his voice. "'Cured' is a big and dangerous claim. Let's not invite more scrutiny."

"'Favorable'? Good God man, what an understatement!" Wakefield boomed.

"I'm downplaying it, yes. Curiosity and suspicion are rising all around me. I'm trying to report this in such a way that I don't further alarm the dean."

"Why don't you just tell Dean Culp that frequency works, quickly, without expense, and without negative effects on the patient. Give the man some credit for being forward-thinking or some such. Get his buy-in—"

A clattering in the lab outside Archer's office startled both men to silence. They rose in concert and rushed to investigate, circling the medical lab in opposite directions.

Archer met up with Wakefield before his office door, bearing broken culture dishes in his hands. "Right outside my office," he said to Wakefield, "this is what I found. Broken Petri dishes, once cleaned and stacked and ready for use. No one around, no one saw anything. A mystery."

"You think someone was listening to us?" a disbelieving Wakefield asked.

"If I said yes, would you again remind me of my paranoid overreactions?"

Wakefield walked to where broken shards cluttered the floor, just around the corner from the open door to Archer's office. If someone had been eavesdropping, they would have heard everything the two men had said. Wakefield turned to Archer and admitted, "Yes, I probably would have. I'd consider every possible *logical* explanation before I'd jump to the conclusion that we were being spied upon."

"Right," Archer responded, extending the broken shards toward him. "I won't try to convince you, as there's no solid proof. But in addition to securing our work away from prying eyes and ears, let's keep all future discussions behind closed doors." The two men returned to Archer's office, shutting the door behind them.

"Adam, I must ask again whether you fully trust your assistant, Henry, to keep our work secret as we've asked? The leak has begun to hemorrhage."

"I've told you before, I trust him. He knows our reasons for secrecy. And again, I ask about your lab assistants. There's plenty of opportunity here as well. And Randall, after all the detailed reporting you've done for the dean? There's not much secrecy left in our secret study, is there? Add to that the human trial and opportunities abound for unwelcome eyes to see for themselves."

"The genie has left the bottle," Archer conceded with a shake of the head. "Each one of our terminal trial participants is an exponential source for wild supposition. But humor me, Adam. Let us at least try to keep whatever lid we can on this for a little while longer until our first human trial is completed. Hopefully its results will indisputably back whatever we claim."

Wakefield bit his tongue, bitterly acquiescing.

§

"Oh Randall, I was certain you'd forgotten. I've been rehearsing excuses for your absence while putting finishing touches on the table. Thank goodness you're home in time."

Elizabeth's words stopped Archer in his tracks at the kitchen door, half in, half out. *In time . . . for what*, he wondered. Trying to conceal his confusion, he stepped to the stove to kiss his wife. "Smells good in here."

He glanced at the wall clock—seven-fifteen—proud of himself for being so early. But in truth, the ongoing demand to explain and defend himself with Wakefield and now Dean Culp had prompted his need for a break.

"Go get cleaned up, quick. Dean Lucian is due at seven-thirty, and he's a stickler for punctuality. Although," Elizabeth mused, recalling her first meeting with him, "you'd never guess it from our first face-to-face, the day I spent out-waiting him. But look where it's gotten me," she added, smiling. "Go on now, Randall. We haven't much time."

"Right, Dean Lucian, fellow Boston transplant. Adam told me about his sour relationship with your brother. Amazing you've overcome that and so much more."

"Thankfully Adam shed light on the situation for me. Thank heavens I ran into him after you stood me up that day following the dean's abusive behavior. It's so nice I get to see Adam more often now that I'm on campus every day."

"You see him on campus 'often'?" Archer asked, feeling unfamiliar suspicion. Was it a pang of jealousy? "I just saw him and he never mentioned running into you. Nor have you as a matter of fact, which does seem unus—" Archer stopped midsentence as his wife whirled on him, wooden spoon in hand upheld like a cudgel. Exasperation darkened her features.

"*I've* told you about it, Randall, our meetings and the proximity of our colleges which encourages them. But you don't recall, do you? You responded more than once how nice it was we *both* could see more of our friend. And yet you have no memory," she stated with disgust. "Well, do you?"

Elizabeth turned back to the food on the stove before abruptly doing another about-face. "It's hard enough having so little of your time with your long and late hours and weekend work. But now we're having conversations you only pretend to participate in? Even when you're here, Randall, you're not here."

She took a deep breath. "It occurs to me that '*we*' might no longer be an apt description of us, Randall. Two ships passing in the proverbial night? Do *we* matter to you, Randall, as well as your work?

"It seems no matter how hard you push yourself," she continued, "you grow less secure about your professional position, not more. And increasingly distracted . . ." Elizabeth steadied herself with effort. "Where does this end, do you suppose, Randall? Where do we end?"

As Archer struggled to process these shocking implications, she exclaimed, "Oh goodness, look at the time. Go! We'll have this conversation later."

Archer made a quick exit to escape the alarming turn in their exchange. He raced up the stairs as the doorbell rang. Exactly seven-thirty, he noted, praying again he'd been saved by the bell. The sudden vision of his shirt button bouncing off the angry face of that bully, Jimmie McGrevey, hastened his ascent.

§

Dinner with Dean Lucian proved to be an enjoyable affair, despite Elizabeth's threatening words preceding it. In addition to the most successful meal Elizabeth had yet produced, the dean did not scrimp on his effusive praise for it and her performance at the College. "I hope you appreciate the talent and determination of this woman, young man."

The dean repeatedly used the term 'young man' to address Archer, thoroughly irritating him. Archer's role throughout dinner was limited to nodding and agreeing as the two discussed the challenges of education within the framework of economic chaos as well as its possible lasting effects on a generation of children. Archer was free to form the convenient conclusion that he'd likely misunderstood his wife earlier. She couldn't seriously have asked if they were still a couple, still important? Insane! *I misheard her,* he decided, *or misunderstood.* Thus he encouraged serious insinuations to fade to non-reality.

As soon as she'd closed the front door behind the departing dean, Archer braced himself, fighting exhaustion and avoiding confrontation by busily clearing the dining table. He stifled a yawn as Elizabeth joined him there. "Go to bed, Randall," she directed. "I can get this. I'm too tired to talk tonight myself, and I don't wish to ruin my wonderful evening. Our married life will have to wait until tomorrow."

Though he couldn't agree more, he hesitated, fearing the trap of non-concern. "Are you sure, Elizabeth? I'll help you clear at least. Though I do agree, it might be best if we talked tomorrow."

"Run along, Randall. You look like you could use a good night's sleep. I too have an early morning. Good night," she tossed over her shoulder as she pushed through the kitchen door, arms laden with dinnerware.

Needing no further convincing, Archer was up the stairs and in bed within moments, snoring loudly long before Elizabeth joined him.

§

The initial human trial of frequency treatment on various terminal diseases produced more than just spectacular test results. It generated the rampant rumors Archer had both feared and predicted.

From the first release among the sixteen terminal patients to the last, all of whom appeared fully recovered, hell broke loose. Hospital staff, medical faculty, interns, residents, and students took note as the condition of the terminal trial participants obviously improved. Despite confining the testing to a restricted area, the patients themselves were glimpsed, as were their loved ones, stopping Dr. Archer in the hallways and stairwells to express deep gratitude with uncontrolled emotion. The alert and curious heard Archer repeatedly referred to as 'a miracle worker' with blessings bestowed upon him for what he'd done for their loved one, not to mention for themselves and their families.

In the end, results from the initial small-group human trial with terminal patients strongly suggested that carefully calibrated electromagnetic frequency exposure halted the progression of each participant's vicious disease. And more, it actually reversed the patients' downward decline to what appeared to be a total recovery of health.

"And it happened so quickly," Wakefield commented as they flipped through the finding sheets kept on each patient. The two scientists sat across from each other in Wakefield's office, door closed. "Only one thing left to do then, Randall."

Archer nodded weakly, speaking the word with Wakefield. "Publish."

"Right-o," Wakefield said, grinning. "Our timing is deplorable, yes. In fact, have you kept abreast of the goings-on in Germany and Russia? Apparently, economic desperation provides a fertile breeding ground for lunatic dictators and extremist factions." Archer didn't have time to comment as Wakefield countered his own point about their dismal timing. "But try to justify any delay to the sixteen terminal patients, as well as their loved ones, who've been given their lives back."

Archer reacted, "It's far too soon to make such claims, Adam! Long-term follow-up on the patients will be required to determine whether frequency treatments are a cure or a temporary reprieve. Unanticipated effects could still develop over time."

"Of course, Dr. Archer," Wakefield facetiously concurred. "Far be it from me to revel in results that could not be better! One hundred percent reversal of terminal diseases. No pain, nausea, discomfort, nor negative effects whatsoever detected in the terminally ill—to date, of course. Fine. But their diseases were brought under control by only a few sessions a week of the treatment. We even watched reversals in mere weeks on those with visible tumors."

Archer thought back to the first introduction of the trial patients to their treatments. Most sat, some were forced to lay, near the cathode ray tube, emitting its undetectable electromagnetic energy at the frequency which had been matched to the vibration rate of each patient's disease-microbe. They waited for something to happen. *'What is that thing, Doc? Looks like an oversized floodlight.' 'Is it on?'* one had asked. *'Am I supposed to feel something? Or hear something?'* asked another. *'Are you sure this bulb contraption is working?'* And when the treatment ended in several minutes, not one hid disbelief. *'All this confidentiality and signed agreements for this, Doc? You sure you know what you're doin'?'*

Archer rose, gathering his papers. "All right, Adam. There are no further tests that will teach us anything we don't already know and haven't tested thoroughly since we began looking through your microscope." He paused. "Heavens, could it really be nine years ago? Yes, we met in 1929, just before the big crash." He huffed. "Yet in another way, it seems like a lifetime ago ..." A completely different life, he realized, when Archer pictured himself back then.

"I'm glad to hear you say we've done all we can, old man. I despaired I would never hear you say those words. You're a good man, Randall old boy, and a fine researcher. I believed it all along. It's been a bumpy ride but, in the long run, an exciting privilege and a true pleasure."

Archer wearily agreed. "That it has, Adam. A most unexpected road." He tidied his papers, aligning the edges meticulously, and placed them on the desk before him. "So I suggest we both try writing up our findings before we collaborate on a professional announcement paper."

Wakefield nodded and the two stood, gripping each other's hands as they shook on it.

Archer exited Physics onto the darkened campus, inhaling deeply the cool night air as he made for his car. Movement out of the corner of his eye caught his attention. He stopped and glanced around. Although he found nothing, he was spooked all over again with the sense he couldn't shake of being watched, followed, and spied upon for almost as long as he'd been working with Wakefield and his microscope. The suspicious lab fire had greatly amplified his paranoia. The hair on his neck rose as he hurried on, suddenly anxious to be home, despite the dire conversation he and his wife had yet to hold.

Somehow that important relationship discussion had been postponed more than once until Archer had all but convinced himself again that he'd imagined her implications. Perhaps Elizabeth's busy life had resolved her insinuation of marital problems. Besides, he rationalized, with the completion of his initial research with Wakefield, his absences and distractions were almost behind them. Should the subject of his overwork and inattention come up again, he'd make certain Elizabeth understood that.

Safely ensconced in his car as he exited the parking garage, Archer breathed a little easier, hope for a bright future stretching ahead for both himself and his wife, somewhat counteracting his dread of the aftermath of published research results.

Somehow it would all work out.

§

Anticipating Archer arriving with a draft of their official research report before they collated it into their final paper to announce their findings, Wakefield bellowed a response to the knock on his office door, "Come! It's unlocked." But the door, swinging wide, laid bare the unexpected. "Elizabeth! Im-imagine seeing you here again. A-another lovely surprise. If you're looking for your husband," he quickly added, "I'm afraid he's not here. I don't generally expect him until evening."

"Hi, Adam," she said, stepping inside. "I was in the neighborhood, so to speak, and thought perhaps you'd let me buy you lunch. I feel we need to talk. Are you free, Dr. Wakefield?"

He studied the agenda on his desk, stalling, before meeting Elizabeth's scrutinizing gaze. That look again, as if divining thoughts which were hardly clear to him. "Well, I have a meeting off campus in an hour and a half. But if you'll walk with me in that direction, I know a place quiet enough to share a bite and really catch up." He rose and grabbed his hat. "'Need to talk' sounds ominous, Elizabeth." When she didn't comment, he adjusted the hat on his head and followed her out.

§

At the small French restaurant where they stopped, it became clear that the *maître d'* made assumptions about the tall, attractive couple. He led them to an intimate table in a secluded corner. "No no," Wakefield protested, embarrassed by the man's presumption. "Have you another larger, more open—"

Elizabeth snickered at his discomfort. "What's a tight space amongst friends, Adam?"

The host admitted, "I'm afraid it's the only table available. Unless you care to wait?"

"I don't have time," Wakefield said. So they slid onto banquettes that met in the corner, knees colliding no matter how they shifted.

"Let's not be silly, Adam," Elizabeth suggested, always amused by his rectitude. "This is fine." They accepted menus before the host left them.

But Wakefield couldn't relax, pressed into the tight space with her. The extreme proximity to Elizabeth Perrish was . . . unnerving. In the forced closeness, her fresh scent heightened his inexplicable discomfort.

"As I said, Adam," she began after they'd ordered and she focused her piercing blue eyes on him, "we need to talk."

"But I don't have much time," he prevaricated, calling over the apron-wearing waiter. "I meant to tell you we're in quite a rush today."

"*Bien sûr, Monsieur,*" the waiter assured, hurrying off.

Elizabeth wasted no time. "Since that day I caught you openly staring at me, Adam, as I crossed campus toward you—"

Wakefield stopped his agitated wriggling. "I was a thousand miles away and forgot myself, that's all."

"Perhaps," she said trying to cross her legs, kicking Wakefield beneath the table in the process. "Adam," her tone compelled him to meet her eyes, "do you know what's always been wrong with you, at least from my point of view?"

He relaxed, replying with a relieved chuckle, "I'm afraid I wouldn't know where to begin."

"You are exactly whom my parents would have chosen for me."

He did a double take. "I, well, perhaps . . . I got on well with your parents, your whole family in fact."

"You said several interesting things when we spoke previously about the fire in Randall's lab." The non-sequitur caused

Wakefield to zero in. "You said scientists search for truth and follow it, regardless of convenience or cost." She held the pale pools of Wakefield's eyes.

And he blinked first. "Your husband thinks that's a prime example of my being cavalier, that I couldn't possibly understand the seamy side of human nature, which one imagines goes double for you, Miss Perrish. Do you think we're out of touch with our troubled world, Elizabeth? Are we 'cavalier'?"

Elizabeth considered. "I hope not. My learning curve has been steep, especially since I started teaching at University Primary. But we are who we are, Adam, a fact which cannot be denied. I've faced a truth that is indeed inconvenient. For me, for Randall, for you. For us all."

Wakefield held his breath, fearing he understood her meaning and at the same time, hoping he did.

"Since I saw the way you looked at me that day, as if you'd discovered precious treasure or beheld an artistic vision so absorbing you couldn't break away, it dawned on me. The way you'd fumbled your handkerchief into my hand after tenderly blotting my tears the last time we met. There was real electricity where you touched me. I felt it. I believe you did as well." She smiled. "This electrical component in the human body you and Randall have been studying—it would appear to be quite powerful. I felt it, Adam, an undeniable jolt of reality.

"And the more I thought about it," she lowered her voice, "suddenly all I wanted was to have your arms around me, feel you again stroking my hair, again inhaling me, then kissing my eyes and ears and lips—"

"We cannot be having this conversation, Elizabeth!" Wakefield reared back, the table wobbling madly with his hasty movement. "Randall is my friend and my partner and *your* husband! You love him, I know you do. And so do I." He attempted to extricate himself from her closeness, only further entangling their limbs above and below the table.

"Yes," Elizabeth agreed calmly, "I do love him, as do you. To be loved for its many complex reasons, it's one thing." She unflinchingly held his eyes with hers. "But to be cherished, Adam. It is quite another.

"Look," she finally blinked, "I've had too much time to analyze my husband, my marriage, and this new life we've undertaken. Randall chose me most likely to throw me and my heritage in the face of those who had belittled him his whole life, starting with his father and brothers whom I've never met. Yes, of course, he loves me in his way, but far bigger forces drive him and always will. He will never stop running nor reaching, as perhaps you can better attest. Sadly, I fear he will never 'arrive' at a place of security.

"But I'm certainly not innocent here," she admitted. "In my own way, I did the very same thing. I chose Randall partly to prove to myself I could live outside my parents' wishes and strictures. And the fact it hurt and disappointed them, even embarrassed them, only added to my infantile need to assert my independence. It didn't have to end as it did with them, Adam. I will forever carry the burden of my father's death on my soul.

"All this is to say," she returned to the conversation again, "I didn't wish for this heartfelt realization, nor to hurt Randall or you, Adam, or myself for that matter. But the truth has presented itself and will not be stuffed back in the bottle."

Her expression and voice softening, Elizabeth stated, "You and I were always a match. I think we've always loved each other. But I was too pigheaded and rebellious, too determined to find my own way, to admit it. That is, until now, when it seems I must." She faced him head-on with her troublesome truth. "I'm sorry, Adam, but I believe you feel the same way about me."

The waiter delivered their food, curious about the now-silent table. "Everything is all right?" They nodded and he backed away.

"Elizabeth—"

She stopped him, pressing her fingers to his lips. "Perhaps I should have kept this to myself. I don't know where it goes from here, if it goes anywhere. But I've discovered I'm like the scientist you described. I found my truth, and with too many regrets already piled up, that truth must find its own way into the world, regardless of 'convenience or cost.'" She dropped her head, so close to him it nearly rested on his shoulder.

Instinctively he caressed her scented hair, his head resting lightly against hers, his eyes tearing up. "Elizabeth," he murmured in her ear. "Oh, Elizabeth—"

She pulled away. "Don't. Don't say anything. We'll talk when we talk, but I'm going. A lot has been strewn across this rather tiny table, and we both need to take a moment to step back."

With that she wriggled her way off the banquette and stood, smoothing her skirt and gazing down at him and their untouched food. The waiter hurried over again. "Something is not to your liking, Mademoiselle?"

"I'm sorry," she muttered to Wakefield, then told the waiter, "I'm afraid I must leave. Wrap up my lunch for my friend here. He's a bachelor. I'm sure he can use it." With that and Wakefield, trapped by tight quarters and struggling to get free, Elizabeth vanished.

§

The damned monthly report. Again.

The overflowing wastebasket indicated the difficulty Archer was experiencing in recording the unprecedented results of the human trial. The terminal patients, without exception, responded positively to the controversial and admittedly little-understood treatment with electromagnetic frequencies.

On the one hand, he wished to subdue the alarm bells his study had already touched off. But at the same time, he struggled to avoid further infuriation of the dean with his obfuscations and omissions. Archer attempted to couch positive trial results and their stunning implications in the least provocative way. Aware he sat on a time bomb, Archer still hoped to delay igniting the fuse.

He scribbled, 'Although findings appear to indicate the eradication of each trial patient's illness, long-term follow-up is required to rule out recurrence of the disease, development of unanticipated after-effects, or—' Archer ripped the page in half and balled up the remnants, tossing them onto the overflowing basket. He'd lifted his pen to begin again when insistent rapping on his office door interrupted. Relieved to have a distraction, he shouted, "Come in," and dropped his pen.

A tall, silver-haired stranger filled the doorway, paint fumes from the lab's reconstruction rushing in around him. "Come in, come in," Archer urged, "and close the door behind you. Those fumes will make you sick."

"Archer," the man said as he stepped inside, his silvery mane glimmering under the overhead lights it nearly brushed against.

"Yes?"

"It has been some time," the well-tailored stranger stated, looming over the seated Archer as his office space shrank with the man's presence. "Let me see now, I left Harvard not long after you, four years ago. And you've been here, way out West, for how long now—five years, is it?"

Archer's jaw dropped. "Dr. Dole?" He leapt up to skirt his desk and extend his hand, taking in the imposing, immaculately-groomed man as they shook. If anything, elapsed time had only increased Dole's towering stature while literally adding lustrous silver to his hair. Self-consciously, Archer worked at the wrinkles in his lab coat with his free hand.

"I'm here on official business," Dole answered, "checking on a few things for the U.S. Medical Doctors Association. I'm addressing the local chapter meeting tonight. Of course you'll be in attendance."

"Oh yes, of course. What's your topic tonight? I haven't had a chance to read up on the meeting."

"I'm speaking on the relatively brief history but rapid rise of pharmaceuticals, and their anticipated effect on medicine going forward. It's sure to be controversial. Manmade drugs and the companies that manufacture them portend massive changes throughout our industry as well as the general population— with everything from vaccines to symptom-controlling forms to outright chemical cures."

Dole's sniggers sounded cynical. "It also suggests a rapid concentration of wealth in a few powerful entities which my Association will insist upon monitoring and controlling. The USMDA intends to educate and assist governmental regula- tory bodies in the establishment of oversight guidelines. As the founding director of the Association, I admit to a personal interest and responsibility. After all, getting our requirements addressed early makes everything proceed more smoothly over time."

"I was of course aware you'd left Harvard, Dr. Dole, and heard you were spearheading the new professional organization. You live in Washington, D.C. now?" Archer asked.

"I do. As you can imagine, Archer, it's critical for me to stay ahead of possible legislation and public opinion as they affect our field."

"Yes, well, please sit down," Archer remembered to offer, clearing the chair of stacked papers before circling back to take a seat behind his desk. "That's what you do at the U.S. Medical Doctors Association? I thought the Association involved itself in medical research and the dissemination of new discoveries throughout the field."

"That too, of course," Dole replied, "but at my level, it's all about knowing how to get things done and through whom. Who you can count on, and why." Again, his cynical chuckle that Archer found off-putting. "I'm proud to report that today the USMDA is an organic whole, controlling the education, the licensing, the certification and re-certification of all its practitioners throughout their careers.

"At the same time, we influence what research and initiatives are funded and which aren't, what gets published and what doesn't, and where most private as well as governmental funding is funneled. It's an enviable structure, Archer—a closed circle that ensures the future for medical professionals like you and me."

"Hmm," Archer huffed, "I had no idea. I thought the USMDA was all about research, like me and this lab. I'll look forward to hearing more about it this evening."

"Mind you, we're not a governmental or regulatory agency, Archer, not officially. We generally rely upon the manufacturer's trials and test results for the products we cover editorially and endorse."

Dole shifted in the chair as if he intended to stay a while. "Good to hear you're attending tonight. I should think it would be a welcome escape from the intricacies and redundancies of lab work. Frankly," Dole glanced around the small office and through its window into the lab, "I never understood the desire to spend one's life in a medical lab. Me, I'm meant for human interaction, both on and behind the scenes. Washington's a perfect environment for me." He smiled at another private thought while Archer awaited an explanation of his presence. "So anyway," Dole began again, "I'm on my way to see Dean Culp but thought too much time had elapsed since we'd said hello."

"Thank you, Dr. Dole, for taking time for me. I'm ... honored."

"Well, you and I go back a long way. You've always been someone I've had my eye on." Archer flashed to the tense interchange between Dole and Della Dolkowski at his pathology ceremony. "And now, you have been making something of a name for yourself, as I'm sure you're aware."

Archer, tuning back in, gazed at him in disbelief. "A-a name for myself? Beyond a few published papers, no. Although my paper on the potential side effects of slide preparation practices used in microscope studies garnered attention. Come to think of it, so did my next paper, which extended those potential effects to the latest technology. In it I conjectured that the electrons used by the new electron microscope could have similar unwanted effects to the chemicals traditionally used on specimen slides." Archer fell silent, guiltily recalling how Wakefield had originally put that thought in his head.

"Anyway, that paper too drew heated debate as well as harsh questions from the dean, who wondered how such speculation aided this College and its benefactors. He forcefully reminded me those benefactors, especially one major pharmaceutical, helped fund my own position."

"He has a point there, Archer. I'm on the Board of S&B Pharmaceuticals, a major backer of this College. As well as your post."

"I—you? I had no idea . . . You mean, Dr. Dole, you had a part in my hiring here?" The statement immediately niggled him. Had Dole maneuvered this behind the scenes? He had boasted about doing such things in his current position. But why?

"No, not exactly, Archer. Oh, I may have contributed a word or two when asked."

"Anyway," Archer eventually returned to the comment at hand, "apart from faculty here and a few people like you whom I knew at Harvard, I'm not aware of others who would recognize my name."

"Far too modest," Dole oozed. "You were quite a standout at Harvard."

Now it was Archer who cynically chuckled. "Yes, until my career prospects evaporated abruptly along with all opportunities for this 'standout.'"

"So you wound up clear out here," Dole said, "as far from the power bases as one can get and still be in the United States. I know under the circumstances I advised you to leave Boston, but given your Brahmin wife, I wondered about such a radical change. She must detest being so far from Boston and all things easy and familiar."

Dole's unexpected mention of Elizabeth and his allusion to her powerful family with whom he had a connection inspired Archer to clam up. Had the Perrish influence materialized before him here in his office in Los Angeles?

Dole breezed on, "I do see Prescott and used to see Bradley Perrish at the Harvard Club in New York from time to time. Part of my job, as I mentioned, is to know the powers behind every line of work which could possibly affect our interests in Washington. Did I hear correctly that the rift between your wife and her family has never been repaired?"

As if he weren't aware, Archer thought, shifting in his seat, feeling like a specimen under study by microscope himself. "My wife's a headstrong woman, Dr. Dole, happily in pursuit of a life of her own making."

"Interesting," Dole commented. "So neither of you have contact with the Perrishes. None of my business, of course. So Archer," Dole leaned in, "as I sit before you with my expansive view of the entire field of medicine around the globe, tell me how you see your future in our field. Is ULA's medical laboratory the answer to all your dreams?"

Archer heard the condescension in Dole's words as he followed Dole's inspection of his cramped office. *Is this all I ever wanted?* Was he settling too cheaply? He finally managed to respond, "I like the medical lab and research, Dr. Dole. It's been my goal since before I entered the field, as you remember. But where I might end up ultimately? Impossible to predict. Given the sorry state of the world at the moment, I'm grateful to be employed and well-paid when so many are destitute and desperate."

"Right. Terrible out there indeed." Dole's tone lightened. "Then it's a good thing I stopped by. Let me toss out an idea that may come straight out of left field as I hear you not thinking big enough, Archer, not nearly big enough."

Dole settled back as best he could in a chair too small for his stately frame. "I'm getting to the stage in life where I'm looking to head out to pasture, Archer. The time is almost upon us, and the USMDA Board and I have been brainstorming the ideal replacement—someone well-educated, brilliant, and reliable, that is, someone we can work with who knows what's expected and how things really function. Like our special arrangement at Harvard, a few unimportant tasks kept confidentially between us, that kind of thing. And I imagine someone only too happy to return to the East Coast, as surely you and your wife would be."

Archer blinked rapidly. *Can he be referring to me in his job?*

"Well, what do you think, Archer? How would you like to become *the* MD in the entire world? Quintupling your salary with an unlimited travel budget? Getting to know all the important people not only in the field of medicine, but in the many other fields which overlap and interact with it? That includes most of the federal bureaucracy as well as government officials in all the important states.

"The job is headquartered in Washington," Dole ran on, "but I'm sure I could wrangle a *pied-à-terre* there if you and your Perrish wife wished to return to Boston. And wouldn't the entire Perrish clan sit up and take note of your return in such a visible and enviable position?"

Dole's insincere smile called to Archer's mind his comments about offending Elizabeth's powerful father, right before he showed Archer out of Harvard and ultimately, Boston. "You . . . are you offering me your job?" Archer stuttered. "Director of the USMDA?"

"Oh no, I can't do that. Only the Board can offer the position. But if I went back to D.C. and told them you'd accept—should it be offered, I think you could fairly well count on it."

Archer envisioned the humbled Perrishes eagerly lining up

to welcome him home, proudly introducing him to high society in Boston and beyond as *the* most influential doctor on the planet. For a moment, he imagined what he'd find upon stepping into Perrish House on Beacon Hill for the very first time. And perhaps he'd return to Pittsburgh after all, just to be certain his brothers and particularly his father hadn't overlooked 'the runt's' meteoric rise far above them all. *Now who's not so smart?*

"And Archer," Dole said, leaning forward conspiratorially, "with what I'm offering you, your wife could start her own school if she wished, without a penny of the Perrish fortune. So what do you have to say?" He sat back confidently, smug with expectancy.

Like a bucket of cold water thrown in his face, Elizabeth's name brought Archer crashing to Earth. They'd never finished the conversation about the marital problems she'd alluded to. *Would she want to move back to Boston? With me?* Archer wondered for the first time since he'd pushed her questioning their marriage far into the background. *Of course she'd be thrilled for me and for the chance to put her interfering family in its place. Wouldn't she?*

"I'm flattered, Dr. Dole. It's tempting, I admit. But I'd have to talk this over with my wife."

"What's to 'talk over'? The two of you would rule Boston society with your position and her family name. Seems to me a quite obvious choice."

"Yes," Archer smiled, imagining becoming an indisputable and untouchable insider, once and for all. "But Elizabeth just began her college degree program here. And her position and students at University Primary are very dear to her, as is our house and particularly the garden she created. I really must . . . I mean we need to discuss it, that's all."

"Nothing you've mentioned cannot be duplicated wherever you land, Archer. Of course she'll understand. Women are far less sentimental than we men give them credit for. There is just one small detail, however. You'd have to be back East within the month."

"The month! Why a month, Dr. Dole? That's—why, that's unreasonable. I have responsibilities which must be wound up and handed off. And in addition to seeing where Elizabeth— that is, to discussing this with my wife, I owe my long-time research partner a conversation as well. The Medical College has been good to me. I'd want to forewarn Dean Culp and get his—"

"Dean Culp will not pose a problem, Archer. Leave him to me. The Directorship starts in a month back East. Nonnegotiable. Take or leave it. But since you brought it up," Dole's tone lost its hard edge, "I have heard inklings of some fantastical project you've been involved with. You forget I'm in the perfect position in which to hear such things. Electrical medicine? New microbes?" he scoffed. "Unbelievable is too tame a word." Dole noticed Archer's eyes widen in alarm. "Ah, so there is some truth to those outlandish rumors then, Archer."

"You've heard all that back in Washington?"

"Evidently." Dole wriggled in the too-small chair, watching Archer intently. "But since you brought it up, as I said, why don't you tell me about this research. Who knows? I might be able to steer your study to related ones out there, or bring in a broader viewpoint to assist you."

"I really wouldn't wish to waste your limited time here on the West Coast, Dr. Dole. Besides, it's still premature, and weren't you on your way to meet Dean Culp?"

"The dean will not mind waiting. Unless you'd prefer I ask him to explain the basis of the rumors leaking from his college."

"No—no, that won't be necessary." Archer glanced down at the report he was preparing for the dean, intending to describe as vaguely as possible the project Dr. Dole now waited to hear about. He turned the page over and sat back with a sigh.

"Well, Dr. Dole," he began, giving himself a moment to think it through, "it started innocently enough by my helping a friend at Harvard—you might remember him, Adam Wakefield?"

"Wakefield, yes . . . yes, the family suffered terribly in the economic Crash. That tall lanky blond, smart as a whip, studying microscopy over at Physics if I recall correctly. In fact, I met him working with you in our lab late one night, correct?"

"That's the man," Archer said, surprised and a little unnerved by such an important person remembering a minor incident from years ago. "He's taken the microscope further than anyone I'm aware of through a number of innovations and technical improvements—"

"I don't need a lecture on microscopy, Archer, unless it's essential to understanding your study."

"In many ways, it is." Archer summarized the lighting techniques and special materials Wakefield had used to reach unprecedented levels of magnification and resolution in the so-called light microscope. It had enabled the two men to experiment with observing diseased blood and tissue specimens as never before—alive and untreated, no additives for enhancing visibility called for or used. He explained how they observed an unknown microbe, smaller than a bacterium, that, even more surprisingly, existed in a similar form in every disease studied, apparently indicative of a disease's most virulent state.

Sensing he was losing his audience to overwhelming detail, Archer quickly summarized the accident involving Wakefield's assistant, Henry, and his wave-frequency-producing device, which had occurred in Wakefield's lab. That incident, he explained, had then led them to observe, then rigorously test, the stunning effects of a range of electromagnetic-wave frequencies on this microbe in individual diseases. It wasn't long until they discovered that when the frequency generated by the ray tube exactly matched the microbe's innate rate of vibration, the exposure appeared to destroy the pathogen without harming surrounding cells.

Archer recapped the four levels of testing and the final out-come—from the original study slides, to Petri dish cultures, to animal testing, and finally to a small human trial on terminal patients. Each stage delivered a corroborating outcome. Regard-less of the underlying disease, after frequency treatment, the microbe proved no longer infectious while its victims appeared to recover full health.

Archer was quick to add that continued study was *absolutely essential* to confirm long-term effects and efficacy.

Dole asked questions from time to time, demonstrating a keen mind and in-depth knowledge beneath his polished bluster. When Archer had finished his rapid summation and satisfied Dole's queries, they both sat back in deep contempla-tion. Having veered far from conventional medical doctrine, Archer worried he'd done more than ruin his chances for the plum job Dole came offering. Had he just botched his best chance at true freedom, safety, and security, or perhaps even for a continued career in medicine?

Then Wakefield entered his warring thoughts. He knew with conviction Wakefield would not be bought as Dole was attempting to do to him. Was it Archer's expertise, or his will-ingness to bargain his soul with the devil as Dole had alluded to, that was on the table here? Hadn't Archer sworn off such behavior forever?

"We don't really know why it works, Dr. Dole," Archer con-cluded, "although Dr. Wakefield has ideas about resonance and the fundamental electrical nature of life itself. The study needs more time, perhaps years before we can be certain—"

"Ironic, wouldn't it be, Archer," Dole interrupted, staring right through Archer until his eyes blinked into focus, "if the man tasked with protecting the future of medicine as taught, practiced, and safeguarded today turned out to be the source of bringing it tumbling down around us? If you have what you imply—a mighty big 'if' I must add—as head of the USMDA, that's precisely what you'd be doing."

Archer gulped as Dole expertly played on his fears. "I've been as careful as I could with this volatile information, Dr. Dole. But truth will out, as they say, and after so many successful tests and retests, it leaks out already. My partner—"

"So," Dole broke in, "have you two thought about patenting this discovery of yours? No, of course you haven't, although patents are the wave of the future in medicine. I could be instrumental to you there. And trust me, if you have what you think you have, there'd be more money in it than you could ever imagine. You could buy the state of Pennsylvania should you choose to go home again."

Suddenly, the entire dazzling and confusing picture cleared. Dole mentioning his roots was the final impetus. He'd always wondered why he'd been selected from the crowd for Dole's special attentions. Dole being related to Miss Della provided another clue. And now, it was all obvious. His humble origins, on evident display in his cheap brown jacket at that introductory lecture made him more likely to be malleable. And hadn't they?

Dole proposed, "Suppose you and I come to an agreement, right here and now. We've always understood each other, Archer. In addition to the lucrative position I offer you which every doctor in the world would jump at, how about I procure the patent for this electro-treatment you've described? And for my efforts utilizing my insider contacts to speed the way, I take say, ten percent of the gross?" Misreading Archer's shock at this turn in the conversation, Dole sweetened his own offer. "Oh all right, Archer, ten percent of the profits."

Archer's whole being went cold under Dole's greedy leer. His internal war intensified. The first thing *the* doctor responsible for protecting the field of medicine had questioned concerned itself with money, ownership, and patents?

Misreading Archer's stunned silence, Dole added, "Look Archer, you're the smartest man in the room, always have been.

And it can't have been easy going up against the entrenched and the privileged. But against long odds, you found a way, and I believe you always will. What I'm offering you is what hard work and brainpower can never provide—social security of the kind Roosevelt is *not* speaking of, freedom from your past and insurance for your future."

Dole scraped his chair back. "I'll presume we have a deal, Dr. Archer, soon-to-be-announced Director of the United States Medical Doctors Association."

Archer stared mutely at the man as he answered his own question. Yes, he had been sought out by this man and his powerful cronies, who intended to control him and their stranglehold on medicine for as long as he held the lofty sounding position of director. In reality he'd be no more than their puppet.

"Well, what's it going to be, Archer? I don't have all day. Dean Culp is waiting, and there's my presentation for tonight's dinner meeting."

Archer's insides churned at risking a job offer he could never duplicate by selling out discoveries he didn't own in the first place, along with selling himself. An unwelcome realization could not be suppressed. *Dole's job is all I could ever ask for, but at a price I swore I would no longer be willing to pay.*

"I simply cannot give you an answer at this time, Dr. Dole," Archer stated as firmly as he could. "Suppose we speak *after* the meeting tonight? It's just a few more hours. I must clear my head *and* talk it over with the few people most affected. After your speech and dinner, we'll finish this conversation. That's not much to ask for a position and decision of such importance."

Dole rose, glaring down his patrician nose at the ingrate. "I offer you the keys to the castle, and yet *you* hesitate?" He picked up the hat he had tossed onto Archer's desk, but paused. "Tell you what I am willing to do, Archer. You tell me *before* the meeting begins, *before* my talk and dinner, what conclusion you've reached. But I warn you, once the meeting comes to order, this offer is forever off the table. You understand?" He turned for the door.

Archer felt his blood draining to his feet when Dole spun back. "And this conversation, it never happened. Strictly off the record. I know you understand. We've always had an understanding, haven't we?"

He shoved the door open, and the noises of a busy laboratory rose and faded as it swung shut behind him. Its final slam underscored the portentous exit of Dr. Errol Dole.

§

"He'd heard all that?" Wakefield marveled, watching the terror in his partner's darting black eyes, his ashen coloring emphasizing it. Archer and Wakefield sat in Wakefield's office where, although its door had been securely closed, Archer continually craned in his seat, double-checking for lurkers and spies.

"It's preposterous what he's offering you, Randall. After all we've been through, all the years, you can't walk away from this research. It's too important and too profound."

"I told him that, Adam. But I don't think you truly understand what a position like his could mean for someone like me. I would never dare dream of something so visible and powerful." *Which would carry me at long last beyond anyone's reach.*

"But the revelations we're sitting on," Wakefield countered, "could mean at least as much or more. Randall, you'd be in the history books for *all time* as *the* doctor who discovered how to use the electrical nature of life to eradicate disease! What's bigger than immortality?

"Besides, you love the lab and the work. You'd flounder in the glad-handing environment you've described as Dole's position, influencing regulators and legislators, manipulating public opinion. Frankly, old man, you are not cut out for it."

"The current director of the USMDA apparently disagrees

with you, Adam. He thinks I'm smart enough to reshape myself into anything I want to be."

"Do you really *want* to be that man," Wakefield questioned, "instead of the doctor responsible for preventing the needless deaths of millions of disease victims who might be saved, not to mention cheaply, quickly, and painlessly?"

"What I *want*," Archer shouted, fists balled as he bolted to his feet, "is for all this to go away! All's I ever *wanted*," he stopped, blushing at his verbal slip, "what I've wanted, Adam, was to leave Pittsburgh as far behind as possible. I wanted to become a noted doctor and run my own medical research laboratory. Of course I hoped for success as a researcher, but this . . . This feels like the undoing of everything I dreamed of, the field I aimed for, and me personally."

Archer paced before Wakefield's desk before speaking. "Dole didn't skimp on his homework, dangling not only money and prestige. He appealed directly to the small-town nobody with a chance to be drafted into the big leagues." Archer stopped and collapsed onto the seat, his tone pleading. "Adam, do you think there is such a thing as true security in this world, at least for the likes of me? Is such a thing even possible?"

He glanced at his new wristwatch, a gift from Elizabeth for their anniversary. "I should talk to Elizabeth before my dinner meeting tonight. This may affect her even more than it affects you, Adam. She must know what's on the table. I owe her at least that much. I'll catch her over at Education."

Archer carefully lined up the stacked pages of the finished paper they'd at last agreed upon, their research findings for publication. He put the bundle into his briefcase. "I'll drop this by the publishing office before my meeting tonight. It's on the way.

"But you are right, Adam. Whatever this costs, personally or professionally, these findings are too important and profound to withhold from the world."

He shut the briefcase with two loud snaps and paused. "No

matter what happens, Adam, I appreciate our friendship and our collaboration. I wish I'd been a better friend, a better person all around, to you and my wife." He stashed away his regrets. "Our working together has been a thrill and a challenge, unpredictable from the outset. Exciting, surprising, frightening . . ." He smiled shakily, shivered, and walked out.

Wakefield raced to catch the closing door. "I'm proud of you, Randall," he shouted after him. "I knew you'd do the right thing. You won't regret it, hard as it may seem now. Don't let that bully intimidate or manipulate you.

"Just do the right thing!"

§

The entire faculty and staff of the Medical College, even men from other sectors of the University as well as its top leaders, were gathering to hear the nationally important speaker of the USMDA at the local chapter meeting as it convened on campus. As he approached the auditorium, Archer's footsteps slowed, then stopped altogether as though he was bolted in place. Eager attendees glided around him like a stubborn and annoying pebble in a swift-flowing stream. He glanced at his new wristwatch. 6:55. He hadn't a moment to lose.

The repeated opening and closing of the doors into the large hall allowed snippets of conversation to escape, underscored by the low rumble of mingling men. He forced himself inside and fixed his eyes on Dole, standing tall in the crowd, surrounded by men hanging on his every word. From his body language, it was clear Dole expected and appreciated being the center of their attention and their world. Archer tried to imagine himself in that role, wondering if a man of short stature could assume such a commanding presence.

Dole's gaze continuously swept the room as he joked and bantered, assessing crowd size or attendees' prominence, or perhaps just when to get started. But once his eyes sped over Archer, they stopped to zero back in.

Archer moved forward toward the men ringing Dole, feigning confidence while his knees threatened to buckle beneath him. When he neared, Dole's face creased into an almost believable smile as he extended his hand. Those gathered reluctantly broke ranks to allow Archer admittance into their circle.

"Dr. Archer, in the flesh!" boomed Dole. "Cutting it rather close, aren't you, Archer? You barely made it in time."

§

Wakefield regretted the telephone he had finally installed in his bungalow when its piercing ring dragged him from the deep sleep it had taken him hours to find.

Although reassured his partner had made the right, the only, decision he could—to go forward with publishing their research findings and reject Dole's offer—still, in the back of his mind, Wakefield worried. Dole had a power over Archer he'd witnessed firsthand. And it nagged on him that Dole was a man who would not be refused. Could Archer withstand not only his own fears for himself and his industry, could he stand up to the added pressure Dole would surely bring to bear?

Unable to find his slippers, Wakefield stumbled barefoot, anxious to halt the grating noise, shouting at the telephone as he neared, "I'm coming. Hold on! Good Lord, what time is it? Hello? This better be important," he threatened the receiver he'd snatched up, the sudden stillness equally jarring.

He recognized Elizabeth instantly, though her voice was like nothing he'd ever heard before—pinched and frightened. He held his breath in order to hear her. "Adam, they've taken him. He was barely breathing. Can you meet me at the hospital? The ambulance just left."

"Elizabeth, what are you saying? Randall? They took

Randall? In an ambulance? Where? To University Hospital? What happened?"

"I don't know. I'd gone to bed before he came home from his dinner meeting. I awakened to a thump and loud crash in our bathroom and found him collapsed on the floor, bleeding where his head hit the tile. And—and he was ... he was turning blue. Blue, Adam!

"I-I tried to wake him, shaking him and shouting his name, but I couldn't. He wouldn't wake up. I called the ambulance. It just left, Adam, for University Hospital. Meet me there. Please. Please."

Wakefield was already unbuttoning his pajama top. "Are you all right to drive, Elizabeth? I can come get you."

"No. Meet me at the emergency entrance as quickly as you can. I'm leaving right now. And Adam, thank you. I have no one else to turn to."

"Of course, Elizabeth, I'll be—" When he heard her click off and the line buzz dead, he slammed the receiver down and ran to his bedroom for street clothes. He would race to Elizabeth and get to the bottom of what had happened to his partner in the few hours since he'd last seen him: leaving his office with their final paper on their long-in-coming research results to drop at the campus publishing office.

CHAPTER FOURTEEN

OUTBREAK

1939

Elizabeth slowly opened the door to Wakefield after his knocking hardened into banging and pounding. It became clear he would not be deterred nor simply go away. He would either force a response or force the door.

Dressed in loose work pants and a work shirt, her hair bound in a scarf, Elizabeth remained in the doorway, avoiding eye contact as Wakefield took in the changes in the woman whom, in mere weeks, had aged.

She read his mind. "I'm aware of how I look, Adam. Which is exactly how I feel."

"You haven't been answering your telephone, Elizabeth. I was worried. I had to come check on you." When she said nothing, he prodded, "May I come in?"

Soundlessly, she stepped back to allow Wakefield to enter an environment completely upended. The only furniture visible from the entryway was the garden seating glimpsed through the French doors at the back of the house. Every other room his eyes scanned stood either empty or piled high with boxes.

"So . . ." Wakefield said, swallowing down another painful loss, "you're leaving."

Elizabeth nodded curtly, then indicated a perch on a box in the living room by alighting on one opposite.

"Elizabeth—"

"Don't. Don't speak, Adam. There's nothing to be said. I'm going back to Boston and that's that. When I telephoned Mother, she described Father's passing and his deep disappointment that I hadn't come back to see him. I can't get him out of my mind. Our sailing expeditions in the bay and beyond. The ease we felt in each other's company." She drifted off on a wave of memory.

"Prescott inferred I'd broken Father's heart, that he started to slip the day I married Randall and knew I wouldn't be coming home. Mother forbade anyone warning me of his decline, but still, she blames me too. I'll never get the chance to say goodbye." Elizabeth met Wakefield's red-eyed stare. "It seems I've destroyed every meaningful relationship I've ever had," adding quietly, "including ours."

"No! Elizabeth, no you have not. I am sorry, but it's not your fault. They cut you off—"

"Under the circumstances," she rushed to speak over him, "Mother has generously invited me to return home. With Prescott living in New York, she's alone now. It's the first time I've heard fear in Mother's voice. Maybe . . . maybe it's not too late for us to start anew. I cannot handle any more regrets that can never be undone."

"Elizabeth, please."

She clambered to her feet. "No, Adam, don't. Just don't." Then she slowly sat again, struggling for words. "The autopsy report said the blood in our bathroom was from the head wound. But the cause of Randall's death was attributed to 'anaphylactic shock,' or a severe allergic reaction. However, the report stressed the exact cause was inconclusive."

Wakefield said, "I didn't know Randall had allergies. To what?"

"He didn't, at least none I knew of. The autopsy doctors weren't sure—something he ate or drank that night most likely. I guess we'll never know. Anyway, the fall he took, causing his bleeding head wound, was secondary to whatever he ingested which triggered the fall . . .

"A number of his fellows at the meeting that night told me Randall was perfectly fine throughout the meeting and well into dinner," Elizabeth reported. "In fact, several said he was more upbeat than they'd ever seen him. Happy. But sometime during the meal, he reported feeling queasy. Moments later Randall rushed from the room, apparently sickening. Since I was asleep when he returned home, I'm unsure of the timing or his condition when he arrived."

"It was a roomful of doctors, Elizabeth. *None* assisted him?"

She shook her head. "I don't know. Maybe they didn't notice, or thought he would vomit up what ailed him."

Wakefield scoffed, but made no further comment. "Elizabeth, I know this is painful. It's painful for me as well. But you must know, I want you to stay. We have to give ourselves a chance. We've waited long enough. Your life has begun to unfold here— your education, your teaching. Us. Please," the rasping in his voice betrayed him, "please reconsider. Please give us a chance."

"I've lost my zeal for teaching," she responded. "I question what I'm qualified to teach anyone. And I'm no longer a faculty wife so there's no more free college education. I cannot support myself on a volunteer's salary."

Her eyes shifted away from his to an unfocused gaze into empty space. "I can't, Adam. We can't. It's completely my fault, I admit it. I acted rashly with you, and for that, I apologize. I somehow feel I'm to blame for not only my father's death, but now my husband's. You should be wary of me."

"But that is not true, Elizabeth. You can't know whether you could have made any difference in either case. You were right about one thing for certain—I've loved you my entire life. And it seems you, me."

"We are not having this conversation, Adam. I've ruined everything, I, who was always so sure she could forge her own way, flaunt all convention, do what I wished. Look where it's gotten me. Where it's gotten us, Adam. And Randall."

She blinked rapidly before meeting his crumbling composure. "I will confess to you that I had just told Randall that I wished to separate since neither of us seemed willing or anxious to sit down like adults and discuss our marriage. But even with that, he seemed to pass it off as something I'd forget about over time.

"We'd grown apart, or perhaps we'd never really been together. You know better than most, Adam, that all Randall really needed or wanted was his profession, and for nothing to stand in the way of his determination to succeed at any cost. He hoped to outrun his past. I feel I symbolized for him the distance he'd traveled, more than truly being his wife, partner, and helpmate.

"And to some degree, vice versa. He represented my independence and ability to choose for myself. Childish, no? Not a strong basis upon which to build a marriage and a life together. So let's not talk about us just now, Adam. I need to grow up and face my choices and their consequences before I make any other life-altering decisions. Or ruin any more relationships."

"Really, Elizabeth?" Wakefield cried in anger, leaping to his feet. "After what you said to me, that we were meant for each other? We were always a match. Always loved each other. You expect me to just forget that now? Let you sneak off when you've admitted your marriage was in trouble for some time? Though poorly timed, now is our opportunity to air our feelings and try to build a life together. Your skulking off to Boston is—it's cruel! How will I get those words of yours out of my head?"

Elizabeth vacillated. He could see it in her sighs and

nervous glances, away and back to him. He pressed his opening, approaching her. "I love you, Elizabeth. And yes, I always have, since the first time your brother introduced us and pulled your pigtails to make you leave us 'men' alone. And that won't change whether you're here in Los Angeles or back in Boston or isolating at the North Pole."

He saw tears brimming in her eyes that matched his own. She rose, tugged the scarf off her head, and as her thick waves cascaded around her shoulders, she took his hand. Wordlessly she pulled him to the stairway. They climbed in tandem.

She hadn't used the master bedroom since Randall's death and opened the only room, a guestroom, still with a bed intact. Once inside, she closed the door and turned to him, taking his face between her hands. He tried to speak, but she shushed him. "No more words, Adam." And sealed her directive with a tender kiss. Wakefield slid his arms around her and pulled her tight against his body, his body reacting immediately. He held and kissed her with an urgency built up over decades, feelings he'd tried but failed to purge. When he attempted to speak, she pressed her finger to his lips, finally leading him to the bed where she began to unbutton his shirt, and he hers.

They fell onto the bed in a tumble of limbs and lips, drinking each other in as if they'd been lost in the desert for a lifetime. As perhaps they had.

Their first lovemaking was rushed and rough, years of hunger barely abating. Afterwards, laying side by side, arms encircled, afraid to let each other go, they began again, more slowly, savoring each other's tastes and scents. Wakefield was moved to tears by the miracle of her beauty and passion. Every time he tried to speak, if only to say her name, she stopped him with either a finger to his lips or a silencing kiss.

At last sated, tired, and content, they lay pressed together like a single body until sleep carried them both to a place beyond death and guilt.

§

Wakefield awoke in a dark and unfamiliar room. When it all rushed back to him, he reached out for Elizabeth in the blackness only to discover himself alone in the bed. He rose, hurried into his clothes, and took the stairs two at a time to find her.

"You've put me behind in my packing, Adam," she quipped until she saw his reaction, his euphoria vanished.

"You're going to Boston? Still?" He glared at her. "My God, Elizabeth, does the cruelty of this world never end?"

Distraught, she led him to the garden where she'd placed a bottle of wine and glasses. They sat nervously beside the gurgling fountain as she poured for them both. "To a love that lasts beyond time and place," she said, raising her glass. Wakefield dropped his head.

The profusion of blooms she'd nurtured from the dirt taunted him. "You're leaving all this? And me?"

She had a hard time controlling the shaking of her hands and sat the wine aside. "I'm leaving the garden furniture for whomever occupies the house next." The tears brimming in her eyes matched his own. "I've done enough gardening." She scanned the area, stopping at a small section of her rose beds where exposed earth lay scarred and barren.

Wakefield followed her gaze. "What happened there?"

She tried to laugh but failed and bit her lip. "I started ripping the garden apart after . . . everything. But the agent who will sell the house came by in time to save the rest. She made me stop, telling me it wouldn't aid in its sale or in anything else."

She swallowed and spoke with difficulty. "I've managed to hurt you unpardonably, Adam, and myself as well. Everyone I touch . . ." She shook back regret. "So yes," she spoke quietly but determinedly, "it's back to Boston and whatever pieces I can salvage there. I shall atone for Randall and my father with whatever time Mother still has. Perhaps then . . ."

The fountain babbled through a long silence until at last Wakefield admitted, "I suppose there really is nothing left here for either one of us any longer."

Distracting herself with a mental inventory of what remained to be packed, Elizabeth finally heard his words. "'Either one of us?'" she repeated. "What are you talking about, Adam? Your work is here. Are you saying you won't be able to finish your project without Randall? Regardless, you run the physics lab, and you're an important member of the faculty. You can still do that, still teach. Or find someone else with whom to resurrect your study with Randall?" Her last word quavered in her throat.

"I'm afraid not, Elizabeth. Not any longer." She stared hard at him, unable to discern his meaning. "Not wishing to add to your problems, but it seems I am no longer welcome at the University of Los Angeles." Her eyes rounded. Her jaw dropped. She gaped in shock and confusion. "I've been fired," he clarified. "I'm unemployed, Elizabeth. Good timing for that too, wouldn't you say."

Her deep blue eyes finally began to blink rapidly. "I-I don't understand. Fired? Whatever for?"

Wakefield squirmed on the metal garden seat. "It's rather a long story, Elizabeth, one I assure you will only add to your already heavy burdens."

"I insist, Adam. Tell me. Tell me now."

Wakefield studied what he could of the home's interior, formerly so elegant and warm, now transformed into a mausoleum to what might have been. Cold, empty, and soon to be abandoned. "If you insist, Elizabeth, but I warn you, it's a lengthy tale."

"I do. I insist. And don't spare any detail."

§

One week earlier on a Monday morning, the telephone had again rung early and insistently. It reminded Wakefield, as he scurried to answer, of Elizabeth's distress call about her husband's collapse and ultimate death.

"Hello. Yes, yes, I understand. What's this about? Right. Fine. I'll be there." Wakefield hung up, hurried to finish his breakfast, and scurried to his automobile for the drive to the University where he'd been called for an emergency faculty meeting.

He knew the moment he stepped into the dean's office that something was terribly wrong. Outside of the Dean of the College of Physics, Wakefield was the only Physics faculty in the room. There were, however, several long-faced strangers forming a semi-circle on either side of the dean, facing a single empty seat placed before his desk. The only friendly face in the room belonged to a security guard at the College, standing off in a corner. He smiled and nodded as Wakefield surveyed his surroundings. "Where is everybody?" he asked the dean. "Am I early?"

"Please take a seat, Dr. Wakefield."

He did as he was told in the only place available, center-circle, repeating, "What is all this, Dean?"

"It seems there have been some irregularities that have caught up with you, Dr. Wakefield." As Wakefield repeated the word 'irregularities,' Dean Grafton spoke over him. "These gentlemen are from University Compliance as well as its Legal Division. Jim, would you please read out the points for Dr. Wakefield."

The youngest man in the room, young enough to be one of his students from the looks of him, stood, cleared his throat, and began to read a list of wrongdoings. Wakefield's mind, careening and stung by incredulity, had difficulty following. "Excuse me, gentlemen," he broke in, "but what have these grievances to do with me?"

Dean Grafton responded, "It has come to our attention that University and College funds have been misappropriated for unapproved research that could have had disastrous consequences for both. Do you deny your participation in animal and human testing of an experimental and wildly unsubstantiated medical treatment which would have required sign-off at my level of this College as well as, amongst others, the University president himself? Further, it would have required these men seated before you to have given their signed approvals of safety procedures to protect the viability of the entire organization, its employees, and its students.

"We've also learned," Dean Grafton continued in a lowered voice, "that you frequently imported contagious disease specimens into your laboratory, which is not outfitted for such materials. That action would also have required prior and expressly written permission, with pre-approved and documented procedures for proper handling, storing, and disposal of said specimens."

The dean slapped dismissively at the paper on his desk from which he had referred and met Wakefield's stunned gaze directly. "Surely you can imagine the damage to the University if students had become ill. What if someone had died from such exposures? The publicity could have caused the entire University to fold. Did you think of that, Adam? These times we live in are demanding enough. We could all have been out on the streets, queuing in the breadlines, begging for work, and taking whatever was offered—a far cry from our lives currently. You knowingly jeopardized all of that? All of us?"

"Dean Grafton, you knew I was working with the College of Medicine to prove my microscope's capabilities, and prove them I did. But what we observed using it carried our research into unexpected realms from the very beginning. I assure you every precaution was taken with study materials. And the fact is, no one became ill. Why are you overplaying the dangers now? The publicity accruing to the University from my microscope alone once its powers are known will do the opposite of what you've implied. They'll be lining up to get into our College.

"Not to mention," Wakefield added, "Dr. Archer of the

Medical Lab is . . . was a meticulous researcher with the highest standards of laboratory safety protocols."

"And yet he is gone," the dean said under his breath. "I am sorry about your friend, Adam. A terrible tragedy. Which only points up the dangers you were not considering."

"Are you implying that Dr. Archer's death is somehow related to our—"

The dean cut in. "At this moment, it is beside the point. You ignored University procedures right and left—there's a long list if you care to hear it all—and I'm afraid I've been left no option but to terminate your employment, effective immediately.

"Such an action is unusual for a tenured position except in clear cases of 'just cause,' which unanimously this has been deemed. You will not be allowed to retrieve anything from your lab or your office. They have been closed off to you from this moment forward. Items of a personal nature will be returned to you by post.

"And now," the dean signaled, "Officer Walker will accompany you to your car and see you off campus. He'll collect the keys to your office, your lab, and the Physics building before you go." The dean stood, joined by the other men in the room as the security guard stepped toward Wakefield. Dean Grafton added, "I'm sorry, Adam," before he exited through an inner door.

Wakefield struggled to his feet, too overcome to make sense of it. "Why are you doing this, Dean Grafton?" he shouted after him. "Why are you painting the worst possible scenario? In order to fire me? All my work here has been outstanding. I've helped put this College and the University on the map! Why? Tell me!"

At the far side of the inner room, the dean conferred with the support team sent to aid him in the firing, ignoring Wakefield's entreaties. The guard nudged his arm. "Come on, Dr. Wakefield, gotta go now." Wakefield followed the man out, too stunned to comprehend.

As they neared the entrance to the College, Wakefield, who knew the guard well, finally began to think. "Alex, I need to get the spare house key I keep in my office. I'm having houseguests. You'd let me pop in for that, wouldn't you?"

"I would, Dr. Wakefield," the guard conceded. "But they ain't there. Everything in your office and much of your lab was moved out over the weekend. I seen it myself. Empty. Cleared out. I'm sorry about all 'a this, Doc."

Wakefield stared at the man, reeling from shock after shock after shock. "Not your fault, Alex. Did you see who did the moving, or where they took everything?" The guard shook his head, and the two proceeded to where Wakefield had parked his car. Once in it, Wakefield rolled down the window to wish the guard well. The man returned the wish and waited for Wakefield to drive off, watching until his automobile had vanished from sight.

But Wakefield's brain had kicked into gear. *All our research. My microscope!* He circled to the other side of campus to see what from their years of exertion might be saved from his partner's laboratory.

As a regular fixture there, Wakefield's presence drew no additional scrutiny as he made his way to the secured frequency area the scientists had been redeveloping since the fire. Its formerly-locked entrance stood ajar and with one glance, Wakefield saw it too had been denuded. Not a trace of their work—animals, equipment, documentation—nothing remained within.

Wakefield's last hope to save any of their research was perhaps in Archer's office. But upon sneaking inside, he was greeted by barrenness. Emptied and wiped clean of its former occupant. Why hadn't he gone ahead with his own suggestion to copy everything and keep it safe and separate somewhere? After the paranoia he'd accused his partner of for years, now who looked the fool?

His heart began to race as he hurried back to his car and

drove from campus, head pounding with the realization that his 'paranoid' partner appeared to have been right all along. And if someone threatened by their discoveries had been spying as Archer had insisted? Might that make his sudden illness and subsequent death at Dole's dinner presentation even more suspicious than it already seemed?

Archer's words echoed in his ears. 'Trust me when I tell you that threatened people are capable of the unspeakable . . .' Including murder? Wakefield questioned. '. . . especially when scrambling to provide for themselves and their families. Or simply to hang onto what they've got, be it wealth, power, or control.'

Even the rich and powerful? Wakefield wondered. *Especially the rich and powerful.*

§

The dull, unfocused eyes which had greeted Wakefield at the front door earlier now blazed with anger. "You're not—" Elizabeth, enraged, accused him, "you cannot be suggesting— Adam! You cannot possibly imply someone *murdered* my husband?"

"You know as well as I do the bind Randall was put in right before his Association meeting. Isn't it too coincidental that on that very night, he suddenly and inexplicably fell ill? And died! You said the coroner's cause of death was inconclusive. Might he have been poisoned? Indeed, you were asked repeatedly about what he ate and drank that night.

"He was a young and healthy man, Elizabeth. I saw him right before he went off to search for you to discuss his decision. He was fine. Perfectly normal!"

Elizabeth stopped him. "What? What are you talking about?"

"Before the USMDA dinner meeting. He left my lab to track you down over at Education and confer with you over what his visitor had that very day come tempting him with. It was a deceptively plum job which outright would have killed our research, or at minimum, endlessly delayed it. His alternative was to sell that research to the man and his powerful cohorts, thus guaranteeing them continued control over the medical field, over our discoveries, and over the lives of millions of disease victims."

Wakefield rubbed his eyes, but his shame would not be rubbed away. "In retrospect, I wish he'd taken the job. But what I said the last time I will ever speak to Randall was precisely the opposite. Ironic, isn't it? I told him to do the right thing. And he had made that very decision, taking our final paper to drop at the publishing office on his way to his meeting. Of course, it too hasn't been seen since."

"Adam." Elizabeth, unable to puzzle ill-fitting pieces together, demanded clarification. "This is not making sense. Randall went looking for me before his medical society meeting the night . . . that night?"

Wakefield, aghast, searched for words. "He— You mean to say he never found you?"

Elizabeth's wide-eyed glare faltered. She looked away before admitting, "I'd left early that day, Adam. I'd gone home to prepare for the night I hoped the two of us might share. I knew you two wouldn't be working to all hours and I planned to stop by your place. I got as far as your driveway, but at the last minute, I simply drove on. I didn't want us to start out that way." She sniffed back her own shame.

"Oh my God," Wakefield cried. "Oh good Lord, and I would not have hesitated to invite you in after the words we'd shared. Imagine me," he scrambled to his feet as if to outrun the truth, "imagine me exhorting Randall to 'do the right thing,' my final words to him forever, when I would have betrayed him in—"

"Don't! Don't torture yourself," Elizabeth commanded. "Nothing happened, and if it had, *I* would have to accept full blame. I spoke first. I acted first. I planned to come to you,

Adam. And I backed down first. Remember that."

Wakefield plunked back onto the garden seat and reached for her hand, but she snatched it away and stood. With him watching helplessly, Elizabeth paced amongst her glorious blooms, which in every season offered scents and colors that were now their own cruel joke. Beauty that inevitably waned with the passing of time.

She seated herself carefully. "Why, Adam? Why would someone want to kill your research and do *murder* to do so?"

"Our discovery would have shaken the entire medical field in a world already suffering. It is that pervasive, that powerful an alternative to how medicine operates today on the narrowly accepted bases of radiation, surgery, and drug treatments for disease.

Your husband repeatedly listed all the folks beyond the obvious medical professionals who would be immediately impacted and potentially destroyed—suppliers of everything from aspirin to bandages to X-ray equipment, even the regulators and related governmental entities tasked with oversight of the field, not to mention the specialized disease charities. Truly the list of interconnected, vested interests is endless.

"The world could not sustain another financial blow of this magnitude, your husband reminded me time and again. And he insisted that those in power would fight with everything they had to hold onto their wealth, influence, and security."

Wakefield gave words to his disturbing conclusion. "I'm afraid these maneuvers by the University to wipe out any trace of our work along with his suspicious death have finally convinced me that Randall was right all along. In fact, he did do the right thing—at my insistence! And he paid with his life."

Only Elizabeth's outrage kept Wakefield from breaking down completely. "It's—it's unbelievable!" she stuttered. "We're talking medical professionals caring more for their wallets than the people they've pledged to save? What about, 'do no harm'?"

"Not all of them, Elizabeth, not even most of the practitioners. The majority of doctors genuinely care for their patients and their life-preserving work. Only the very few in key positions of power and control could make such overarching decisions about the future of the field.

"But keep in mind doctors' education, training, licensing, and recertification are held in the hands of those few who apparently work the system in every direction—up, down, and sideways. They control both the industry along with the regulators who *should* provide supervision and oversight. Yet these blatant conflicts of interest proliferate!" Wakefield shouted, furious all over again. "How long can anyone, any organization no matter how powerful, squelch the truth? Lord, how I wish I had the answer to that question."

Elizabeth covered her mouth as if to stifle a scream. She choked out, "Is the world really so terrible a place, Adam? So selfish? So brutal?"

"Randall was right about that too. It is—at least when monetary sums beyond comprehension like those we were talking about are at stake." He managed a sad smile. "He told me you and I couldn't fathom it. Again Randall appears to have been right."

Elizabeth collapsed forward in her seat, burying her head in her hands and weeping. Silent heaving deepened into cries and moans, then desperate gasps, as her pain convulsed her. Wakefield could no longer keep the distance she'd imposed and came to her, pulling her to him from his perch on the arm of her chair. He held her close as she cried with abandon, leaning his head on hers, dampening her hair with his own inconsolable tears.

Shock, grief, regret—a storm of emotions—eventually exhausted them both. Elizabeth sat up, gently extricating herself from Wakefield's arms, drying her eyes, and staring up at him. "I'm afraid, Adam," she sniffed, "I'm afraid for you. If there are those who would stop at nothing—"

"I'll be all right," he proclaimed unconvincingly. "I'll land, well, somewhere. But from this day forward, my priority will be to bring the conspirators—those with their eyes and ears everywhere, their hands pulling every string—to justice. If it takes the rest of my life, I will see them pay!

"Every time I relive Randall's words, recounting his meeting with Dr. Dole, my heart rate triples. The man bragged about his power and reach, not just over all of medicine, but over regulators and government officials, medical and drug companies, and over many in associated fields.

"That's where I plan to start, Elizabeth, with Dole, the USMDA, and his cronies, to track down the culprits in this conspiracy to suppress life-saving science by eliminating all those who stand in their way. I swear, even if it takes the rest of my days."

"Oh Adam," she lifted her wet and streaming face toward his, "I'm running away, to Perrish House and Boston, to the protection of my family. Who will protect you?"

The finality of Elizabeth's words squelched the last of Wakefield's hopes. "I've lost you both," he cried, finally crushed beneath the full weight of his defeat. "And what's been unleashed on this miserable world or when this travesty might end, if it ends . . . is anyone's guess."

Elizabeth wrapped her arms around him, whispering over his sobs, "Oh Adam, I'm so sorry. Sorry for this suffering world. Sorry for us.

"But then," she concluded wearily, "when have such words ever been enough."

THE END

ACKNOWLEDGEMENTS

I wish to thank two experts for their unwavering sense of humor, patience, and insights as I struggled to understand both aspects of medicine and physics. Their patience cannot be overstated.

The late Dr. Paul Coleman, PhD/professor in Space Physics from UCLA, a decorated NASA and Los Alamos veteran, Paul was as kind and as humble as he was accomplished and brilliant. I'm sure our conversations left him stunned and amused at my attempted re-phrasings.

Dr. Arthur (Hank) Williams, MD, McGill Medical School, Montreal, Canada, Pathology Residency and Hematopathology Fellowship, USC, Los Angeles. Thank you, Hank, for allowing me time in your medical labs, views through your microscopes, and cringes at the jarred body parts I kept my distance from in your laboratory.

Both experts helped me to translate into plain English, to the extent such a thing is possible, their expert knowledge and deep understanding. I am forever grateful to you both, and for your friendship.

I must also thank my early readers who toiled right along with me to shape this challenging subject matter into a novel, or a series of novels, which also required novelistic basics: suspense and intrigue, difficult relationships, and all the background matters—jobs, homes, relationships that run the emotional gamut—that make up a real or a fictional life. Dr. James J. Owens, author and Associate Professor of Clinical Management Communications, the Marshall School of Business, USC; and Nancy Ellen Dodd, MFA, MPW, author and writing instructor whose expertise in structure and character proved invaluable. Thank you for our years of collaboration since USC, and for the years to come.

And to my friends and collaborators at BooksForward/BooksFluent who made the words and intentions behind them correct, clear, and presentable. My earliest partners, Julie Schoerke and Marissa de Cuir, whose long-term encouragement bridged flagging moments until we reached our goal. Hannah Robertson's team delivered tireless suggestions and endless energy as the book physically developed from editing, layout, design and cover art, and myriad details. Editors Emily Colin and Kate Leboff were sticklers in very different ways, both appreciated and necessary. The publicity team, starting with Brittany Kennell and Angelle Barbazon, worked their magic to get the word out and books in minds and hands. Book-making is a long and demanding process but much more fun with competent and dependable people every step of the way. Thank you to you and your teams.

Partial Reading List for those interested in furthering their understanding of the underlying science in *The Human Trial*

We Are Electric, Sally Adee

The Body Electric, Robert O. Becker, MD and Gary Seldon

The Field, Lynne McTaggart

The Rife Handbook, Nenah Sylver, PhD

Cancer Wars, Robert N. Proctor

The Cancer Cure That Worked, Barry Lynes

Rife's World of Electromedicine, Barry Lynes

Life on the Edge, The Coming of Age of Quantum Biology, Johnjoe McFadden and Jim Al-Khalili

Bioelectromagnetic Healing, Thomas Valone, PhD

Made in the USA
Las Vegas, NV
22 September 2023

77958309R00163